Lock Down Publications and Ca$h
Presents

SON OF A

DOPEFIEND

My Story Written in Blood

By

RENTA

First Edition 2023

Printed in the United States of America

This is a work of fiction. Names, characters, places, and incidents either are products of the author's imagination or are used fictitiously. Any similarity to actual events or locales or persons, living or dead, is entirely coincidental.

Lock Down Publications
P.O. Box 944
Stockbridge, GA 30281
www.lockdownpublications.com

Like our page on Facebook: Lock Down Publications
www.facebook.com/lockdownpublications.ldp

Cover design and layout by: Dynasty Cover Me
Book interior design by: Shawn Walker
Edited by: Tisha Andrews

Stay Connected with Us!

Text **LOCKDOWN** to 22828 to stay up-to-date with new releases, sneak peaks, contests and more…

Like our page on Facebook:
Lock Down Publications

Join Lock Down Publications/The New Era Reading Group

Visit our website:
www.lockdownpublications.com

Follow us on Instagram:
Lock Down Publications

Email Us: We want to hear from you!

Acknowledgements

What's the business, world! Maaannn, where do I start? So much has happened since we last vibed, I'd be here all day if I were to open my wounds and reveal to you the tale of each scar. So, I'll merely say to you that I've learned a lot! I wrote this book in the dark, fam—literally! After a while, I didn't think I'd be able to see beyond the bullshit in order to complete it, yet here we are!

Muhammad Ali was absolute to say there is no such thing as Impossible! *Impossible is Impossible!* It's also impassable.

We create possibilities by our drive and having faith in our path to its reality. In the same breath, we have a tendency to set imaginary boundaries and limitations but with less effort. A simple thought — *Impossible* renders us immobile. That one word creates a barrier, a highway to a road called *impassable*. Yet, impassable is a word with no truth. To declare impossible a reality is simply to admit that you lack ambition!

It reveals how mentally weak you are because when we think of George W. Carver, Oprah, Ida B. Wells, Nelson Mandela, Barack and or every other individual that defied the laws of the word *Impossible*, you have to see that impossible is truly impossible!

I hail from the mud—my mom's was a drug addict that defiled her integrity in order to epitomize the depth of a woman. An oxymoron but feel me, my mama was my Queen. Though she smoked crack cocaine, I learned the virtue of a woman versus the beauty of her. Queen sold her body at times to provide, teaching me how to be a man while she is high! In my eyes, no one could have done it better.

I give my first acknowledgment to God for being *within* me even when I felt he was absent! I praise you cause you watch over gangstas and babies alike.

Ruth "Black" Ridge—*R.I.P.* I love you, baby, and will mourn you 'till I join you.

Drea, never forget that you're a Queen. Know that you're great and without you, I'd still be thinking impossible is impossible. Be happy and know that I salute you.

Mama Helen, you stood with me forever and a day and as I reflect on the breed of woman you are, I can only hope that everyone that ever gets the pleasure of knowing you, understands what rare truly means. I love you, Queen!

Cash? Peace, my G! This one for the books, my nigga. You rocked wit' me when all I had was a vision. I owe you one, playboy! LPD and all the authors under the umbrella— Keep pushing, fam. We're the best that do it and it won't be anyone after us.

Dunte, Papa, Too Black, Thug, Lil K, Big J, Lil C, Pacman, Tru, E-Man, Lil Woo. Early like lo3 Gang Gang Gang, Big Compton, Juvie, Paublo, and the entire gang, gang, gang—*It's too many* to name! I love you boys. I ain't even gotta say it! From the trap to bookstores across the globe!

Last but not least, the most important part of my family— my fans! The love is 100! I wanna thank ya'll for thuggin' with me. Without y'all, there would be no me, and as we change the story, we'll keep rockin' em with the truth! Tell the world, *welcome to the greatest show on earth—our show!*

Impossible is impossible.

Prologue
Entry 1:
February 15th

Dear, whoever is reading this

Since you are, it means that I'm either dead or better off so. So, either or, I want you to stop reading this as of now! This book was never meant for you to read. This book holds the secrets of an emancipated black woman that are hers alone to reflect on.

This book is an account of every defilement, every sordid detail, and every mistake I've ever made. This is a diary that you shouldn't be reading, and if you have even the smallest shred of respect for a woman's right to secrecy, close this book, and bury it.

Yet, if you do choose to read it, judge not my sins, but try to understand that as I inscribed these words, I was a stranger to even myself. Every man that I've ever fucked wasn't for my enjoyment, or the pleasurable euphoria that most women seek while being intimate with the opposite sex.

I've given myself to men that saw me as nothin' more than a piece of pussy. A momentary escape from their boring housewives who lost their fire of being his fantasy in reality. I've sold my soul for a high that wouldn't last longer than my pain would. I've manipulated my way through life because once I've became numb to the call of my heart, I found it was easier to forget the things that once made me smile.

Memories are the greatest treasure one can hold sacred, yet with those reflections of the past comes a self-created enemy. An enemy that's internal and will drown you within dark waters of melancholy. My heart is a deserted island that I can't seem to swim from. Makes me wonder if God and the devil are the same people.

Messiah—my heaven—my son? If I'm so unlucky for you to have opened this book, King, then I am a woman born with the wrong destiny. I don't know how I'll be remembered. Maybe you'll remember me for all the love I've given—the sacrifices. I've taught you and loved you to the best of my abilities.

Yet, even after that proclamation, maybe you'll simply remember me for being a whore—a drug addict that lied, stole, and sold me short for what was never meant or worth to be obtained. No matter how you remember me, never pity me, baby. I lived!

Yes, I was a whore if that entailed me doing what I had to do to survive, but what does that say of a God that would forget his angel in the ghetto? Yet I don't blame God for anything. Well, maybe for the lie the Bible told of him always being on time. That's a bald-faced lie, Messiah!

From the moment my husband's blood stained my hands, I needed God, but he never showed. Possibly, he meant to be on time but got lost within the many other prayers he had to listen to. Either or, I don't know how to love anymore, baby,

I lost my heart somewhere along the many roads I've traveled. So, I began this diary not to be remembered but because I'm barely holding on to a thread of my sanity— a thread of hope that isn't strong enough to withstand a gentle kiss of the wind.

I'm recording every moment and event of our life, Messiah, so in the event of this thin thread snapping, maybe I can find repentance within these pages. If there's a God and at this time in my life, I'm not too sure, maybe he'll soften his heart to the cries of a black woman trapped in a world of savage men.

If you ever find this diary, Messiah, the last two pages will be blank. They're for you to complete the story. You must, because for you to be reading this, it means I'm dead and the dead can't tell no tales, baby.

Mama

****

The end of the beginning —2010

The charcoal gray trench coat flapped open and flowed behind him with each step he took. The black silk dress shirt he wore was tucked neatly into the waist of his black Tom Ford slacks, that were tailored to perfection and rested gently upon the top of the soft-skinned crocodiles that covered his feet. With each step he took, the butt of the Glock .17 irritated him as it dug into his back. The walk down the highly polished hall seemed to last forever as Messiah stared at his reflection that seemed trapped inside the glow of the waxed floor. The fluorescent lights made the day seem drearier than it was and it caused him to sigh before losing fascination with the blurry form of himself. Taking in the whispered life on the second floor of the hospital wing at Parkland Hospital in North Dallas; the same hospital he was born in, he allowed his feet to carry him to his destination.

His heart ached to the point he inadvertently returned his gaze to the glossy floor, his thoughts becoming a wicked tornado inside the walls of his mind, spinning so fast they threatened to snap his sense of sanity in half.

Every thought was tainted with regrets—*How'd shit get so ugly? SunJay? Pimpin? Justice? Mama! Shit crazy, fam.* Thought after thought clashed like rival warriors inside his head. Yet, Messiah was too old to believe in a life without pain. He was a product of the ghetto and knew life didn't always make sense, but that realization wasn't a consolation to the internal chaos that surged through him. Messiah inhaled a deep breath of sterile air as his thoughts played in his head like a tragic movie.

He was so much in a daze that he hadn't realized he'd reached his destination until he looked up in surprise — Room *288*. All it would take was for him to walk through that door and he'd step into the waters of past and present. Yet, he merely stood there. Messiah yearned to see her—to talk to her—to laugh with her about the crazy times, but life was vindictive.

He had to mentally prepare himself for crushed hope. His eyes were trained on the door handle and at that moment, he realized he'd been holding his breath. Messiah's lungs begged for release before he exhaled in a slow, long whoosh of air.

"Shit's crazy," he whispered to himself. He'd been back and forth from the streets to that room for the past eight months and with each visit, he lost a little more of himself. The vibration of his phone snatching him from his thoughts, Messiah took it off his hip and opened the text,

SunJay is back in the city. I won't kill him. Well, not yet. Next time its rock-a-bye-baby.

Messiah allowed his eyes to scan his surroundings; Keisha was known to pop up in strange places. He ignored the message. He was more concerned with his Queen; the woman on the other side of that door needed him.

On the other side of that door was his mentor—his soul. Yet, as she laid somewhere in that room, mentally deteriorating, Messiah had to swallow the reality of even superwoman having her days when she didn't feel so super.

As if just remembering he held it, Messiah firmed his hold on the black book he held. His cold eyes drifted to it as he reflected on every possible hope it held on its pages. It resembled a thick Bible, but it was merely a book; a book that only he and the woman on the other side of that door knew of its contents.

Even after the doctors told him there was nothing they could do without a matching donor, Messiah knew the words that stained the pages of that book was the medicine no man could prescribe or create. He knew sometimes—just sometimes, the most potent medicine derived from the love of a person that truly gave a damn.

Exasperated, Messiah rubbed a manicured hand over his bald head before placing that same hand on the surface of the door. His heart cried a crooked melody as he stepped forward and rested his forehead against the cool wood.

"Remember me, Queen. *Please,*" he plead while willing his love to her. "Remember your—"

His words were interrupted by the soft click of the door as it slowly opened. A cool breeze escaped from the room as Messiah stood erect and took in the woman that stood in the doorway. She was a creature of understated beauty and as he took her in with a penetrating gaze, he was sure she caught a glimpse of the lion that stared out from the darkness of his eyes.

In another time, Messiah would have poured her a potent sip of game, but that part of his life was now buried beneath a mound of vows he'd made to his wife Justice. Yet, while he would honor those vows, he admitted to himself that the woman had curves of temptation hidden beneath her white nurse's scrubs.

The tag clipped to her left breast pocket read *Lawson,* but due to the hue of her skin, Messiah had his own name for her. A name that made her blush each time it slipped from his lips—*Coffe.*

She stood frozen in surprise as she hugged a clipboard to her chest.

"Umm. Hey, you! How long have you been out here? You scared me, Mr. Ridge." She smiled sheepishly.

Coffe always seemed nervous in his presence, but the lust in her eyes was evident in her stare. It was more of the unsurety of her heart, however, that stirred the emotional tide inside of her. She'd heard so much of his exploits and though her heart warned her that one night of pleasure could lead to a tropical storm of destruction, the curiosity—the call of her pussy made her battle with rationality.

Messiah was aware of the effect he had on her and though he was no longer a connoisseur of women, he could still hear the slut in Coffe calling to the animal in him. Coffe held her smile and though it was the last thing he wanted to do, he reciprocated the gesture with a wistful smile that didn't quite reach his eyes.

"Peace, Coffe. I've seen better days, but I was once told that before the brightest day is the darkest hour," he responded with an indifferent shrug of his shoulders. "Guess it's just my hour." Messiah glanced past her. "How is she?" he asked.

Coffe's hazel eyes followed his gaze before returning to him. Her smile was bright, but Messiah recognized what lied just beyond the surface—the truth. Nothing had changed. Coffe stepped to the side before gesturing for him to enter.

"Why don't we see if she recognizes you today," she whispered before taking his hand and leading him into the room. "Mrs. Ridge, someone's here to see you, honey," she announced as the door closed behind them with a gentle click.

The only light source in the room came from the window that was next to the bed, and standing before it, was a gorgeous dark-complected woman gazing out the partially parted curtains. She turned upon hearing Coffe's announcement.

"Oh my, Coffe, why didn't you tell me you'd be bringing Mr. Bald and Handsome to visit me, girl? I look a mess!" The ebony woman complained before snatching the silk scarf off her head, and without an iota of shame, loosened the sash on her robe.

She did it just enough that a generous amount of cleavage was revealed. Messiah noticed that her thick mane of hair looked healthier since the last time he'd saw it, and he knew it was due to the tender love and care Justice invested when she came to visit.

That was one of the many reasons he loved her; Justice was a rida. She had his back when noone else seemed to give a fuck. He made a mental note to thank her for helping to restore the woman's once brittle hair. A weak smile touched his lips.

"What's the business, mama? I see you bringing sexy back," he teased her. She blushed from the compliment, but the frustration on her face was evident.

"Mama? Haven't I told you bout that *mama* mess, suga? What you trying to say? I look old?"

She frowned before glancing down at her bosom, and adjusting her breast with a pout to her lips. The woman's name was Ruth Ridge, but the streets knew her as Black Diamond or *Black* for short. She was Messiah's mother, and had been held in that hospital room for the past eight months.

Eight months since she'd been found face down in a dirty alley with blunt trauma to the back of her head and her heart barely beating. The doctors found the spirit of cocaine swimming inside her bloodstream and that coincided with the officer's report that claimed she'd been in that alley getting high when someone snuck up behind her and hit her over the head.

The next time Black Diamond opened her eyes, she was disoriented, her mind blank, and her heart rotting. Messiah's Queen was living out her last days and couldn't recognize her own son, and that truth ate at his sanity. Coffe recognized his torment and it was contagious; her heart went out to him.

"Mrs. Ridge, why don't you show Messiah what you found earlier?" she proposed.

Black's eyes became slits. "Girl, what I tell you 'bout that Mrs. Ridge craziness!" she exclaimed with a roll her eyes. "Who is Mrs. Ridge anyway?" Black inquired with a crude look on her face. "My name is Black Diamond! Black..." she paused and gestured to her lower self. "Black with the fat cat to some," she sang.

Coffe was embarrassed, but Messiah laughed deeply. Out of all the shit she could've remembered, she held tightly to the memories of herself that to some would be better off forgotten. But to him, she was just being— *mama.*

He understood to those who'd never had to brave the cold winters of a calloused ghetto, it was abnormal to see the fucked up shit those conditions birthed into the men, women, and children of that reality. The slums had a way of stealing the innocence from people and for a black mother that had to play the role of mother and father, that alone created a rose that blossomed from the concrete.

Black reached down into the pocket of her robe and pulled out a wrinkled photograph, before gazing at it with a look of confusion. "I found this in my things last night. It's— It's a photo of..." Her words trailed as she searched for the right words. "It's a picture of —" Again her words abandoned her.

She waved the picture in a dramatic sweep, and Messiah laid the book on the floor before making his way to her. He extended his hand as he and his mother's eyes met.

"May I see it?" he asked softly. For a moment, Black only stared at him; her eyes studious.

"I've seen you somewhere—met you somewhere before," her words unsure, as her expression danced on the brink of recognition.

Messiah held his breath, Hope creeping into his nature, but he feared the emptiness disappointment leaves in its wake, so he waited before playing it safe.

"Yea, I'm the same dude that's been comin' up here to—"

"No!" she stopped him with a raised palm. "No, I've met you someplace other than here. I—I knew you at some point in my life and you—you were—" Black fought for the words, but couldn't find them. "I don't know where, nor when, but *maybe* you were one of my John's. Did we fuck?" she asked hopefully.

Messiah flinched at her words but held tight to every ounce of strength he could muster. He smiled a sad smile before taking the picture from her outstretched hand. "Naw, ma, I was taught to never trick and I can assure you that we've never slept together."

His eyes fell to the wrinkled picture. It was aged and time had eaten away at the image, but he'd recognize it anywhere. His heart clenched without his consent. The picture told a story of times passed—a time when God seemed to give a damn 'bout people from the mud. Messiah stared at it—the people frozen in time on the paper.

A dark-skinned man with mischievous eyes and a contagious smile stared back at him. At six-two, Cedric was a handsome man with soft hands. He was a conman that possessed a good heart. There was a woman—a beautiful woman and two children in the photo with him and with only a glance, one could tell they were his most prized possessions. The picture was taken a day before Christmas, proving that the Grinch was real and as Messiah ran his fingertips over the aged photo, he longed to go back to those simple times. His eyes found Coffe watching him. She smiled before nodding her head in encouragement.

Coffe knew Messiah loved his Queen with his soul, but even more, she understood that love was the only true medicine capable of resurrecting lost memories. Coffe headed for the door.

"You be good, girl. Later, I'll braid your hair real pretty-like," she told Black, while waving over her shoulder.

Messiah waited until he heard the click of the door closing before taking Black's hand in his and leading her to the edge of the bed, nodding for her to take a seat. Black was hesitant at first, but it was something about the handsome stranger that she trusted, so she sat.

She was certain she'd met him before but couldn't remember where. *Somewhere* deep in her consciousness, she knew he was telling her the truth and that only made her *hate* the sickness that had stolen her memory. Messiah's eyes were fixated on the young girl in the picture; Da'Shia, his sister, was somewhere out in the big cold world. Again, he ran his finger over the surface of the aged photo before looking up at his mother—the woman that didn't recognize her own seed.

Black didn't understand why he was so entranced with the picture. *Maybe he knows those people, but what's so special about them?* she wondered.

"Do you know these people, ma..." he caught himself. "Black?" he corrected.

Black leaned forward—her eyes deviated from him to the picture. She didn't know who the people in the picture were nor did she give a damn; what she wanted was her life back! Black wanted those doctors to fix her old heart.

Am I gonna die here? Why can't I remember anything other than selling my body? Why?

She couldn't tame the raging river of her thoughts. Black shook her head to let him know she didn't recognize any of the people in the picture. Erecting herself, she studied him; his eyes searched the photo as if there was something there he'd find.

Black's eyes fell to the black book that rested on the floor. She may have lost her memory, but a woman's intuition was an internal compass that would never fail her. She knew the answers to her questions resided on the pages of that book. Every time Messiah read from it, it set flame to her spirit.

At times, she had snippets of movie-like memories, but she kept that revelation to herself. She *needed* the pages of that book to do what the doctors seemed incapable of.

"This picture is a moment of perfection, Queen, love frozen in time. The man in this picture was my father. His name was Cedric," Messiah spoke with a sadness tinging his words. His eyes studied her for a reaction, but there was none.

He smiled a weak smile before continuing. "The woman's name is Ruth, but she's better known as Black. She's a special kind of woman and when life shitted on her, she turned it to gold."

He laughed at his own words, then slid his coat off and took a seat in the chair by the bed. He had to adjust the burner so he could sit comfortably.

"The little girl in this photo is Da'Shia and I think she may have grown up to be a very beautiful girl, but God had a different plan for her than he did me."

His words gave life to a horrible scene in Black's mind; gunshots erupted in her head, causing her to flinch, but since Messiah's gaze was on the photo, he missed the effect his words had on her.

"The boy's name is Messiah and Black loved her son with all her heart." He was confident in the declaration. Black bore witness to the clouds that converged in his eyes, yet she sat silently. She didn't miss the play on words, associating his and her names with the boy and woman in the photo.

Could it be true? Is he merely attempting to make the story more personal for my entertainment or is the handsome man sitting before me a creation of my womb?

Black toyed with the possibilities. Still, she said nothing. She studied his features and to her astonishment, the resemblance to her was uncanny. His chocolate skin, his big round eyes, his nose — they were reflections of her own. The observation unnerved her, but she showed no sign of recognition.

Black's eyes were blank, but her mind was grasping for *something* of her past. It was a scene without faces. She watched in a daze as Messiah tucked the photo inside the pocket of his coat and retrieved the black book.

Black held her breath at the sight of it. The velvet covering gave life to the scene in her head; a scene of a faceless woman scribbling a cursive script onto the pages of a book that looked identical to the one Messiah now held. She stared down at the book as he opened it, her breathing becoming choppy at the sight of the calligraphy—*It was hers!*

"I want to start this from the beginning, just in case you missed anything. It's a tale of pimps and hoes — love and a black woman's sacrifice." Messiah brought her out of her reverie. Her eyes were unblinking as he spoke.

"This is my mother's diary, her account of every day of her and my journey. It begins in the year of *1985*, the year crack cocaine became an epidemic that helped destroy *every* black community across the south." Messiah leaned back in his chair and crossed his left leg over his right. "This was during the time Ronald Reagan created an insane hustle dubbed Reaganomics, and the hood became an inescapable Juggernaut." Messiah paused to look up at her. His eyes were filled with a mixture of love and what some would classify as pride. "This is our story, ma, the tale of *The Son of a Dope Fiend.*"

Chapter 1
1985

"Pay attention, son. The eyes are quick, but the con is slicker," Messiah's old man whispered closely to his ear. They were standing by the luggage claim in DFW airport and it was crowded, filled with the bustle of travelers that were flying in or out of town for the last holidays of the year.

No one paid much attention to the man and child that paid so much attention to them. It was two weeks 'til Christmas and Messiah's young mind spun at the thought of boarding a plane. It had been a dream of his ever since he'd learned that the fast-moving lights in the sky weren't shooting stars, but an invention of men.

At nine years of age, Messiah was more in tune with life than most children his age, and it was due to his parents being set on making him a man before his time. They hid nothing from him and taught him the trades of survival that would one day become more of a provider for him than they could ever be.

Cedric's eyes scanned the bustling crowd, searching for a target; that day he was gonna introduce his son to something he'd never forget. He owed him that. Cedric felt he didn't have much more time with the boy — his gambling habits and steep debts had brought him to the end of his rope and he knew the dice wouldn't land in his favor much longer.

Suddenly, his eyes narrowed as he spotted a man of potential. A slender pale-skinned man in a tailored suit was deep in the conversation he was having on his cell phone.

It was the year of eighty-five and the only people that could afford the big devices were either privileged white people or drug lords, so, without taking his eyes away from his prey, Cedric kneeled down beside his son and spoke in his ear. "Now, don't forget what I told you, Messiah. Stay as close to me as possible and when I move…" Cedric paused to make sure the man hadn't switched directions before he continued.

"Whatever I hand you, put it in your jacket and walk that way." He pointed towards the exit. "Remember where I told you to meet me?" he quizzed. Messiah nodded as his young eyes followed his father's intense stare, and spotting the polished-looking Caucasian man, he returned his gaze to his pops.

"Yea, pop, you said to meet you by the doors." He said, and Cedric patted him on the back before standing and heading in his target's direction. Messiah followed, but his little feet were no match for the long strides of his father.

He had to jog to keep up with him, but by the time he matched his old man's pace, things happened in such a blur, his young mind couldn't comprehend the scene before him. His father crashed into the white man with a calculated trip of the feet.

The white man's phone clattered to the floor as Cedric spun slightly and dropped something at Messiah's feet. It landed with a thud, but Messiah was so in a trance that he merely stood in place; shocked!

"Goddammit! What the hell is wrong with you!" the white man spat as Cedric held up his hands apologetically. As he tried to explain how he'd tripped, Cedric's fast eyes diverted to another man in a cashmere sweater that was a few steps away. His quick eyes fell to the bulge in the man's right pocket before returning to the first victim of the day.

Yet, his mind raced with a thirst for what caused the approaching man's pocket to bulge that way. In seconds, he had a ploy, but it would take the first mark's assistance. Timing it perfectly, Cedric got in raw form.

"Did you hear me, bozo? What the fuck! Are you dumb or—" the white man said before Cedric stepped up in his face, his lips puckered as if he was going for a kiss.

"You're just so cute!" he spoke between mock kisses and just as he anticipated, the man's face contorted in disgust before he pushed Cedric with all his might.

Though he was as weak as a breeze, Cedric used his reaction to his benefit. He threw himself backward just as the man in the cashmere sweater was passing him, and spinning until they were face-to-face, they collided with enough force to cause both men to make a fast descent to the floor. Cedric landed on top of the man and as they crashed, his hand slipped into the man's pocket.

He grasped the bulge before slipping his hand out with the impact of the fall, and rolling to the side, his hands were quick as he slipped the wallet into his coat pocket.

"You're a fucking, sicko!" the first mark shouted before disappearing into the crowd of onlookers.

Unbeknownst to him, he'd just been a party to a crime. Cedric climbed to his feet, the feeling of accomplishment strong as he dusted himself off, but it dissolved as the airport's security rushed over.

"What's going here!" a potbellied, white rent-a-cop demanded. Rushing over to Cedric, his eyes were accusatory as one of his personnel helped the older white victim to his feet.

"No, no. It wasn't that young man's fault, someone pushed him into me!" He gave Cedric a smile before turning his eyes to the officer. "I'm fine, I'm fine; as I said, it wasn't his fault."

The officer frowned as he looked from the older gentleman to Cedric. He wanted so badly to haul Cedric off to a cold cell for having the gall to touch his fellow Caucasian, but it was out of his hands.

"I—I'm sorry, officer. I wasn't paying attention to where I was going and someone pushed me into him," Cedric fed off what the other man said.

He had an apologetic expression on his face as he walked over to his victim and shook his hand.

"My apologies, sir." He offered, and the potbellied security became red-faced as his suspicious eyes drifted to Messiah, who'd just stuffed the wallet his father tossed at his feet down the sleeve of his polyester coat.

"Is that your kid?" the fat officer asked. Messiah's young mind raced, as he tried to comprehend his first introduction to crookery. Yet, he knew there was a lesson to be learned.

"Oh my God! There you are, son. I've been lookin' all over for you!" Cedric's shrill voice caught everyone off guard. He rushed over to Messiah and wrapped him in a tight embrace as if he'd been reunited with the boy after years of being separated.

Cedric held Messiah at arm's length and inspected him, "Don't you ever do that to me again! The airport isn't a place to play hide and seek! You had me worried sick!" he scolded, and Messiah's eyes grew wide in shock. He didn't understand his father's game, and tears came to his young eyes.

"I'm—I'm sorry, pop. I know you told me to meet—"

"I've found him! This is the reason I was so distracted. He's my son!" Cedric spoke over him so he wouldn't give them up.

The officer smiled as Cedric's eyes found the man in the cashmere sweater. He was patting his pockets with a look of confusion on his face. With that, Cedric and his boy made a hasty retreat before things got funky. Messiah didn't know it at the time, but he'd always remember his father and the day he used him as bait.

***

21

Next Morning

"Justice, Jah betta get yuh behind ready for school, yuh know Joseph will bruise yuh backside for yuh laziness. I tell yuh no more!" Mrs. Leah, Justice's mom demanded in her thick Trinidadian tongue.

Justice was curled up beneath the quilt her grandmother Ellen made for her; it was thick with different color patchwork that represented her homeland of Trinidad. It was a cold morning and she hated the thought of climbing from the warmth of her bed but knew that her parents wouldn't hear any of that. She huffed her way out the bed and stumbled her way to the hallway bathroom.

"I'm up, ma! I'm up!" she declared as the aroma of Mrs. Leah's cooking permeated the air. Justice's stomach growled at the thought of the pan sausages, cheese eggs, and sliced mangos that she knew would be on the table when she finished her hygiene.

Yet, frustration instantly overtook her when she tried the door. Justice banged on the door to the bathroom in an attempt to be heard over the music that blasted from the inside, but her urgency went unheard as Cleo sang along with their homeland melodies. Justice stomped her feet.

"Hurry up, Cleo! I have to get ready for school!" she whined as she bounced from one foot to the other. She and her sister Cleo were only a year apart and though they were close, Justice hated when her sister used up all the hot water.

"Wah yuh doin all de yelling for, girl?" The masculine voice calmed her tantrum. Her father JoJo wasn't a big man, but his reputation as being a dangerous man was noted throughout the section of Dallas – Ft. Worth.

Though he was a no-nonsense kinda man, Justice was the apple of his eye. A daddy's girl at heart, she turned to face him with a pout.

"Pa, Cleo is using up all the hot water again and she knows I gotta get ready for school," she whined. JoJo smiled at his youngest daughter. He loved his little princess, but he

knew she had a tendency to use his as a weapon against her siblings.

He squatted down to her level before taking her pretty face into his hands before pushing a loose curl away from her right eye and giving her his most charming smile.

"There are two bathrooms in the house, yuh know?" His words were laced with laughter. Studying her, pride surged through him as he thought of how far she'd come from being that fragile little girl she used to be. Justice was a fighter.

In the early stages of her life, she'd battled with asthma and severe fluctuation in weight, but even with the few ailments, anyone that had ever come into contact with the child knew she was a special creature. Justice studied her father with confusion etched into her expression; skeptical, she searched for trickery in his offer. Finding none, she inhaled deeply as her eyes went wild in shock .

"Yuh, mean I can use you and mama's tub?" she asked excitedly. Justice knew her mother would forbid it, yet here her father was offering her the chance to be rebellious. She giggled as JoJo tickled her.

"Hurry, mama. Go clean yuh self before yuh mother kills the both of us," he whispered as if they were sharing the world's biggest secret.

Justice glanced behind her before turning her searching eyes back to him. She loved her old man with all she had and though she was too young to understand the tests of marriage, Justice knew there was something off between mother and father.

She'd passed by her mother's room too many times and heard her whimpering, and sensed the turmoil between them. She'd also noticed how JoJo had been absent from home more often than not. JoJo studied her; he knew his babies, and there was something bothering his daughter.

Justice was usually very outspoken, but he could tell whatever it was that stilled her tongue was deep. Since they'd made the move from Trinidad to the States, JoJo noticed how the culture difference unnerved her, that coupled with his job as an offshore welder keeping him away from home had an effect on his baby girl.

His eyes took in her features; Justice would grow to be a beautiful woman, but it was the darker side of her that bothered him. She'd started having visions, visions that his mother had the gift of. Rather the gift was a curse or not, he had no idea, but he feared for her. He saw so much of his mother in his daughter. The cinnamon skin tone and her untamable mop of curls that tumbled about her head.

"What is it, mama? Yuh worried? What troubles yuh?" he inquired.

Justice dropped her eyes to the floor before replying, "Will yuh be home when I get home from school?"

The doubt in her small voice cut at the exterior of JoJo's heart, and at that moment he vowed to himself that he'd fix things with his wife and find a job that didn't keep him away from home as much. Using his thumbs to wipe the sleep from the corners of her eyes.

"I'll be here, yuh know. But yuh mama gonna beat yuh if yuh not ready for school. Hurry now, Justice, I'll keep her occupied until yuh done."

Justice nodded with a big smile on her face before running off to take advantage of the once in a lifetime opportunity. JoJo shook his head slightly as his thoughts turned over in his head. I'll have to keep an eye on that one.

***

"Messiah, mama said get yo' ass out that bed!" Da'Shia six-year-old voice penetrated his rest. Messiah cracked his eyes open, to find sunlight shining through his bedroom window, but that wasn't what caused him to put the pillow over his head. It was the pair of crusty feet that were inches from his face.

His best friend had stayed the night and SunJay's ashy ass feet always seemed to find their way by his nostrils. The two boys had grown up together; pallets on the floor and peanut butter and jelly sandwiches had forged a bond between the two that was as thick as mud.

"Da'Shia Marcella, you betta watch yo' mouth before I beat yo' ass!" Their mother's voice was a brief distraction from the dry toes by his head, yet Messiah groaned.

He'd told SunJay on numerous occasions about the stink of his feet, but SunJay was a seed of the Butta Beans projects. He never seemed to notice the ratchet smell of his own toes. Slowly, Messiah eased from the bed; he knew SunJay was a heavy sleeper, so Da'Shia's wakeup call wasn't enough to rouse him.

As silently as possible, Messiah snuck to the bathroom and found a tube of toothpaste. He smiled wickedly before returning to the room with the same care he'd used to exit. The smile grew wicked on his dark face in anticipation of some retribution.

SunJay's hand was palm up on the bed – his face exposed as he drooled. Messiah snuck over to him and slowly squeezed a big glob of the white paste into his friend's palm. That done, he retrieved one of SunJay's dirty socks from off the floor.

Messiah cringed at the stiffness of the material, the stench was so strange, it bordered the smell of old corn chips and the stink of sweat. Messiah swirled it around SunJay's face as he himself held his free hand to his mouth to stifle his laughter.

SunJay snorted deeply as his face frowned at the foul smell, and Messiah lowered the sock a bit more until the tip of it grazed SunJay's nose. The frown on his boy's face deepened before the smell and irritation pushed him to do exactly what Messiah expected.

Impulsively, SunJay swatted at his nose. His hand made a squishing sound as the toothpaste smeared on his face.

Messiah burst into laughter at the sights of his friend's face, it was too much to bear.

SunJay's eyes shot open; surprise and confusion contorting his features as he studied his hand. It only took a moment for him to figure out what had happened; They'd played the, "whoever goes to sleep first," game for years. After a moment of reflection, his eyes traveled to Messiah, and without warning, SunJay leapt from the bed, and balled his little fist.

"I'm finna beat yo ass, nigga!" he growled before taking a wild swing at Messiah's exposed face. Messiah tried to dodge the unexpected blow, but SunJay was fast.

His fist connected with Messiah's face in a wet sound of skin and toothpaste. SunJay tried to follow up with a wild hook, but Messiah weaved and began to defend himself. Both boys fought their damnedest, but with a lucky jab to the nose, SunJay caused blood to burst from Messiah's nostrils. The crimson liquid shot everywhere, and SunJay stepped back in triumph.

"Yea, I told you! I told you!" he chanted in victory. Messiah used the back of his hand to wipe the blood away. He was furious.

"I'm gonna get you for that, SunJay." He spat. SunJay was fearless with slits for eyes as he stuck his chest out.

"I ain't scared of—" he was in the midst of saying when Messiah rushed him and tackled him to the floor. They landed in a tornado of flailing blows with Messiah landing on top.

SunJay tried to push him off, but Messiah was a vicious cub. He reared his fist back as far as it would go and just when revenge would have been his, a searing pain slashed across his back. Messiah rolled away from SunJay just in time to avoid the long switch his mother swung against SunJay's bare stomach. Both boys screamed bloody murder, but Ruth was relentless as she worked the flexible stick.

"What I tell you bad mothfuckas 'bout all that fighting each other!" she yelled, emphasizing each word with a swing.

SunJay wasn't trying to hear that shit; he found his refuge underneath the bed, leaving Messiah to face the madwoman alone. She whooped his ass until the switch broke and just when she was about to slip off her house shoe to finish the job— "That's enough, Ruth, the lil niggas learned their lesson." Cedric, Messiah's pops intervened.

He leaned against the doorframe with a Kool's cigarette dangling from between his lips, and smoke swirling before his face. Sweating, Ruth turned to him. "Well, you betta teach them to be more civilized, Cedric. Look at the mess these two heathens made!" she shouted, pointing heatedly at the blood, toothpaste, and disarray of the room.

Cedric allowed his eyes to take in the mess before looking back to his Queen. "I got it from here, suga. Let me have a heart to heart with them," he spoke with the cigarette bouncing between his lips.

His eyes fell to his weeping son as Ruth rolled her eyes and turned for the door, but she was on her way out when she paused to glance back at her son. "Your black ass is grounded!" She jabbed a finger into her palm. "School and bring yo' ass right back to this house. If you make the slightest detour, Imma beat yo' ass all over again," she vowed before glaring at her husband. "And don't think you're gonna save his bad ass from every one of these ass-whoopings 'cause you not," she fumed before storming out the room.

Cedric and Messiah watched her leave before the older man laughed. "Jay, get yo bad ass out from under that bed!" he demanded before walking into the room and taking a seat on the edge of the bed."

SunJay crawled from underneath it, his eyes searching for his godmother. He looked to Cedric who merely dumped the ashes from his cigarette in the palm of his hand. "Sit down," he demanded while making eye contact with them. His eyes settled on Messiah.

"Lil nigga, do you know how hard me and you mama had to work for this shit in here?" he waved his hand in a wide-sweeping gesture. Messiah rubbed the spots on his body that were welting before nodding his head. Cedric laughed a hard laugh. "No you don't, boy. Quit lying!"

He chuckled as he looked around the room. He recalled every con—every crooked move he'd had to make to ensure that Messiah had more security than he had as a lil' nigga. "You boys gonna have enough enemies in this life that's gonna try and shed y'all's blood, for y'all to be shedding each others. I understand that boys gonna be boys and sometimes it takes bloodshed to thicken the bond, but never hurt each other to the point that there's no room for forgiveness."

He locked eyes with the two boys before setting his gaze on SunJay. "You're like a son to me, J, and you and my boy gonna be something hard to deal with one day. I don't know if I'll be around much longer and y'all gonna have to take care of each other," he revealed before standing and heading for the door.

Messiah was curious as he climbed to his feet. "What you mean, pop? Where you gonna go?"

Cedric kept his back to them in order to hide the storm building in his eyes; There was no way to explain the cost of the streets to two nine-year-olds. Cedric owed Gator, the neighborhood's kingpin. Everyone in the city of Dallas knew how vicious he could be when his money was tampered with, and Cedric owed him a hundred thousand dolla debt. A hundred thousand that he didn't have. Cedric stood still—silent for a few seconds before responding.

"Get yourself ready for school, Messiah and son?" he called. Messiah was disturbed by his father's words as he and SunJay watched the man's shoulders slouch.

"Yea, pa?"

"Always watch ova ya moms, boy. When no one else is there for you, even when God ain't movin' fast enough for your taste, your mama will be the one to love you through the good, bad, and fucked up shit life throws at you. You hear me boy?" Cedric asked, glancing over his shoulder at him.

Messiah looked to SunJay with questions dancing in his young eyes, and SunJay shrugged his bony shoulders with the same confused expression. "Do you hear me, Messiah!" Cedric was persistent. Messiah knew something wasn't right but wasn't in the mood for another ass whooping.

"Yea, pop. I hear you." He acknowledged, and Cedric nodded. He couldn't teach one of the most powerful lessons that every man had to learn on their own; the lesson that even Gangstas shed tears.

***

Erasmo S. Elementary was only a few blocks from Messiah's house, but he and SunJay always seemed to make the walk longer. Beckley was a long street that led to a lot of troublesome spots in Oak Cliff, and since Messiah and his folks stayed directly across the street from the Beckley recreation center, he had a front row seat to everything that transpired on or near the slums of "Deuce-deuce Beckley".

He and SunJay loved observing the operations of the hood, and there was a new neighbor in town that was stealing the beauty from the struggle until all the beauty was gone and all that was left was the struggle.

Crack cocaine had hit Dallas/Fort Worth with a vengeance and neither child nor parent was safe. Messiah and SunJay waited for the light to change before racing across Beckley towards the HiHo corner store. It was ritual for them to meet there with their friends before going to school.

*"Nigga, you slow! I'm the fastest cat in the hood!"
SunJay shouted as they crossed the street.*

*They were out of breath but Messiah shrugged his
indifference. SunJay was more competitive than him, and
most times he was too competitive.*

*"Hi, Messiah," a soft voice caused Messiah to turn, and
he beheld her. "Yuh walkin me to school, right?" Justice
asked sheepishly.*

*Messiah tried to play it cool, but his heart was beating
out his chest; he'd had a crush on the pretty island girl ever
since she and her people moved to the hood a year ago. He
tried to show her, but always ended up being clumsy, so he
decided to let fate run its course.*

*"Ye—yea, Justice. I'll walk with you." He fumbled over
his words, and Justice blushed.*

*"Messiah and Justice sittin' in a tree, K-I-S-S-I-N-G.
First came—"*

*"Shut up, Porsha!" Justice snapped, pinching her best
friend's arm.*

*Porsha laughed. "Ouch!" She slapped Justice's hand
away. Turning her eyes to Messiah, Porsha snaked her neck
with a dramatic roll of her eyes. "I know Justice ain't the
only one you see!" Her words were sharp as she placed her
hands on her hips.*

*Porsha was as fast as they came. At eleven-years old,
anybody with a set of eyes could see she'd grow up to be a
slut. Her mom's kept her dressed in the newest trends and it
seemed she encouraged her daughter to grow up too fast.
Porsha's clothes were always too tight or too small.*

*Messiah nodded at her real cool like. "What's up,
Porsha?" She smiled at him.*

*"Pink. Nice." SunJay's voice rose from below, and all
eyes fell to him. SunJay's mannish ass had went to his hands
and knees to peek under her skirt. Porsha slapped him in the
back of the head.*

"Nasty ass!" she shouted as SunJay rolled away laughing.

Porsha was embarrassed he'd revealed the color of her panties, but the bell above the entrance of the store jingling, rescued her from the moment. A tall man with a Jherri curl hair flowing backward exited the store. Skin the hue of lemonade gave him a dirty look. But the excessive gold chains and rings that glistened from his neck and fists was what stole the young group's attention.

The purple Velour unit he wore was fresh as he stood there smacking his lips with grease and hot sauce glistening from the wing basket he'd gotten from the store. Blow was Gator's underboss, a wild cat from East Dallas projects that had a savage hustle game.

He'd just bitten into a chicken wing when a dark-skinned, unkempt woman approached him. With merely a glance, one could see the fading beauty she was trading for the need to get high.

"Hey, Blow, you workin', baby?" she asked with a quick glance in the kids' direction. She turned her hungry eyes back to Blow as she began rocking from foot to foot as if she couldn't stand still.

Blow's quick eyes fell to her feet, disgust etching into his facial features. She was barefoot and her feet were so dirty that they matched the concrete.

"Bitch, what I tell you 'bout steppin' to me like this? I told you I don't hug corners nomo!" Blow spat.

The dingy woman's eyes were pleading, her head swiveling from one side to the other as if she anticipated the police jumping out at any moment.

"I know, I know, baby. But I need my medicine!" She reached down into her soiled pocket and pulled out a few filthy bills. Slowly, she counted seven dollars.

"One—two—three." She glanced up at Blow nervously. *"Four—five—six—seven,"* she continued, before quickly flipping the bills over and recounting them. She then looked

31

up at an amused Blow. "I got fourteen bucks, daddy, but I got you. You know tomorrow is the first and my check will be in," she pleaded.

Blow squinted his eyes, knowing the woman didn't have a job. Laughing, he raised his left eyebrow. "What check you got comin', Debra K?" The question rattled her for only a moment before she counted off three fingers.

"Boy, I got the check comin' from my ole job; they still owe me 'bout two checks. I also got a white man with one leg that gets his disability check early. Oh, I got a check comin' from the Dart bus company for a settlement," she smiled a rotten smile and Blow chuckled before trying to walk past her. Yet, she jumped in from of him.

"Please, Blow. I'll do anything!" She cupped her hands in a praying gesture.

Blow spat on the ground before taking another wing from the basket dinner. He bit into it as he allowed his eyes to molest the woman's curves. She wore a stained T-shirt and a dirty pair of pants, and even though her odor told the tale of missed showers, the woman's curves were something that the drugs had yet to corrode. Blow sucked the bone of the stripped chicken wing as he studied her.

"Follow me, Debra K., and you better make this shit worth it!" he caved. Tossing the bone to the ground, Blow turned and headed for a midnight blue Fleetwood Cadillac that squatted on gold dipped Dayton's.

He slid into the driver's seat and motioned for the woman to get in. Messiah and his friends watched in fascination, but SunJay was star struck. Even at that young age, he craved the flash and dash that came with being a hustla, yet Messiah was more observant.

He too was in awe of the jewels and nice car, but he wondered more of what the woman was gonna trade for her moment of euphoria.

"Come on, y'all. We gonna be late for school!" Justice shouted as her and Porsha turned and headed off.

Though Justice paid the pair in the car no mind, her friend Porsha was intrigued with the hunger she'd witnessed in Blow's eyes when the dirty woman said she'd do anything!

"Y'all go ahead, me and Messiah will catch up with y'all," SunJay responded as he placed a hand on Messiah's arm to stop him from following the girls. Justice saw the move, but kept her pace.

"Messiah? Mrs. Ruth gonna whoop yuh butt! Imma tell too!" she shouted over her shoulder before she and Porsha disappeared around the corner.

Messiah was heated SunJay made him miss his chance at walking with Justice, but before he could voice his frustration, the window rolled down on the driver's side of the car.

"SunJay, Messiah? You lil niggas come here." Blow demanded.

He'd watched the boys run wild around the hood and determined long ago that SunJay would grow to be the gangsta and Messiah the breadwinner. The two boys walked over to the driver's side of the sleek car and were stunned at what their young eyes were seeing.

Blow was unfazed by exploiting the young lions to the primal nature of the streets. He greedily tore into the last wing before tossing the empty basket out onto the pavement. Blow sucked the hot sauce from his fingers as both boys stared, transfixed at the woman's head bobbing up and down in his lap.

She worked vigorously, taking all of him in as he used his hand to hold her head down. The sounds of her gagging seemed to excite him, and Blow smiled wickedly before acknowledging Messiah and SunJay.

"You boys get in! Hell you standin' out there looking crazy for!" he laughed, snapping the boys out their trance. Rushing to the back, the boys got in before Messiah slammed the car door. Blow's angry eyes found his in the rearview mirror.

"Say, cat daddy, watch how you handle my shit," he admonished. Messiah didn't know what to say, so he said nothin'. He stared back at Blow with an indifferent gaze until the older man smiled. "It's cool, lil man, I know you didn't mean no harm. How's that conning ass father of yours?" He inquired.

Messiah had seen his father and Blow fraternizing a time or two, so he didn't recognize the hint of evil in the man's tone. "My pops ok, he just got a bunch of money at the airport too!" Messiah bragged, never knowing he was feeding an apple to a serpent.

Blow's grin widened. That was news to him because just two days ago, Cedric told Gator he needed a lil more time to make good on his debt.

"Oh really!" he chuckled. "That's real good to hear, young Messiah." Blow's words were tense as his gaze dropped to the bobbing head in his lap. The tingling sensation that started in his toes was now racing through his body, causing him to grit his teeth.

"Shit, woman. You sho know how to get your money's worth!" he growled before grabbing a fistful of her nappy hair and bucking his hips.

Blow's explosion was powerful. His seed shot from him in a gush of heat as the anticipating woman gulped and swallowed his essence without wasting a drop. SunJay was so entranced with the act that he leaned forward and stuck his head between the front seats, his eyes diverted from Blow's strange expression to the woman's tongue cleaning his flaccidness.

"That's enough, woman! I won't have enough for my own woman if you suck me dry!" Blow pushed her away, before smiling appreciatively as he fixed himself. Debra K held the wrinkled bills out to him.

"You still want this, honey?" Blow cringed at the few bills.

"Naw, give it to the boys," he gestured to the backseat before reaching under his seat and pulling out a zip lock bag and examining its contents.

Messiah and SunJay stared at the bag in fascination. SunJay's face was a mask of confusion, assuming the beige substance was some sort of bread, but Messiah's attention was on something totally different. His young eyes were on the thirst that resonated in the woman's stare. She stared at the whitish brown rock as if it were Jesus descending from heaven. Blow held it up so all could see.

"You lil niggas know what this is?" He made eye contact with them through the rearview. Both Messiah and SunJay vigorously shook their heads "no". Blow smiled. "This that shit that's gonna make you boys very rich one day!" he exclaimed with a chuckle.

Blow opened the bag and broke a small chunk off the mountain, using his thumbnail to chip the chunk into three pieces. He gave a small rock to Debra K, then demanded she take out her straight shoota.

After she complied, he told her to smoke right there in front of them. As strange as the request was, the woman had no shame as she loaded the pipe and leaned toward Blow who'd pulled his lighter from his pocket and struck a flame.

Messiah watched in a trance as the glass valve turned black with smoke before Debra K sucked it into her lungs and held it. Her eyes widened as big as an owls as she held the putrid smoke a little longer before suddenly doing the most unpredictable thing. Exhaling, lady flung the door open, and without so much as a word, bolted from her seat.

The boys stared bewilderedly as she disappeared around the corner, but Blow exploded into laughter after seeing the effects the potency of the drug had on her. SunJay smiled though he was naïve to what was so funny, but Messiah's expression was that of frustration. Blow handed each boy a piece of the rock, and as soon as it touched SunJay's palm, he felt the power of its nature.

"That's crack, young blood. The new world's order, and I'm gonna show you lil niggas how to get you some lunch money." Blow chuckled. Yet, Messiah wasn't as intrigued with the drug as SunJay was. Blow noticed he had a frown on his face, and confused, he wanted to know what the young boy's problem was.

"What's happenin', main man? Why yo' face all balled up?" he asked. Messiah looked in the direction the crazy lady had ran.

"That lady—you told her to give us the money, but she took it!" he replied.

Blow frowned in confusion until he remembered the seven crumbled bills Debra K had offered him. At that, Blow exploded into laughter; Messiah was gonna be a sho nuff bread winner one day. That he was sure of.

Chapter 2

It was a hot day in Oak Cliff, Texas and Ruth was taking advantage of her time alone. She'd cleaned every room in the house and had to open most of the windows to rid it of the heavy scents of Pine-Sol and bleach. Feeling sexy as she sat gazing out the picture window, Ruth sipped a glass of coke made stronger with a splash of Hennessy Cedric kept in his stash.

A Newport long cigarette dangled lazily from between her fingers as she lounged in a thin silk robe. With nothing else separating her feminine attributes from the kiss of the air circulating through the house, her nakedness made her feel liberated. Ruth's mind ran wild, everything in life seemed to be going good for her and her family.

Though things could have been better, she was taught to never shun small beginnings. As she watched the comings and goings of the neighborhood, she shook her head in dismay at the scene of two young girls that wore clothes small enough for her six-year old daughter.

She watched a car pull up beside them and after whatever words were exchanged, one of the girls got into the car. As it pulled away, Ruth noticed the older white man looking around nervously as he navigated the vehicle into traffic. The young girls looked as if they belonged in school at that hour, but with a glance, one could see that the rough streets had stolen the innocence from them.

Ruth inhaled deeply from the cigarette before fanning the cherry red nail polish she'd just applied to her toes. God is love, she thought of the two young girls, and only after she was sure the polish was dry, did she go check on the smothered pork chops and cream corn she had simmering on the stove. Betty Wright's soulful voice filled the house as she hummed along.

"I'm trembling, waiting for you to walk in. You said you'd be gentle with me," she sang along in a good mood. Cedric had left that morning and said he'd be out of town for a few days. She didn't know what his slick ass did on those two-day excursions, but whatever he was up to, he'd always return in one piece with a pocketful of money.

Ruth was raised to play her position—Let a man be a man, Eddie Ruth. As long as he takes care of the household, and respects you, you let that man be a man, baby. She could still hear her mama's voice. She remembered watching her mother get all dolled up with nowhere to go, but as Ruth grew older, she realized her mother was showing her that a woman was the representation of her man.

Ruth smiled as she lowered the fire under the simmering meat.

—I wanna play big girl and put on a sexy smile, but I know so very little bout what love is—

Betty's words made her giggle as she glanced at the clock. Her kids were at school, but Ruth knew she only had a few more hours before it was back to being mama. Solitude was scarce, but she wouldn't trade her babies for the world.

With that in mind, she dried her hand on the dishtowel, and headed to get her discarded drink. The smell of potpourri was the first thing that caught her attention when she entered the living room, but that wasn't what caused her heartbeat to accelerate.

Gazing out the window, Ruth took a big gulp from her cup as she watched the dark blue Cadillac pull to the curb in front of the house. Before she could wrap her mind around what could have brought Blow to her neck of the woods, the answer stole her breath—trouble!

Before the piss yellow brotha ever showed up to the house with Cedric about six months ago, Ruth had been hearing his name whispered in the streets and salons around the city. Blow was a crazy son of a bitch. The stories she'd heard of him were tainted by tales of bloodshed, and rather true or myth, they scared the hell out of her.

Through lowered lashes, Ruth watched Blow slide his six foot two frame out the car and gaze up and down the street before heading for the house. If she was to be honest with herself, she could admit that Blow was a handsome man. His stride was confident as he walked onto the porch and before she could step away from the window, he spotted her. Ruth waved with her fingers before going to the door, and swinging it open.

"Mr. Blow, what brings you 'round these parts where the poor folks stay?" She smiled up at him.

Blow's eyes were predatory as they rolled over her body. Ruth felt a chill run through her and only then did she remember she was naked underneath the thin material of her robe.

She cursed herself for being so sassy, and careless as to answer the door in that state. Blow's eyes lingered a little too long on her protruding nipples, making her feel uncomfortable. Ruth crossed her arms over chest.

"Can I help you, Blow?" she asked with an attitude. Blow licked his pink lips before giving her his brightest smile.

"Ye—Yes, I was wondering if ya ole man was here, but seeing his car ain't here, I figured I've missed him." He said, but Ruth was far from naïve. Blow sensed it when she frowned and glanced to the driveway before returning her suspicious eyes to him.

"You didn't figure that out before you pulled your car up to the curb, brotha?" she retorted. Blow had to contain the

animal within him. He wasn't used to people speaking so boldly to him, especially women.

His eyes took in the slim woman. Ruth was chocolate beauty. Being five ten classified a woman as a stallion, and Ruth had a curly afro that made Blow wonder if her lower lips were surrounded by the same sort of texture. Her sharp eyes were smoky as Blow smiled a tight smile.

"Movin' too fast, that's all. When will you be expecting him back?" he asked.

Ruth bounced her left leg with impatience, the act causing the already too short robe to ride up her thighs, giving him a view of the trail that lead to a paradise that any sane man would sell his soul to venture to. Lust seeped into Blow's stare and Ruth's next words led her directly into the tangled web of his fantasies.

"He was posed to be back a few minutes ago, but I'm sure he'll be back soon enough. Maybe you should come back later when—"

"I'll just wait. You don't mind, do ya?" Blow cut her off. Ruth's face betrayed her, her deceit had backfired, and not wanting to get on the man's bad side, she figured she'd have to play her lie out. Blow saw her indecision. "I'll only wait for a while. I have other things to do than to be sittin' round waiting on Ced's slick ass."

He played his role with a quick glance at the expensive watch he wore. The move had the desired effect and Ruth's apprehension lowered some. Though she was still leery of him, she had to play the lie out.

"Well?" Blow questioned before running his fingers through his long hair. "You gonna let me in or leave me to roast out her under this hot sun?"

As if she'd just remembered he was standing there, Ruth stepped to the side.

"Oh, my goodness. Come on in, Blow." Little did she know, she'd just saved herself from being slapped across the face. Gator's money was somewhere in that house and Blow

wanted it, but neither him nor Ruth could have imagined the cost of him leaving with it.

***

The room was smoky, the dim lights casting a shadow over the five men sitting at the table in the back room of Maxwell's gambling shack.

Cedric had a pile of colorful poker chips in front of him and the day had been good to him. If that last hand of Texas Hold Em played out in his favor, he'd leave seventy-five thousand dollars richer. He'd gambled the rent money and the loot he owed Gator.

He'd learned long ago that the only way for a man worth his weight in gold to get his hand on that gold, was for him to understand that the end of the rainbow sometimes ended deep in the trenches.

Sometimes a man has to take the risk of losin' his first dollar in order to obtain his first million, his father always told him. Cedric glanced at his cards before his sharp eyes touched each player at the table. When he was sure he had everyone's attention, he tossed a five-hundred dollar chip onto the pile in the middle of the table. Bo Jackson huffed beside him.

"Man, I'm all in! Yo' lucky ass must've eaten a bowl of Lucky Charms before you came, Ced!"

Though the atmosphere was tense, the men shared a needed laugh. Pimpin Maxwell had been hosting those games for years, and every Friday afternoon, good drinks flowed while muhfuckas sold their souls for the devil's dreams of being rich.

Four men stood around in the background. They were security, but the most menacing in the room was a big grizzly bear of a man known as Bear. He was the doorman and the Mossberg pump he held threateningly simmered the anxious

41

men that played for the type of bread that would be hard for any man to take a loss with.

With the ante raised, Chong, the Asian mob boss, folded. The same went for Tru out of Eastwood, and Black Rat of west Dallas Gator Boys. The stakes were too high to take the risk on a bluff. Cedric was so high off the three men's reaction that he reached for the pile of chips.

"It was nice playing this here game with you good fellas, but I think it's time I cash out while lady luck still got her legs open," he spoke with laughter in his voice, but a scarred hand fell on top of his with so much force that the chips and liquor glasses shook from the impact.

"You may wanna steady your quick fingers, country boy. We ain't all buying that chicken shit bluff you just tried to feed us!" a deep scratchy voice growled from across the table.

Pistol Pete was a six foot four guerrilla with the evidence of his occupation permanently carved into the skin of his face. A thick fold of skin ran from the left side of his face to his ear from a knife wound he'd incurred in a street battle. Using his free hand, Pistol Pete dropped a green poker chip in a separate pile, before leaning forward and showing his stained teeth.

"I take your bet and raise you a G," he challenged. Pistol Pete and Cedric glared at each other in defiance. Cedric's eyes strayed to Bear. The big man blew a stream of smoke from his lungs before pulling the Black & Mild from between his teeth.

Cedric's eyes returned to Pistol Pete's stained grin. Sweat beaded on the bridge of his nose as the room awaited his call, and having to pry his hand from beneath Pete's, he retrieved his cards. He studied them before his gaze lifted, finding Pistol Pete staring at him like a famished jackal. Cedric became apprehensive, but knew he had to take his chances on winning it all or losing it all. His life depended on it.

"House calls for your bet, Ced. Your black ass gonna either shit or get off the pot?" Pimpin Maxwell pushed him to make his decision.

The room was electric as Cedric wiped sweat from his forehead. Pistol Pete's chuckle was mocking as he lifted his glass and downed the shot of Jack Daniels. With a shaking hand, Cedric tossed his chip onto the new pile. He studied Pistol Pete for signs of bluffing, but saw nothing! The big man was unreadable.

Take the chance on losin' a dollar in order to obtain your first million. He could hear his father's voice in his head.

"Drop out, big man. You called this shit storm, so it's on you to end it," he challenged.

Pistol Pete's face instantly frowned. The bully in him wanting to force Cedric to reveal his hand first, but the sound of Bear pumping a round into the chamber drew all eyes to the big man. Yet, it was Pimpin Maxwell that spoke.

"House calls for your hand, big fella. Let's not get any blood on all those colorful chips." His voice resonated from somewhere in the thick fog of cigar smoke.

The temperature in the room shot up as Pistol Pete's eyes turned in the direction the voice came from.

"You threatenin' me, ole man?" he hissed. The silence was thick as the smoke parted, and Pimpin Maxwell stepped forward.

The dull light of the room reflected off the blade of the sharp switchblade he used to clean underneath his nails. Pimpin's deep stare left his nails and slowly found Pistol Pete. Though Pimpin Maxwell wasn't a big man, his reputation as a sho nuff gun slinger made him seem like a giant.

"Now, Pete, we've been knowin' each other since Coco-Cola came in a glass bottle. When have you ever known me to threaten a man?" he inquired with a crooked grin. Pimpin Maxwell used the knife to make his point. "This here is a respectable place of business, cat daddy. My place of

business! Now, I'm gonna call your hand once more, old friend."

For a moment the room held a deadly silence. Pistol Pete wanted to put his gangsta down but knew anything other than lying down his cards would be fatal. He rested the cards on the table as all eyes fell to them.

"Jack high flush!" Pimping Maxwell called before pointing the knife at Cedric. Cedric's expression was sour and that gave Pistol Pete the impression that he'd won.

"You bluffin, muthafu—" he was saying before Cedric revealed his hand. Three deuces stared up at the room.

"Three deuces!" Maxwell shouted before slapping him on the back.

Everyone congratulated Cedric, but Pistol Pete had murda in his eyes as Cedric stood to leave. Anybody with eyes could see he didn't intend on allowing the smaller man to leave with his earnings. Pistol Pete stood and in the midst of reaching to retrieve his coat, the barrel of the Mossberg dug into his back. He paused, his eyes finding those of a nonchalant Pimpin Maxwell.

"Ced, you gone and get out of here, old playa. I'm sure you have a lot of things to do wit' all that their cheese," he spoke before placing an unlit cigar between his teeth. He nodded at Pistol Pete.

"You have a seat, big fella."

***

"A hundred thousand dollars! Oh no, Mister. You must be mistaken. My husband doesn't owe nobody no hundred thousand big ones!" Ruth spat matter of factly. She knew Blow had to be jivin' her with his nonsense.

A hundred thousand dollars! she thought, as Blow pulled a huge .357 from inside his waistband and laid it on the coffee table. It was a scare tactic that had the desired effect as he explained how Cedric's heavy gambling and borrowed

44

money debts had gotten him in some deep shit with some heavy people.

Blow witnessed the fear blossom in her eyes at the sight of the big gun and like an animal, he fed on it. "Listen, Ruth, I ain't got no reason to lie to you. I have much more important shit to do with my time than to waste my breath," he retrieved the gun before rising from the couch.

Ruth stood with her back to him, and stepping behind her, Blow leaned forward and inhaled deeply. "Umph, umph, umph! Sweet as spring day," he whispered. Ruth spun to face him before placing her palms on his chest and gently pushing him back. He was invading her space and Ruth wouldn't tolerate anyone disrespecting her household. "I think you need to leave. I'll give my husband the message and tell him you came by, but—" Blow's hand was so quick that she didn't understand what had happened until the sting of her jaw transcended into a hungry pain. Blow had slapped her with brute force and by the time she had the mind to return the favor, he had the big gun aimed at her.

"Bitch, pay attention or pay in blood! I'm sure you've heard the stories and yes, my reputation does proceed me!" He smiled evilly. Ruth glared at him, heaven and hell melting into oceans in her eyes before running a race down her pretty face.

Blow's heart held no pity, and he kept the business end of the pistol trained on her as he stepped into her space.

"Listen, I didn't mean to hurt you, baby doll, but I need you to take my next words as serious as you would the preacher tellin' you that Jesus is on his way back, riding on a cloud and all that good shit." His words were soft as he used his free hand to lift her chin so they'd be eye to eye.

"Now, I know you love that good for nothin', quick handed sucka, but he owes my boss some big cheese and I can't leave here without something to show for it. Dig me, Ruth. This is the kicker. We both know that sneaky mothafucka ain't got one red penny of that money left or have

you been lying for him?" He played on what they both knew was the truth.

Yet Ruth's defiance clawed its way to the top. She slapped his hand away before snorting deep and spitting a thick wad of saliva in his face. "Damn you, you high yella Devil!" she screamed her anger from her spirit.

Surprised, Blow stepped back and used his palm to wipe her spit from his face. He made sure he had her attention before he used his tongue to clean his hand.

"You know what…" He paused before walking back up to her and placing the barrel of the revolver under her chin. "I'm gonna give you a few options." His eyes rolled over her as he held up a finger. "You can die for that no good nigga of yours?" he hissed with a smile before holding up two fingers. "You can sacrifice your son?"

He tilted his head to the left as he analyzed her reaction, but she said nothing—showed nothing. Three fingers raised, Blow narrowed his eyes.

"I can wait right here for ole Ceddie boy to get in and then blow his brains out the back of his head as soon as he steps through that door?" Blow paused, but this time he stole a portion of Ruth's dignity. Without so much as a warning, his hand was a flush of movement as it found its way between her legs and palmed her pussy. "Your last option—you can buy that nigga some more time! Bitch, that's more options than the state of Texas gives a known felon. Pick your poison."

Chapter 3

"I got the high that'll take you to the sky!" a tall slim kid said before a nervous woman approached him. She wore a dingy trench coat even though the weather was too hot for such a thing.

"Let me see what you got, baby I want a bolo for thirty," she spoke before licking her dry lips.

Slim surveyed his surroundings before reaching behind and into his pants. The smoker watched as he retrieved the sack of drugs from between his ass cheeks. The savage move didn't bother her. She'd grown accustomed to the strange places the young block huggers hid their drugs in case of unexpected police visits. Slim pulled out a sandwich bag containing an assortment of beige stones.

"This that shit straight from the coca plant, baby girl. This strong like that shit Frank Lucas was up there sellin' in New York, but it don't make you all sleepy and shit," he boasted.

A skeptical look etched into the woman's features. She'd just begun the dance with crack and ever since her first two step with the unforgiving drug, she knew she'd be chasing that form of euphoria for the rest of her career of dancing with the rock stars. With a quick eye, she scanned the various sized rocks in the young man's outstretched hand as he impatiently glanced around.

"Let me see this one," she said and lifted a rock from the pile, before placing it in her mouth. *"Let me taste this shit to*

47

make sure it's real." She mumbled , and when she spit the stone back into her hand, it was noticeably smaller. "Naw. That shit fake!" she shouted and frowned.

Slim glanced down and noticed the missing piece and commenced to beating her ass. All the while, the eyes of adolescence captured every moment.

"Man, I hate school!" SunJay huffed as he and Messiah walked home from school. His young eyes were hungry as he watched the beginning of the crack epidemic unfold before his eyes. If he only knew then, that fast money was only a prelude to a horror movie that couldn't be contained, maybe he would've understood that being poor was merely a seasonal reality.

"SunJay, you always complainin', foo. School ain't that bad." Messiah laughed before sticking his foot out to trip him. SunJay saw the move and pushed him before he could follow through.

"I don't care what you talm'bout, Messiah. One day, I'm gonna quit school and..." His words trailed off as he revealed that he didn't have the slightest idea as to what he'd do next. Messiah laughed.

"And what, smart ass? What you gonna do after you quit school?" he jived him before shooting a quick jab at SunJay's midsection.

The question was neglected as the two boys slap boxed. They'd grown up fighting and their bond was solidified by busted lips and bruised egos.

"Y'all play too much!" a sweet young voice brought the match to an end. Messiah's eyes lit up at the sight of Justice, and SunJay laughed at the heat in his boys' eyes.

"Yea, and Messiah loves you!" he shouted with a laugh as Messiah pushed him. Porsha smiled; she too could see the intensity in Justice's gaze whenever Messiah was around.

The group began to walk toward Beckley Recreation Center. "I'm tellin' you, Messiah, I'm gonna be the biggest dope boy in the city!" SunJay professed with passion as he watched the older kids on the lock chase cars for the sale of their wares. "I think this stuff Blow gave us will—" he was in the midst of saying when Messiah elbowed him. Justice saw the move.

"What stuff, SunJay? What you talkin' about?" she asked. Messiah gave his friend a sharp look that made SunJay divert his eyes toward HiHo. Young hustlas hustled as if it was legal.

"Nothing," SunJay whispered. "I ain't talm 'bout nothing." Messiah was his savior.

"What you gonna be when you grow up, Justice?" Justice looked from one to the other; she knew they were hiding something. Her suspicious gaze trailed to Messiah, her eyes narrowing when he looked away guiltily.

"I'm gonna be just like that woman right there—the girl that makes boys go crazy over her and give her all their money!" Porsha spoke with admiration swimming in her eyes.

Messiah's gaze followed her outstretched finger, and not too far away from them, at the intersection of Beckley and Sanger, a white Monte Carlo pulled to the curb. A beautiful dark-skinned creature climbed from the passenger's side and after placing a large pair of sunglasses on her face, she turned to speak to whomever the driver was.

Messiah couldn't help but notice the thickness of her legs that descended from beneath a fire red mini dress. The instant he took in her sex appeal, Messiah knew there was something special about the woman. "Special in a vulgar way". She leaned inside of the window to retrieve something from the driver as she smiled at something that was said, and Messiah caught a brief glimpse of the small roll of bills before she stuffed them down into her bra. The car pulled away from the curb and disappeared into traffic, and before the woman turned and strolled away, she spotted the group of adolescents that watched her harsh reality of self-

preservation. She waved before turning and searching for her next trick.

"My mama told me that girls like her do nasty stuff for money," Justice said, bringing them out of their trance.

Messiah's eyes found hers before traveling to find Porsha. To his surprise, she stared back at him with an understanding that a child her age shouldn't have ever had an understanding of. She ignored Justice's statement.

"What you gonna be when you grow up, Messiah?" she asked. The group reached the playground behind the rec center as SunJay reached down to pick up a fallen branch, and pointed it at Messiah.

"Yea, what you gonna be when you grow up, Messiah?" he mimicked Porsha in a girlish voice.

Laughter resonated through the group as Messiah thought on it for a minute. After a brief moment, forever was born from his promise. Messiah's eyes connected with Justice's, and without blinking, he made a vow that would seal his fate. "I'm gonna be a boss when I grow up."

***

The old Chevy eased into the driveway, and Cedric had to double check his surroundings to make sure he was at the right house. The beautiful Cadillac threw him off as he wondered who it belonged to, but as soon as realization dawned on him, a chill ran down his spine. He hastily attempted to jump out the car without putting it in park, and it began rolling backwards. Cedric scuffed the top of his gators before finally getting the car into park, and bolting from the driver's seat, he only had one thing on his mind. I gotta get to Ruth!

He knew Blow was a snake in an expensive pair of gator shoes and him showing up to his home meant trouble. Cedric rushed to the door and found it locked. Using his key, he attempted to move as silently as possible, but the chain at the top of the door revealed that whomever had locked it wanted absolute privacy.

He didn't want to wake the dead, so he swiftly made his way around the house, gambling on the element of surprise working in his favor. He eased his thirty-eight special from the small of his back as he glanced around to ensure no one was watching, before he crept to the back door and tried the handle.

Eureka! he thought as it turned and eased the door open. Slipping into the kitchen, the aroma of simmering food greeted him, but it was the soft sounds of Betty Wright that contradicted any sense of danger.

Tonight, is the night that you make me a woman. You said you'd be gentle with me and I hope you will...

The soul oozed from the singer's voice. Confusion was a parasite inside him as he crept through the house he'd risked his life to provide for his family. Every step he took was torture, but it was Ruth's soft moans—the same sweet melodies he'd stroked from her for decades that navigated him to the place his soul would betray him at.

***

2010 - The Present

Messiah paused to study her. Black's eyes were distant for a moment, but the soft hum that emitted from her mouth sent chills through his body. It was Betty Wright's "Tonight is The Night!" Just as it started, silence took its place, leaving the mind to reflect. Messiah dropped his gaze, battling with what only time could heal.

The era of 1985-1986 was when muhfuckas down south was making the transition from stickin' needles in their arms in an attempt at chasin' that opium high, to stuffing their dignity and rent money into a pipe, searching for heaven within the putrid smoke of crack cocaine, and Messiah was a witness to the destruction of that Juggernaut that hunted

51

the ghettos all over America. As he watched Black find her way back from days passed, he wondered how God could promise Noah, the man in the Bible, that he'd never again allow a flood to destroy the world. Yet he forgot 'bout the niggas in the slums that could've never prepared themselves for the hurricane of crack cocaine.

Messiah gently closed the black book. His eyes studied his mother; she was a woman that had stood tall in a world, and time dominated by savage men.

"What—what happened next?" Her words were so low that Messiah had to make sure he wasn't imagining them.

"Did Ruth fuck Blow to save her family or—or did she sacrifices her life for theirs?" Curiosity slipped from Blacks lips.

Messiah smiled, "Which option would you have chosen?"

Black seemed to think on it for a moment, and while staring down at her hands, the answer came from her as she met the gaze of her son. "I would have acted as if I'd give him some, then gotten my hand on that gun and blew his brains out!" she spat as if she were back in that moment in time.

Messiah stood with a tired look on his face. "Well, we'll save that part of the story for tomorrow, Queen. Right now you need rest."

He laughed at the frustration on her face, before strolling over to help her into bed. The mental journey of the past had stolen her energy, and Messiah could always tell when her mind needed rest. It was her posture.

"But I'm not tired!" she pouted. Messiah smiled down at her before adjusting her robe and pulling the hospital sheet up to her chin.

"One day you're gonna remember doing this same thing for a boy that you loved dearly," he whispered before Black slapped his hands away.

"Stop fussin' over me and give me a real answer!" she demanded. She was still glowering when the door to her room slowly opened.

"Ms. Ridge, it's time for your meds, baby." Coffe's voice was low but strong. Both Messiah's and Black's eyes turned to her, and she smiled brightly as she held up a small paper cup.

"I don't mean to interrupt, but duty calls." She sashayed over to them as Messiah slid into his coat before collecting the black book.

"You good, Ms. Lady. I was just on my way out!" he acknowledged. As Coffe fed Black her pills, her vision fell to Messiah's hand.

"I see you've been reading her stories from the Bible, one day I'll have to sit in on one of your sermons." She smiled at him. A choking sound brought their eyes to Black in alarm.

"Are you ok, honey!" Coffe inquired, before helping her sit up and patting her back. Black sipped from the glass of water Coffe always kept full by her bed before clearing her throat.

"Yes, I'm ok, sweetie. Those lil pills just went down the wrong way. That's all." Her eyes went to Messiah who was making his way to the door after seeing she was safe.

"Messiah?" she called to him, her eyes not missing the bulge that was evident at the small of his back. Messiah paused and glanced at her from over his shoulder. He hated watching his super woman being fed meds as if she were some kind of crazy woman.

"Yea?" he spoke over his shoulder.

"You still haven't answered my question. What option did Ruth choose? Come on, don't leave me hangin' like that!" she whined.

Messiah smiled, persistence had always been one of his mother's strong points. He opened the door but before stepping out into the hall, Messiah left her with a jewel she'd

53

once given him when he was younger; a time he was more impatient.

"Patience is like bakin' a cake; you can't keep openin' that oven door, checkin' to see if that cake is done or not. Stop allowin' your anticipation to override time." Messiah's voice trailed off as he slipped from the room.

If he would have stayed for merely a few more seconds, he would have witnessed the moment of reflection his words had ignited. Bittersweet portions of Black's memories resurfaced as soft words slipped from her lips.

" 'Cause if you do, that cake gonna come out flat, just like your expectations of it. It's gonna be your fault because you were trying to rush time," she said, completing the old proverb.

A sad smile quirked the corners of her lips as her eyes found the confused expression on Coffe's face.

"What—what did you just say?" she asked Black. The older woman merely smiled as she rested her head against the pillow. Before her eyes drifted closed, she patted Coffe's hand.

"Oh, it's nothin', baby. I was just remembering an old proverb taught by an old fool.

***

A thick swirl of smoke snaked around SunJay's wild hair as he stood leaning against the cocaine white Corvette ZR1. The sports car vibrated with bass as the sounds of Trap boy Freddy's "Trap Scars" blasted from the fifteen-inch speakers in the trunk. SunJay was surrounded by a pack of shooters that itched to get it on.

He and Murda had snuck into the city a few hours ago, but rather than going to Dallas where Gator's reach was long, he figured the wild section of Stop Six projects would be a safe haven until they'd built a strong defense to face off with their foes.

The strange aroma of K2 hovered in their midst as drugs and money switched hands; the hustle didn't stop although each man surrounding them knew of the potential danger of thuggin' with Murda and SunJay. They were trained to go and all eyes were alert just in case the devil decided to make an appearance.

SunJay appeared calm. Yet, he was a man on the edge of a steep cliff and with the slightest shift of the wind he could evolve into a hail of bullets. Bloodshed called from the cracks in the streets of the metroplex and a trail of spent shell casings led to him and his shooters.

The vibration of his phone stole his attention, but before he reached for the horn, his eyes scanned the streets. Other than the kids of the ghetto running wild and the illicit activities going on in the breeze ways, everything appeared normal. SunJay grinned when he saw Lil Evil's number flash across the screen; he'd just sold the homie a brick of Girl and was surprised to see him back so quickly.

"The business, my G. You ready for another—"

"Noooo, honey," a sweet Jamaican dialect cut him off. SunJay's blood froze in his veins as his heart went out to Lil Evil's family. He knew the boy had died a horrible death. "De only thing him boy ready for is de morgue," she spat.

Keisha was deadly as she was sexy; she was a black Belladonna that oozed poison after every climax. SunJay was frantic as he snatched the burna off his waist, and Murda witnessing the action followed suit. Though he didn't know what the business was, he knew what the look in SunJay's eyes meant—danger!

He glanced around to see if he could spot the threat, and his alertness set off the rest of their circle. SunJay tightened his grip on the handle of the steel. He fucked wit' the boy Evil and wanted revenge. Heat radiated in his eyes as he and Murda's eyes locked in; they both knew the business.

"Bitch, you and your family are gonna die and—"

"Shsssh!" Keisha whispered into the phone. "Listen, can't you hear it, SunJay," she taunted him, but SunJay only heard the music that raged from the speakers of the Vette.

He signaled to one of his young boys to turn the music down before tapping Murda's shoulder. "I don't hear shit, bitch but—"

"Listen!" Keisha hissed like a deadly snake and that's when they noticed it.

At that moment, every detail of his surroundings became acute. SunJay's eyes bulged as a lime colored dot crawled up his leg, it paused on his crotch area, danced on his stomach, before finally finding residence between his eyes. Murda's eyes were wild as his high evaporated. He and SunJay knew that all it would take was the slightest pressure on the trigger and his spirit would be snatched from his body.

SunJay's life was caught inside the web of a hungry Black Widow and she was toying with her prey, while Keisha humming a strange melody in SunJay's ear.

"La, da, da, daa." Death colored each note as she began to sing of a girl in Kingston that had the power of seducing snakes. SunJay's nerves were at war as he gave a signal to his killers who stood there perplexed with their tools out.

Everyone's eyes were on the mark of death that shined in the middle of their boss's head. Frustration tainted Murda's expression as he signaled for them to snap out their trance and go find the treat. In seconds, all but one had dispersed in different directions.

A young boy they referred to as Loco was stuck, as high as Mars as he stood there oblivious to the Reaper's presence. That unawareness would cost him a fee too steep to pay the gatekeeper.

"It's de sound of death, SunJay. Him silent, him efficient. You were warned to stay out de metroplex, and Jah know I dance wid de devil, boy, but here Jah and him boy Murda stand," Keisha spoke through gritted teeth. The infrared played with SunJay's vision as his heart threatened to

hammer though his chest. "Twenty-four hours, SunJay. Jah and him boy have twenty-four hours to leave Dallas Fort Worth or Jah dead, mon. Hear me, pussy boy? Dead, mon," she vowed before the line went dead.

How the fuck they know I'm home! he thought before taking the phone away from his ear. He was about to clip it back to his hip when it vibrated with a text message. By de way, Messiah sends his love. It read with an emoji blowing a kiss.

SunJay's eyes lifted to find Murda staring at him curiously, and without warning, SunJay began to swat at his face as if he could rid it of the soft glow of the laser.

"Where it's at, bleed. You still see it?" he screamed, feeling like insects were crawling over his skin.

"Where's what, homie, fuck wrong wit' fam?" Loco's lazy voice asked, bringing their eyes to him.

Both men's eyes were wild as they found the green dot crawling up his neck. The Reaper wanted blood and as the infrared settled between the windows to Loco's soul, both SunJay and Murda was helpless to prevent the bloodletting.

"What?" Loco questioned when he saw the looks on their faces.

"Loco, listen, fam—" Murda began before a twin bead of light shown in his right eye as if he was being warned. He swallowed his words. Loco was on the verge of laughing, he assumed it was the toon blunts—another name for K2, they'd been blowing that had them wigging. He chuckled before relighting the half a stick he had left.

Fuck wrong wit these boys? he wondered— "If y'all boys can't handle this gas, y'all need to leave it alone, fam."

He laughed before taking a deep pull from the blunt. Yet, it was only when his vision recaptured them that he noticed the green dot dancing over Murda's face. The blunt fell from his lips.

"Saaaayyy, brah! There's a—" That's as far as he got before a silent popping sound disturbed his explanation. The

impact of the bullet rocked Loco's head back, causing a bloody, maggot-like matter to splash against the right side of Murda's face. Both he and Sunjay watched as gravity pulled the dead man headfirst to the pavement.

Chapter 4

Messiah reclined in plush interior of the backseat of a luxury vehicle, his eyes digesting the extravagance of every detail. From the white upholstering, the mini bar, and on down to the glossy wood grain that surrounded him, it was perfection, and with a sly smile, he brought the crystal glass to his face and inhaled the rich aroma of the aged cognac before taking a gentle sip.

He laughed to himself as he reflected. Not too long ago he was merely a poor nigga from the slums, but things had changed. He no longer dreamed of better days; Messiah was a boss, yet, the opulence caused him to frown as a deep regret dimmed his pride of self-accomplishment.

Damn, SunJay. This was posed to be us! he thought of his estranged brotha. With one last gaze around, Messiah exhaled.

"Money ain't everything," he whispered. As he reflected on how far he'd come from being that lil nigga that thought he'd had it all figured out, he admitted to himself that he'd been a fool all along. That was his reality as he parlayed in the back of his Bentley Bentayga, gazing out the window at a ragged man in tattered clothes.

"Should I let him know you wanna speak to him, daddy?" Paradise asked from the driver's seat. She was a stunning beauty with flawless skin. The African and Dutch blood in her veins gave her an exotic look that drove men over the

edge and that's one of the reasons she was also one of Messiahs top earners.

Messiah's eyes shot to her as if she'd just insulted his mother. "Bitch, did I tell you to do so? Furthermore, you know betta than to offer yourself or the service of your lips to any man without compensation. That includes cheap words, hoe," he spat before returning his gaze to the dirty man that stood outside of the HiHo store.

The man had once been one of the biggest names in the city before he fell from grace. Crack had stolen his money, cars, and hoes, and as Messiah took in Pimpin Maxwell's disheveled appearance, his heart hurt. Messiah watched as a group of young brothas walked up to the old pimp with laughter in their voice, and he had to crack the window in order to hear the exchange between them and his mentor

"What's good, Pimpin Maxwell? What you know good, OG?" the eldest of the group acknowledged, while extending his fist to the old man. Maxwell smiled a snaggle toothed smile, causing the solitary gold tooth in his mouth to reflect the sun as his scarred fist bumped the younger man's.

"Watch out now, Slick. Ain't nothin' changed 'bout ole Pimpin Maxwell's mojo but my hoe flow," he shot before doing a funky two step.

Messiah smiled a sad smile as he watched the exchange between the two different generations. He couldn't comprehend how the dirty man that stood out there could be the same man that had helped shape him into a Bonafide playa. One of the younger boys tapped his friend on the shoulder before turning to Pimpin Maxwell.

"Say, Maxwell, spit some of that pimp shit you always kickin'! That shit be fa real!" he shouted excitedly. Pimpin Maxwell smiled before extending his hand. Everybody knew his philosophy.

The game was meant to be sold, not told. The group of young boys laughed before the eldest took a quick glance around before reaching down into his pants. The other two youngins were alert as he pulled something from inside his boxers.

The group was attentive as the boy opened the sandwich bag and pulled a small stone from the pile of others. He handed it to the older man before he and his boys stood guard as Pimpin Maxwell pulled out a glass pipe, loaded the rock onto its tip and lit it.

All eyes were drawn to the tip of the pipe as it turned beet red under the flames, and Pimpin Maxwell sucked the foul smoke into his lungs. The boys stared in fascination as he held the funky smoke in, until his eyes went buck, and he exhaled in a dramatic breath. Pimpin Maxwell smacked his lips a few times as if savoring the drug

"That's some good shit, youngin, but it's nothin' like that Ray Charles shit we had back in the day," he stated before sticking his chest out as if he were the most dignified smoker in the world. Maxwell pointed the burnt end of the pipe at them as if it were a Magic wand.

"You lil niggas listen close 'cause I'm 'bout to learn you something," he jazzed before wiping himself down. "Once upon a time on the stroll, there was one of the world's slickest niggas, dapper Dan, head to toe in snakeskin. All he ever wanted was a stable of bad hoes, and a candy red Cadillac.

For that compensation, he mastered his conversation... until he was able to talk the skin off an animal's back. He vowed to get his hoes to the stroll whether they had to walk 'til they broke the heels on their stilettos, ran a marathon, or got his money in the Sahara desert arriving hunch back on a camel's back." Pimpin Maxwell paused to wipe sweat from his forehead.

The boys were caught in his concert as he performed with a flourish of his hands. "See, the Bible taught us the first lesson of a rogue hoe when that slick ass snake stepped to Eve. See, Adam was a square, so the only sustenance he could give the hoe was food, water, and a bed of leaves." Pimpin popped his collar.

"But that ole snake knew the truth about the tree of good and evil, and recognized the hoe in Eve. Knowing she had the potential to be a bonafied Jane. He scoped her before he approached her, and the moment Eve laid her eyes on that snake-skinned suit, she'd fallen victim to his game.

That ole snake slid up on the dame and said, "Hoe, why you standin' there gazin' awestruck at that tree, when you could be out there in that garden makin' a pimp rich!"

Eve looked at the ole snake as if he'd lost his ever lastin' mind before her lips parted and disrespected his spit. "No— no, ole snake,' God said: 'Thou shall not eat from the tree of good and evil or thou will be one dead bitch!"

As Pimpin Maxwell spit his jewels, a strange sensation washed over him; the feeling of being watched! And it was only after the feeling took root, that he spotted the snoop! The champagne-colored Bentley sat idly by the curb of the store.

Maxwell attempted to see through the tinted windows, but to no avail. The luxury truck was out of place in the hood, but he knew someone important was watching his show. So, with a smirk, he returned his attention to the boys, knowing they were merely lost in his fancy words and failing to grasp the jewels he spit.

"That cunning serpent laughed at the silly hoe. 'Bitch, God lied to your pretty eyes, but here's the grandest truth known to man. So, listen close, hoe, so your virgin ears can understand. God knows as surely as the wind blows that if you ate of that tree, you won't die, but your eyes and ears will be opened to see...the power of dick and pussy and you'll be open to some bonafide game from a pimp like me. I have a glorious room for you in a palace in Dallas— a closet filled with furs, minks, and baby, I'm talkin' Russian sables! All you gotta do is accept this here game and you'll be the object of stories and fables."

As Pimpin Maxwell spoke, his eyes captured a high yella stallion sliding from the driver's side of the truck, before strutting her fine ass to the back door. Curious, Maxwell's audience turned to see what had the old hustla's attention, and as soon as their eyes beheld the beauty and the beauty of that truck, their jaws dropped.

A dark bald-headed playa climbed out the back seat, his presence powerful as he stood next to the buxom beauty. Maxwell's chest filled with pride at the sight of his protégé.

Messiah sure done come a long way, he thought before bringing his spiel to an end. "Eve and the serpent— the first sin known to man. They'll say I deceived you with my tongue, and they'll speak of how you sold your soul for a piece of fruit. Yet, no one will acknowledge that God lied, but I gave you the truth, nor will muhfuckas speak of how you were standing naked out here in public when a pimp like me peeped the hoe in a girl like you!"

Pimpin Maxwell clapped the tallest boy on the back before leaving the young boy's slack jawed and lusting for that boss shit Messiah was on.

***

"Mama, mama! Look what I did!" Karma, her and Messiah's five-year-old daughter squealed as she ran into the laundry room.

Justice laughed after seeing her child frantically waving her coloring book.

"Hold on, baby, mama gonna look at it in a second. Let me—" she was in the midst of saying before noticing the red juice stains on Karma's clothes. "Are you serious, Karma!" she demanded as her eyes narrowed.

She'd changed her daughter twice already, but somehow Karma kept finding ways to keep her busy. Justice shook her head. "I got something for yuh bad ass!" she said as she tossed her last load of clothes into the washer.

Karma's excitement evaporated when she saw the stern expression on Justice's face. "I sorry, mama! I sorry!" she pleaded with watery eyes.

As she gave Karma the evil eyes, Justice had to fight to keep the smile from her lips. She could never stay mad at her baby.

"I sorry my butt, little girl. I got something for your bad ass," she declared. Fear ignited in the little girl's eyes until she noticed the playful mischief in her mother's smile. Her eyes got big when Justice formed claws with her fingers. "It's bubble time!" Justice growled.

Karma burst into laughter as she turned to run but was scooped up into her mother's arms. Justice kissed the top of her head as she headed for the bathroom. "Yuh father will be home soon and you'll be his problem then. For now, let's get you cleaned up; can't have you making me look like an unfit mother," she spoke in Karma's ear.

They'd made it to the top of the spiral staircase when the doorbell rang. Ms. Rosa, their housekeeper, exited the kitchen drying her hands on a dishtowel.

"I got it, Mrs. Ridge!" she shouted, and Justice smiled down at the older woman. She'd loved Ms. Rosa. She been a friend of the family since Justice was a little girl and now she was their housekeeper, as well as Karma's nanny.

Ms. Rosa pulled the door open and greeted the visitors, but after a brief exchange, she frowned. Justice observed the woman's posture become defensive before heated words were exchanged.

Alarmed, Justice headed down the stairs to investigate, but paused with a shocked expression on her face when sudden evil slipped into the room. A whispered pressure sounded before a spray of blood misted the air, and Ms. Rosa stumbled back as if someone punched her.

"What's wrong, Mami? Why you scared?" Karma's voice swam into the fog of her mind as Justice stared in horror. "Mami, what's wrong with Ms. Rosa!" Karma cried as Ms.

Rosa slightly turned as if she were attempting to flee, before crumbling to the marble floor.

When she landed, Justice noticed a dark hole in the center of her forehead, where a thick trickle of blood ran down her pretty face. When the visitor strolled into the foyer, their eyes met and a smile formed on the visitor's face.

"Hey, Justice. We need to talk."

***

While admiring the interior of the truck, Pimpin wanted so badly to pull the straight shooter from his pocket and smoke his disappointment away.

"You wanna know something, OG?" Messiah's voice was a bridge that stretched across the chasm of Pimpin Maxwell's urges, allowing him to separate the man in him from the fiend.

Pimpin's orbs trailed to him as he poured three knuckles of aged cognac into two separate shot glasses before handing him one.

"I was watching a compilation of all Richard Pryor's earliest standups and that cat was one funny muhfucka!" His words were low. Distant. Messiah took a sip from his glass. "The man was a success during the time black people were finally waking up to the fact of us being a superior race. You know..." His eyes trailed to the window. The city of Dallas, Texas flew by in a blur as Paradise pushed the SUV to its limit on 635.

"In August of 1963, Martin Luther King was talm'bout having a dream durin' his march on Washington, never knowing he'd get assassinated before he could see his dream turn to reality."

Shaking his head in dismay, he reflected on the perfect words to convey an imperfect truth. Without looking away from the skyline, he held up eight fingers. "Eight years after that speech in that same month, George Jackson was murdered in San Quentin while tryin' to escape those crackas torture."

Messiah's eyes found Paradise staring at him through the review mirror; she wanted to know where he was going with his tale just as bad as Pimpin Maxwell.

"Maxwell," Messiah called to him before turning his attention to the big ball of lights that sat atop of reunion tower. "On that same day, of August twenty first, my mother was born."

Messiah's words were bitter as he chuckled to himself. Using his pointer finger to stir the amber liquid in his glass, his eyes slowly turned to his mentor. "A few years after, here comes this nigga Richard Pryor. The man's jokes were so crazy that the same white folks that hated the mere color of his skin, fell in love with his humor."

Both men downed their drinks, and Messiah grimaced from the smooth fire before refilling their glasses. "You wanna know what made Pryor so hilarious, ole head?" he asked without waiting for a response. "Pryor's stand ups were so colorful because he told the truth of what it was like to be a dope fiend. In those jokes, Richard Pryor was introducing muhfuckas to the reality of free basin!

The man's jokes became the common ground niggas and peckerwoods used find that unity amongst races that Martin spoke 'bout in his Dream speech. Nobody knew the reality he'd create." Messiah emphasized his point with a pointed finger.

He saw Pimpin Maxwell stiffen from his reflection in the window. Messiah smiled to himself before taking a generous sip from his drink, and turning to study the man he once admired. Tilting his glass slightly in Pimpin Maxwell's direction, he gave his mentor the real.

"What homie couldn't have foresaw was that almost half a century later, our people are still chasin' that monster he introduced them to in those jokes. The only difference now is cocaine is no longer the rich white folks' drug of choice."

He swallowed the rest of his drink and sat the glass down before looking Pimpin Maxwell up and down in disgust. "Now it's rocked up and the people's self-appointed slave master!" he spat.

Pimpin Maxwell's pride cracked into a million pieces as he threw his drink back in one gulp. The liquid fire cascaded down his throat, leaving behind a tingling trail. He was the first to break the stare as he turned and gazed out the window. Tears of shame swam in his eyes as his reflection stared back at him from the tinted glass.

"You can judge all you want, cat daddy, but sometimes— sometimes, Messiah, life is a bitch with no loyalty. No matter how good you fuck her, nor no matter how well you treat her, one day she's gonna fuck over you with no remorse." Pimpin Maxwell's voice caught in his throat as he fought to hold on to the little bit of dignity he had left.

Without warning, Pimpin Maxwell's pride was nonexistent as he pulled out the burnt pipe he'd sold his soul to. He stared at it before allowing his heart to slip from his lips.

"The reflection of an ugly woman is one she hates to look at. Medusa was once a bad bitch, but in the end, Perseus defeated her with her very own reflection," he whispered. "Men live and die by the same vanity"—

The click of the safety being released on a pistol caused Pimpin Maxwell's head to shoot up and his attention to capture Messiah. The long tunnel of the barrel was dark as he stared into it, but Pimpin laughed bitterly before looking passed it and into Messiah's depths.

"Can't you see, young blood, I've been dead since the day I sold my soul. Messiah, a bullet can't do nothin' to me that this here pipe ain't already done to me."

He handed over the last ounce of his dignity. Pimpin Maxwell leaned forward and placed his forehead against the tip of the gun, and Messiah's eyes became pools of black water as he contemplated knocking his mentor's brains out

67

his head. Seconds seemed like eternity before he exhaled a deep breath and spun the tool around his finger until the handle faced Pimpin Maxwell.

"You still know how to use one of these, ole man?" he probed. Confusion played over Pimpin's face before he gingerly took the tool from Messiah's hand, and cocked it. Admiring its dull polish, a crooked smile formed onto his face.

"How could I forget, youngin? It's just like pimpin," he said and laughed before his eyes flickered to Messiah. "Once it's in your blood, it's in you," he confirmed as Messiah leaned back in his seat and rested his head against the head rest.

"Good, because you may need it to kill SunJay," he revealed.

Chapter 5

In these types of situations, one can never tell, Ms. Ridge, but if we can't find you a new heart..." the Asian doctor's words trailed. Black liked him. Dr. Sung's heart was pure and he truly cared about his patients. As he studied her for a reaction, he couldn't help but feel sorry for her. He'd grown fond of the brazen black woman after having watched her fight her way back from a coma, only to wake to the betrayal of her own body.

Black's mind was blank, but her most unforgiving reality was found within the truth; her heart was rotting with every second of the day. Dr. Sung studied her charts, reading over the notes from x-ray they'd done earlier that morning.

"There are donors—we merely have to find one that—"

"Don't!" Black cut him off with a raised palm and a disappointed glint in her eyes. "Don't play on my intelligence, Doctor." She allowed her stare to speak for her as her gaze went from him to Coffe. "Don't attempt to feed me no bullshit false promises or tell me that all will be well, Dr. Sung. I've been admitted to this hospital because there's something wrong with more than simply my memory. It doesn't take a physician to tell me that."

She sat on the edge of the hospital bed, she crossed her legs and gave them her brightest smile. "Doctor, I can't remember anything of my former life other than selling my pussy to survive." Black couldn't tame the seductive laughter that slipped from her at the sight of their expressions. "How

69

cruel can God be? No matter how hard I try, no matter how much I yearn to recapture just the smallest of memories, I— I can't."

A hurt look eased into her expression as she shook her head slightly, her eyes falling to the linoleum floor. "No matter how much you want to give me hope, Dr. Sung, it's your job to keep it real with me," she whispered before her eyes lifted to find the doctor staring at her with pity in his gaze. She hated it! She smiled a big artificial smile and spread her arms wide. "So?"

Doctor Sung admired her resilience, and with resolve blossoming, he nodded his understanding. Strolling over to the x-ray spectroscope, he spoke over his shoulder as he tacked the x-rays onto the board.

"Nurse Lawson, could you cut the lights, please?" he addressed Coffe before the lights went out. The doctor used a pointer stick to indicate a section of the first image. "These two images are of your brain and heart, but this first one is the only one worth speaking on." He glanced back to see if she followed him. "This is your heart, Ms. Ridge, and this right here—" he used the stick to point at the lower part of the image. "—this middle part is called the left ventricle. Its sole purpose is to receive arterial blood from the left atrium and—"

"Doc?" Black cut him off. "You have to dumb this down for me. Keep the Harvard words and just tell me what's going on with me. Am I gonna die?" She sat up straighter before crossing her arms over breast. "I'm a big girl. I can take it."

Dr. Sung nodded his understanding before turning back to the x-ray. "Your brain – the memory loss is a common occurrence with patients that awakens from a comatose state. Most often than not, memory loss is a symptom, but the only cure for that is time and a lot of love."

He looked from the image and found her stare. She nodded to let him know she followed him, and Doctor Sung turned back to the images with a sad smile. "Now, this blurry spot, Ms. Ridge, this is where your heart has begun to deteriorate. My guess is its due to your heavy drug use and poor care of your health," Dr. Sung stated before nodding to Coffe to turn the lights back on.

As soon as Coffe turned the lights back on, the small Asian man walked over to Black who had to fight the urge to look away.

"What I'm saying, Ms. Ridge, is that your brain will be fine. It merely takes time." He paused before placing his hand on her shoulder. Dr. Sung stared her deep in the eyes – "But your heart, if we don't hurry you up the donors list, your heart will expire before the time you need to regain those precious memories you crave so deeply."

***

Pimpin Maxwell stood staring with his mouth agape before his eyes found Messiah.

"This ain't good, young blood. This shit ain't—"

"Shut the fuck up!" Messiah raged with spittle flying from his mouth. "Let me think. Just let me think for a minute," he whispered.

Mrs. Rosa's blood pooled around their feet as he and Maxwell stood in the foyer of his home, their eyes trained on the older lady's twisted body. The hole in her head had gelled over and as Messiah stared into her vacant eyes, he wondered why people died with their eyes open as if the Reaper wanted them to witness their last moments on earth.

Messiah's heart was freezing in his chest, he could literally feel it blackening. He could feel the evil seeping into the only section of himself the streets hadn't yet tainted. His eyes were bloodshot as he turned his sights on the three men that he'd entrusted his family's wellbeing to.

He paid all three good money for security, but it was his relative Josh, the eldest and more respected one of the three that he felt the most disappointment in.

"Explain to me, J, how someone—anyone, could gain entry to my castle and not only murder a woman that's been like a mother to me, but also snatch up my—" he stopped, choking up at the mere thought of Justice's name.

Messiah fought to tame the volcano inside him that boiled just beyond the surface. He couldn't formulate the words that made his wife and daughter's kidnapping a reality. He rubbed his hands down his face as if he were attempting to wipe away invisible tears.

"How the fuck did someone live to snatch my only reasons for living right from under the noses of not only trained killas, but also the man that vowed to protect them with his very own life!" he spat in a deadly tone.

Messiah and his cousin stared at each other in a clash of reflection, both men remembering the promise. Josh fidgeted.

"I—I was out getting some things Justice needed from the store and when I returned, this—this is what I found," he stuttered as he nodded to Mrs. Rosa's cold form.

Messiah stared at him for a few seconds before a bright smile contradicted the wounded animal that stared back from his irises.

"It's Gucci, fam. I understand that in this life we live, we can't prepare for everything, no matter how calculated we are." His eyes touched each of the three men before he made his decision.

"E-man, you and Miko get this mess cleaned up," he demanded, nodding to the body. *"Be good to her, homie. That's family."*

His eyes then met his older cousin's. *"Josh, you get some of the men together and y'all get out in the trenches and see what you can dig up on the disrespectful mu'fuckas that violated my house! I want my family back like yesterday, Blackman, or you'll be the first example for the streets."*

Josh moved without question. Pulling his phone from his pocket, in seconds he was barking instructions into the *receiver. Messiah moved as swift as a panther, as he eased the steel into his palm. Pimpin Maxwell witnessed the act, but before he could wrap his mind around what was about to transpire, Messiah's finger squeezed the trigger – boom - boom – boom!*

Three shots sung their deadly tune, the gun jumping with each explosion. Josh's head burst open as he pitched forward and fell headlong to the ground as Messiah calmly walked over to the dead man, thick, blurry tears slowly zig-zagged down the right side of his dark cheek.

He hurt internally, not only for his stolen family, but also his aunt that he knew would mourn her slain son. E-man and Niko were petrified; each man wondered who'd be next as Messiah's finger molested the trigger twice more.

"For the lives of my family, someone has to answer in blood," he whispered before his black eyes found Maxwell. "For them to get passed the gate and up on those I trusted to guard my family, OG, that tells me that whoever committed this sin had to be someone my guys trusted. This was an inside job, Pimpin Maxwell, and betrayal is suicide!

* * *

Two Days Later

Black sat in the hospital's outside garden with her knees pulled up to her chest. Her gaze was fixated on a bright yellow and black butterfly that had just landed on a tulip. Its big wings fluttered as a gentle breeze cooled the days heat. Her mind was miles away, and only when a shadow hovered over her did she realize she had company.

She looked up to find a well-dressed Messiah, but the pure white linen suit he wore contradicted the rugged unshaven appearance of the man. He held the black book in his right hand, but it was his eyes that stole her breath away. They were tired, cold, and filled with a sadness that Black drowned within.

She steadied herself as she climbed to her feet and studied him, hating the hurt in his eyes. She wondered what could be so bad that it caused the usually well-poised man to unmask the raw emotion they both knew was best kept hidden from the eyes of this cold world.

Without much thought, she pulled him into a tight embrace, and it was at that moment, in that enclosed garden where her heart was decaying by the seconds, something special happened. As Messiah held on to her as if she was his only life source, he cried. The man cried the melody that only a gangsta that had finally realized the true debt of the streets could cry.

As Black held him and took in his pain, a moment of reflection rocked her galaxy.

"Mama, mama. I'm home! The little boy screamed as he ran through the house with SunJay at his heels. She looked up from the dying man in her arms—her teary eyes capturing the ones of her son and his friend in an unspoken tale of cold days to come.

"Mama, mama. Are you ok?" A hoarse voice penetrated the fog, and as if being pulled from a distant place, Black came back to the present. When her and Messiah's eyes collided, she flinched before hurriedly releasing him, and taking a step back. Pressing a hand to her chest in shock, she became short winded. Concerned, Messiah studied her, but her mind was miles away.

Those eyes—the little boy—it was Messiah in his younger years. The woman—it was the same woman she'd seen in that old wrinkled picture. It was me! she thought.

"Talk to me, ma! Do I need to get the doctor?" Messiah asked, while already turning to go find help. Black reached out and grabbed his sleeve .

"No, I'm ok, baby. I—I just…" Her words trailed before she waved him off and composed herself. Their eyes danced—"Are you ok?" she inquired. She'd found a piece of

her past in that brief reflection and her heart felt suddenly heavy.

Messiah wiped his tears with the sleeve of his suit jacket but didn't attempt to mask the turmoil that sailed through his veins. He slightly shook his head "no" before taking a seat on the ground and gazing out at the mass array of flowers the hospital used as a therapeutic treatment for their patients.

"They took them, Ma. They stole what means the most to me," he whispered as his eyes became lakes.

Messiah's vision was drowned in murky waters as he gritted his teeth. But he lost that war as twin rivers raced down his face.

"Who—who is they, Messiah? Who did they take?" Black asked perplexed. Messiah watched the yellow butterfly lift its wings, flapping as it hovered in place. Rather than answer her, he patted the ground next to him and opened the book. At that moment, a strange thought struck him.

If you want to hide something from a black man, put it in a book. The old adage sparked an urge in him to read the story of the Black book. For some strange reason, he knew he'd find the answers to his problems there—inside the story his mother had recorded on those pages.

***

1985

The smell of sex greeted him as he pushed the door to his room open. Slowly, as if in a lucid state, Cedric watched the door swing inwardly and that's where he found the greatest betrayal he'd ever experienced.

"Nooo, Ruth. Not you," he whispered as his heart cracked in every piece.

He stood there stuck in place as Blow pounded himself into the treasure he thought he'd never have to share. Having Ruth doggy style, Blow's trousers were down his ankles, and he had Ruth's robe bunched up around her waist. Their backs were to him as Blow reached forward and grabbed a handful of her curly Afro, and with each stroke he spat a different vulgar word of bliss. "Shit! Goddammit, woman," he growled as Ruth moaned.

"Hu—Hurry and oh, hurry up and nut, Blow!" she cried out in a heartbroken cry, but to Cedric she was encouraging the madman. From his standpoint, the act appeared receptive—intimacy! Yet, only if he would have walked a little closer, he would've witnessed the wetness of Ruth's face as tears escaped her eyes.

She hated herself for what was taking place, but in her mind, it was a small price to pay for the safety of her family. "I'm gonna kill you snake sons a bitches!" Acid fell from Cedric's mouth. The temperature in the room shot up as Blow rolled away from Ruth while she scampered to cover herself.

"Oh my God! Ced, what are you doing here? I—"

"Bitch, this my house. What you mean what I'm doing here?" he spat as his vision blurred.

Ruth's heart broke at the water in his eyes. She couldn't believe she'd sinned against the only man she loved. "I—I didn't mean it like that, I—it's not what it looks like!" Ruth stumbled over her words. Cedric snorted a bitter laugh.

Why is it that whenever a mu'fucka gets caught doin wrong, the first thing they say is it's not what it looks like! he wondered.

The gun shook in his hand as he swung it back and forth between Ruth and Blow. Ruth hurriedly lowered her robe while attempting to explain, but her words sounded like gibberish. Cedric's broken heart couldn't grasp rational thinking as the gun trembled.

They all knew that of all the foul characteristics of Cedric's nature, being a killer wasn't one of them, and that alone gave Blow courage. "Now, Ced? Don't you do nothin' stupid, cat daddy. You know how these hoes are," he said, *trying for a rational plea, but his words only pushed Cedric over the edge.*

"I loved you, Ruth," he admitted before swinging the gun towards Blow, and squeezing his eyes shut, he pulled the trigger.

Click, click.

Confusion and fear were powerful as his lids cracked open and he eye'd the gun perplexed. What the hell? he wondered. Slapping the pistol against his palm, he tried to figure out why it didn't fire, but that was his worst mistake.

"Cedric, nooo!" Ruth's frantic scream was the last thing he heard before the loud explosion of Blow's gun echoed in his ears.

The first bullet tore into his stomach and just as he doubled over, the second one ripped into his shoulder. Cedric crumbled to the floor as Blow yanked his pants up proper, fastening them while cursing himself for not hearing Cedric enter the house.

Now he had to kill him and explain to Gator how his little head had caused him to murder the one that was in debt to him. As soon as he was proper, Blow turned to finish Cedric off. He lifted the burna with the intent of getting the job done, but Ruth truly loved her dude.

"Nooo!" she screamed as soon as Blow squeezed the trigger.

She'd caught him off guard when she jumped in front of Cedric. At the last moment, Blow's aim diverted a bit, but not enough! Ruth screamed in agony as the slug grazed her, but luckily, that's all it did.

She felt the burn at her side as she fell to her knees clutching the wound. It was minor but surprise and never being that close to death before caused her to hyperventilate.

"Please, please. We'll get you your money. I have kids. We—" Her words got lost in her throat as her eyes misted up. She struggled for the words that could soften the heart of the devil.

Blow studied her. Knowing he was on borrowed time. Someone had to have heard the shots and called the police and going to jail wasn't on his agenda. His eyes were piercing as he and Ruth faced off; her mind raced with thoughts of it being her last day on earth while his mind was on a totally different plane.

Damn, she has some good snatch, he thought as he weighed his options. "How do I know you won't rat to the pigs the moment I leave?" he asked.

Ruth saw hope, and in that hope, she vowed on her son's and daughter's life to keep her mouth shut. "I'll tell them that someone tried to rob us and Cedric tried to be a hero. I'll tell them that the robber had on a mask. Just please just leave!" she begged.

Blow was hesitant, his gut screaming for him to eliminate the possibility of a future witness, but after a moment's deliberation, he went against his it. With a threat to return if she so much as mumbled a word of what transpired in that room, Blow left behind ruined life.

As soon as she heard the sound of burning rubber, Ruth hurried to the phone beside their bed and called 911. "We need help! My husband has been shot by a robber! Please!" She cried, but when Cedric gasped for air, the phone fell from her hands. Dazed, she rushed over to him and fell to her knees. Her heartache was far deeper than her physical wound. Cedric was fighting for breath as thick trails of blood bubbled from between his lips. Ruth knew he wouldn't live long enough for the paramedics to get there, so she did the only thing her heart allowed her to do.

Gently pulling Cedric's head into her lap, she cradled him as she prayed. "It's—it's cold, Ruth," Cedric whispered before coughing a spray of blood into the atmosphere. Ruth rocked him back and forth as she cried.

"It's gonna be alright, baby. You'll be okay, Ced. Just— just don't talk." Her voice was thick with internal pain. The distant sounds of sirens made her smile even though she

knew the war was lost; the ambulance wouldn't make it on time.

"Show my—my boy how to survive." Cedric's weak voice confirmed her suspicious.

She stared down at him as her tears fell and splashed against his face. His lips were a bluish color when he smiled at her, but just as quick as the smile came, it vanished, giving birth to a sadness in his gaze.

"Why, Ruth? Why you betray me, baby?" he whispered so low she almost didn't hear him.

Ruth's tears were plentiful as they bathe her face. She tried to explain that her act wasn't one of betrayal, but one of love and sacrifice, but Messiah's voice echoing from the living room made her pause and look up.

"Mama, I'm home!" he screamed. She could hear him and SunJay racing through the house, their laughter, a strange addition to the heartache residing in that room.

"Messiah! Don't come in here, baby." She didn't want her son to see his old man in that condition. Ruth knew death was a permanent stain on one's soul; it couldn't be washed away no matter how many times one scrubbed it or prayed.

"Mama, what you doing in—" Messiah ran into the room but pulled up short when he found his first introduction to a broken heart.

Tears blurred his vision as he stared down at this mother holding and rocking the only man he knew as Superman. SunJay wasn't paying attention to his friend's silence until he stepped into the room.

"Why you—" He way saying before the scene before him robbed him of his innocence. Cedric was just as much his father as he was Messiah's, and that shit did something to the young child that years later would be his justification for the darkness in his heart.

"I'm soooo sorry, baby. I'm so, so sorry!" Ruth cried as her eyes bore into her boys.

With blood staining her robe, she harbored the pain in Cedric's eyes when he asked his last question, and she wanted him to know that she'd never cross him like that. Her eyes dropped to his in an attempt to convey just that, but as her eyes looked into his, no matter how hard she searched, she couldn't find his spirit there. Cedric had checked out on them without saying bye.

Entry 2
The walls of a man's mind can become a cage that imprisons him; they'll speak to the soul of that man. It's a room that will show the reflection of one's self even though it's a room with no mirrors.

Chapter 6

2 years later – 1987

As Messiah stood on the corner of Illinois Street, it was three in the a.m. and the night was frigid. He cupped his numb fingers in front of his mouth and blew warm breath on them in hopes of regaining feeling, but that only served to make them moist.

The night was filled with shadows and the fiends were out seeking that momentary escape from their problems. Danger danced in the air of the night as Messiah exchanged vice for compensation. Killers, robbers, and predators—pimps, hoes, and other night walkers hugged the corners of those trenches as if they were long lost lovers reunited after years of being apart.

But the truth was, neither man, woman, nor street corner gave a damn about even the smallest conception of love. It was 'bout the love and greed of the all mighty dollar and at that time of night in the section of Oak Cliff the natives knew as "The States", not even the devil was respected.

"Say, what you doin' out here, lil daddy? You too young to be out here on these cold streets this late at night," a foul unkempt man asked as he approached him.

Messiah observed him from suspicious eyes; He'd never seen the man 'round those parts and just by the man's posture, Messiah could tell he was a shady cat. Subconsciously, Messiah took a step back, but it only served to enflame the stranger's motive.

Yet, if the strange man's eyes would've been more observant than filled with greed, maybe he would've recognized the man staring at him from those adolescent eyes.

Maybe if the evil intent in him weren't so great, he would've noticed SunJay slip from the darkness with the small .22 clutched tightly in his hand.

"Let me see what you got there, lil man, I'll give it right back. I promise." The rugged man tried to sound convincing. Messiah could see SunJay lurking.

"I ain't got nothin, man. You need to keep it pushin', Mister." The fear in his young eyes empowered the older man and as quick as the strike of a viper, his scarred fingers were around Messiah's slim neck.

The young boy's eyes grew as large as an owl as the dirty cat used his free hand to pry his fingers open and snatch the last few baggies of dope Messiah had left from his pack. An ugly grin stretched across the man's face once he saw the beige stones.

Bingo! he thought, and knew where there were drugs, the money wasn't too far away. He was elated. The game God gotta be smiling down on me for me to have stumbled cross a lick so easy! he thought. "Where the money at, lil nigga? You gonna either give it to me or I'm gonna—" POW! The shot echoed through the night.

The man's eyes grew large before the drugs slipped from his hand and he was forced to release Messiah. With a shocked expression plastered on his face, he reached for the burning sensation that seemed to be intensify in the center of his back.

Confused, he turned to face off with his attacker, and what he found stunned him. SunJay smiled up at him as he aimed the small pistol.

"He told you to leave him alone, but you wanted to be a bully," he whispered. As he held the tool steady, SunJay looked like an overgrown chucky doll as he stepped forward

and aimed a little lower than his intended mark; just like the big homie, Juvenile, taught him.

"You little piece of shit, I'm—" the man began, but SunJay smiled sinisterly before his finger twitched on the trigger once, twice, three times.

Each bullet struck the man high in the chest, but the fourth and fatal shot struck him in the throat. Instantly, the man's hands shot to his neck, blood poured from him, and in a desperate attempt, he tried to turn and run, but he only made it a couple of steps before collapsing.

"Help!" Justice screamed hoarsely as she shot up in bed. Her eyes were frantic as she surveyed her surroundings, and sweat glistened on her brown skin, causing her nightgown to stick to her. She tried to calm the wild beating of her heart.

It was just a dream, Justice. Just a dream, she told herself, but knew her dreams were never merely just dreams! Her grandmother had the gift of premonition as well, it seemed to only develop in one out of each era of their family. Sometimes the gift skipped around for decades, but it always came. Justice's had came early , and she hated it.

Glancing to the alarm clock, a moan escaped her lips. 2:34 a.m., school was hours away and she'd barely fallen asleep. Justice slipped from her warm bed before pulling the moist nightgown over her head, and hurrying into a pair of sweats and t-shirt, she searched for her coat.

Spotting it, she slid it on before glancing back at her bedroom door to ensure it was closed. She headed to her window and pushed it open, the cold breath of the night stealing her breath.

Justice shook it off before climbing as silently as possible, she knew that if Leah or JoJo caught her sneaking out the house, she'd be the walking testimony of a true ass whoopin'. Yet, as soon as her small feet touched the ground, caution and fear evaporated.

She had to find Messiah and warn him. It was dark— scary on the cold streets of Oak Cliff as she ran up Sanger, passed the gym and headed for Illinois Street. Her breath clouded in front of her as she bent the corner.

It always surprised her to see how active the streets were that late into the night. Her family tried to protect her from that harsh reality of life, but her love for Messiah slowly but surely introduced her to the uglier sides of shit.

Ever since his old man was slain, Messiah and his family struggled. Justice hated the hand life had dealt the young boy and as she raced up the block, she knew inside her small heart that shit would only get worse the second she saw Illinois.

"Justice! Justice! What you doin out here at this time of night, girl!" a concerned voice called to her.

Justice slowed her stride, panic resonating within her as she recognized the woman's voice. Turning, she watched the tall dark-skinned woman approach her. It was Mrs. Black, Messiah's mother.

The pretty woman wore clothes that were so short and tight that Justice wondered if they once belonged to a girl much shorter and smaller. Outside of the banana yellow dress she wore, the only thing that protected Black from the cold was a thick faux fur, and the heels she wore were so high that Justice couldn't understand how she walked in them. Yet, beyond her wonder, Justice felt a deep sadness to see how far Black had fallen from grace.

After the death of her husband, times had gotten hard for Ruth and no job wanted an inexperienced, Black woman. Black became desperate and, in the end, began to search for love in all the wrong places.

Life was stealing her self-worth and Black had given into the notion of by any means necessary. She begged God for help, but he seemed to ignore her pleas. Not even a full year after her husband's death, CPS had taken her baby girl away, and if Messiah hadn't been staying at SunJay's, he'd have been taken too.

Heartbroken, lost and in despair, Black wandered right into the sick intentions of Sauvé. The rest was history, and as Justice drank in the woman's beauty, she wondered how God could allow an angel to fall from grace only to land in the filth of the ghetto.

Black placed a long cigarette between her lips and inhaled deeply. The red glow on the tip of it grew bright before she exhaled a long stream of smoke.

"Lil girl, JoJo would beat yo' sneaky ass if he found out you were out here in these streets. How old are you now, Justice, ten?" she asked as she studied the younger girl.

Justice fidgeted. "No, ma'am. I'm eleven now, Mrs. Ruth," she responded. Black nodded before shivering slightly, the night's chill was vicious but there was work to be done. She pulled her coat a little tighter.

"You need to turn your lil ass right on back around and get back to that house before Leah or JoJo finds you gone. These streets ain't no place for no eleven-year-old, baby. Believe me," she warned with a hint of mirth in her tone.

Black liked Justice, she could tell that she was different from the other fast-tailed, young girls of the ghetto. It was something—something about the young girl she couldn't quite put her finger on.

"I—I can't, Ms. Black. I have to find Messiah," Justice whined as she impatiently moved from one foot to the other.

She seemed nervous but even more, her glancing from Black to the direction she hoped Messiah to be, caused Black's eyes to narrow. She wondered if she and Messiah were fuckin'.

"What's wrong, Justice? What that lil bad mu'fucka do now?"

Justice was about to respond when a brown Buick pulled to the curb and the passenger's window rolled down. "You workin' or what, suga?" a gold toothed, Jheri curl wearing cat called out.

Black's eyes narrowed in suspicion as she studied him. "Hey there, handsome, one's nice, but twos a trip to heaven." A sugary sweet voice stole their attention, as a thick, white woman approached from around the corner. Creamy was gorgeous, and being one of Sauvé's top earners made her and Black fast friends.

"It depends," Jheri curl responded skeptically. Creamy smiled big as she winked at Black.

"Depends on what, suga? It's either you want to treat yourself or you're gonna cheat yourself."

She seduced him as she strode over to the open window. Black's dark eyes trailed from the reality she'd fallen so deep into until they found the beautiful, young girl that was staring—witnessing the lower levels of life a woman would travel to in order to provide.

Their eyes met, and Black was still woman enough to feel shame at what she'd become as she took a drag from the now short cigarette.

"Messiah's lil black ass is up on Illinois with SunJay," she spoke around a lungful of smoke. For a split second, Justice could see the pain of a black woman exuding from her stare as they studied each other in a moment of understanding.

Black knew it was foul of her to allow her eleven-year-old son to be out in the wee hours doing what they both knew he was doing, but Messiah had to grow up the best way he could. The boy had to find his niche in life since he'd learned young that mama and daddy wouldn't be there forever.

"Come on, Black. You know Sauvé will be around soon, so let's get this quota, girl!" Creamy spoke over her shoulder as she slid into the passenger's side and gave Jeri curl her most seductive smile.

Black watched as the man handed Creamy a few bills before the white woman reached over, pulled out his limp dick, and went to work. With a sad nod of her head, Black looked from the truth of what her life had become and found Justice once more.

"Tell my baby I said mama loves him and I'll see him when I get back home, and Justice?" she called to the young girl before turning and heading for the car. "Hurry and get back to your house before you give JoJo a heart attack," she spoke over her shoulder before climbing into the back seat of the car to turn her last trick of the night.

***

"Man, you not ready yet!" SunJay spat before blowing on his hands and rubbing them together. The chill of the night caused his teeth to chatter. He'd sold almost half his pack, but had lost the hunger of the hustle when the night had grown cold and unforgiving.

Gunshots sang out in the distance causing both boys to look in the direction the sounds of death came from. Yet, it was a common occurrence in the city, so neither boy knew the fear that should have been present in the company of dark times.

"Man, you still got work, SunJay. You lazy, dawg," Messiah laughed after making a sale to a white woman.

"Bro, if you don't hurry up, I'm gonna leave you. It's too cold, Messiah!" SunJay pouted and buried his hands in his pockets.

Messiah opened his frozen fingers, he had ten more dubs to sell and he'd be finished with his entire pack. Wiping snot from his nose, Messiah looked to his boy. SunJay had grown to become a young wolf, but at times, he complained too much.

"Nigga, I don't need you to hold my hand, go home!" he shot, and SunJay's stare instantly became heated.

"Who you talking to, boy?"

Messiah laughed, knowing what would get his brother's blood flowing. "I'm saying, bro. You soundin' like a lil bitch right now. Hurry up, Messiah. Imma leave you. It's cold, Messiah!" he teased, mimicking his boy in a girl's voice.

SunJay instantly posted up on him. "Nigga, I'll show you who's the bitch! Step into my square, fool!" he challenged before knuckling up.

Messiah was seconds from obliging him when the panic of a familiar voice filled the air. "Messiah! Messiah!" Justice screamed as she ran towards them.

Both boys dropped their hands and turned in surprise. They both knew Justice had no business being out at that time of night, and for her to risk the wrath of JoJo, it had to be something bad. She was out of breath when she reached them, sweat causing her skin to almost glow under the streetlights. Messiah rushed over to her and stared perplexed.

"What you doin out here, Red?" he asked, addressing her by the name he'd affectionately given her because the hue of her skin always bordered the color.

Justice caught her breath before responding. "You—we need to leave here. I had a bad dream, Messiah," she rambled.

Messiah's young eyes studied hers. He was the only one outside of her parents that she'd confided her deepest secrets to. And even though she'd never went in depth of how her dreams worked, Messiah trusted her more than he trusted anyone in life. He nodded his head.

"A'ight, ma. Give me a few more minutes to get these last few—" – he said before Justice latched onto his arm.

"No!" she demanded in defiance. The heat in her eyes was one Messiah had grown to understand; it meant she wasn't tryin' to hear shit and wanted what she wanted.

"Man, Justice, chill! Ain't nothin gonna happen to us, especially while I got this!" SunJay said, before reaching underneath his shirt and pulling a black .22 from his waist.

Messiah's mouth fell open at the sight of the gun, but Justice froze in horror. Her breathing quickened as flashes of her dream streaked through her mind like flashes of lighting during a storm. Messiah had to hold on to her to keep her from falling.

"Put that up, SunJay! You scaring my girl, fool!" he spat. SunJay laughed as he tucked the pistol back under his shirt.

"Man, let's go!" he responded before turning and walking off without waiting on a response. Messiah turned Justice to face him.

"You ok, Red?" Justice nodded her acknowledgement before glancing around. The street was silent—almost deserted outside of a few bums. Maybe she'd overreacted. Maybe her dream had been merely that—a dream. She felt foolish as her eyes met Messiah's.

"We need to get you back to your house before Mrs. Leah or JoJo finds you gone – you know they'll blame me." He smiled before taking her small hand into his, and turning to follow SunJay. But just as they were leaving, a gruff voice caused Messiah to pause and look back.

"What y'all doin' out here this time of night, lil daddy?"

Messiah observed the unkempt looking man as he approached them. The hair on the back of Justice's neck stood up as she slowly turned to meet the eyes of the same man she'd saw in her dreams.

Messiah felt her tense beside him and gave her a quick glance before returning his stare to the shady appearance of the stranger. He'd never seen the man before and wondered why Justice was so affected by the man's presence. Wishing SunJay hadn't left, he noted when the man's hungry stare fell to the piece of the sandwich bag that was evident in his small fist.

"Let me see what you got there, lil man. I'll give it right back." The rugged man tried his shot, but Messiah's apprehension caused him to take a step back.

"Run, Messiah! Run!" Justice's sudden scream was like a horror flick playing in slow motion as a look of surprise

registered on the man's ugly face. The young girl's scream confused him, but he knew he had to act fast.

His hand was a blur as he reached for the young boy's throat, but Justice pulled Messiah's arm as hard as she could, causing the man's hand to come up short. The two kids bolted into the night and just as he was about to give chase, a loud popping sound tainted the night, followed by a searing pain at the center of his back.

Surprised, the would-be robber reached for the intensifying pain in his back as he turned to see what was going on. He could feel the blood pouring down, but what caused him to panic was the evil sneer on SunJay's face.

"You shoulda left them alone," he whispered as he aimed a fraction lower than his intended target.

"You, lil piece of shit. I'm gonna—" he said, stepping to the young boy. SunJay's laughter was drowned out by the explosion of the gun as he squeezed the trigger not once, not twice but three times, each bullet knocking blood from the man's upper chest.

The fourth shot hit him in the throat and as he began to fall to the stained pavement, SunJay stared wide-eyed—fear and fascination becoming one as he watched the life leave his first body.

"Come on, Brah! We gotta go!" Messiah shouted as he snatched him by the arm. He and Justice had stopped when they heard the shots. Justice knew the conclusion and warned Messiah to go back for his boy. Now, all three raced towards their place of safety, but SunJay couldn't get the thirst of his first murder out of his mind. He felt invincible!

***

Porsha slept in her panties and a long t-shirt, and being a wild sleeper, part of her blanket had slipped away from her body. At thirteen-years old, she was blossoming early. That was a curse to a girl born to an absent father and a mother that was so blinded by love, she pretended not to be privy to the sins of her live-in boyfriend, Rock.

That night, just like every other night that Porsha's mother went to work on the graveyard shift at the hospital, Rock snuck into the girl's room and stared at the form of Porsha.

He was a sick dude, and was convinced his perversions were helping the girls body blossom. He never contemplated what his sins would create in the girl, a thirst too powerful for any one man to quench!

***

Entry 3:

Some of the most vital pieces of game I've ever learned in life is what I want you to hold as dear to you as a gangsta does his gun. Never fall in love, Messiah. Love is a fool's game with invisible heartaches. You can't see them in the beginning because love in the beginning is a beautiful storm with soft rain and irrational promises.

Love will blindfold you, baby. It will convince you that you're supposed to love your significant other more than you love yourself. You'll eventually become so consumed by it that while being in love, and giving all you have to that person, when they kiss you softly on the neck, you won't feel their fangs sink into you.

You'll be oblivious to the poison they've injected into you until there's no more you, but a whole lot of them. That's the truth of an actual vampire. Messiah, true love died back in the 50s and late 60s. A time of our great grandmothers.

A time it wasn't natural for a black woman to not be married. A time period when it was dangerous to be alone because seeing strange fruit hanging from oak trees was a reminder of the pledge of till death do us part.

True love died with the black power fist—it died when your father was stolen from me. Never forget my next words, child 'cause they'll be your only sense of faithfulness along this wild journey of life.

A man is a dirty dog that has no qualms with doing his dirt in public, but a woman is a sneaky bitch that you'll never figure out. Have you ever noticed that a dog will shit and piss in public, not caring who's watching as if the world was his personal restroom?

Yet, how many times have noticed a cat shit? Sure, you've seen its droppings, Messiah, but you've never caught the feline in the act. The feline has more etiquette than the beast. Women are sneakier. My point is, baby, no matter how docile or well-mannered some women appear, they have secrets.

There's only ten percent of woman that are strong enough to tame their pussy and that's because they were bred to be virtuous. Their mother or father invested that into them over time. The other ninety percent of women could care less for self-value.

They'd rather get ahead rather than be respected. Messiah, there's only one woman that will never leave or forsake you. There's only one person, period, who will stand by your side no matter the weather, son. That once in a lifetime kind of woman's name is your game!

She's your experience, the one you sit and learn from while enduring those growing pains. She'll get you food and shelter when your stomach is touching your back, and she'll find you refuge from those dark nights.

Your game is your con, your hustle. She's the only one that will stand solid rather you win, lose or draw. She'll never cheat because she's you. So, always master your game, baby. Add to her. Make love to her.

If you never forget a heartache or betrayal, if you never forget the pearls you obtained from life, you'll grow to understand success. You're gonna meet thousands of women that will claim to love you with all their souls, Messiah, but no one has ever seen the soul nor know if it truly exists.

Quiet your heart and create a castle in your mind. Love is a beautiful notion for a man that believes in fairy tales, son, but one thing about fairytales is that they're all based off a sort of magic. Whenever someone is trying to make you believe in a fairytale, all you have to do is ask yourself when was the last time you've ever witness true magic?

Mama

Chapter 7

1987

"Whore," Sauvé spat as he counted the wrinkled bills for the third time. His hot stare lifted from the money and fell upon Creamy "What's this?" he hissed with a perplexed look on his face.

She shivered. "I know, daddy. I know it's chump change compared to what I usually bring in, but it was a bad night and that scumbag Detective Spinks was out patrolling the stroll. Lavish's girl Strawberry was arrested tonight and I thought—"

Smack!

Sauvé's hand swept across her face with brute force. Spit flew from her mouth along with the excuse she was attempting to use for slacking, and the sound of flesh against flesh echoed throughout the house, causing Black to flinch in the midst of slipping her foot into her heel.

She watched as Creamy rubbed the side of her face that he'd back-handed. Her eyes fell to the floor as they clouded over, but Sauvé's cold heart held no compassion as he stepped in her space.

"Whore, I ain't asked you to think, blink, or shrink on my cash flow." He had a disgusted look on his face as he looked down at the money. "Look at this pitiful shit!" he shouted before throwing the sweaty bills in her face.

Black knew how crazy he could get when he felt slighted and she wanted no parts of it. She quickly slipped the remaining heel onto her foot and attempted to stand, but Sauvé's sharp eyes caused her to plop back down onto the couch cushion.

Even though Creamy was a top-notch bitch and brought in no less than twelve or thirteen hundred a night, Sauvé felt he had to keep his Stacy Adams in his girl's asses to keep them motivated. His philosophy was "one lazy hoe would create two lazy hoes and before one realized it, the entire stable would be sleepin' instead of freakin'."

"Sasha, Candy—you hoes get your asses out here and I'm talkin' speed of light fast," he demanded the audience of the other two women in his stable.

Candy was the first to appear from the back room, as naked as Eve was in the Garden of Eden. Her pretty titties and freshly waxed lowers lips caused Sauvé to pause in admiration.

"Yes, Daddy? I was just getting ready to—"

"Quiet, hoe. Ain't nobody asked you to move your lips," he growled. Sauvé was a sure chump for pretty women with sex appeal, and that was one of the many sins of his pimpin'.

When a nigga keeps his dick in his hoe, she's bound to lose respect for him as a bonafide mack and begin to see in him the same traits she sees in every other sucka thats a wussy for some good pussy—a trick!

Candy's expression was one of confusion. She'd assumed Sauvé had called her to see what was taking her so long to get ready for work, but as her eyes took in the red hand print on the side of Creamy's face, she turned her gaze to Black for an explanation.

Black quickly shook her head in warning; she'd hate for her wife-in-law to be next. The twenty-three year old was way too pretty to be subjected to Sauvé's guerilla tactics.

The young Puerto Rican girl was slightly bowlegged with a permanent tan. Her long black hair hung just inches from the beginning of her waist and even though she was slim *thick, the plump ass that she'd been blessed with was enough for any man to seek a tryst for the right price.*

"I was just doin' my makeup, papi. I swear," Sasha rambled as she rushed into the room having the same impression as Candy, before she witnessed the handprint on the side of Creamy's face.

Sasha was a five-foot six model thin white girl. She wasn't as blessed as the others in terms of body or soul, but what she lacked in structure, she made up for in beauty and an untamed sexual liberation. Sasha was more outlandish than most porn stars.

Her eyes were quick as she assessed the scene before her. As she studied the bruise that had formed on the side of Creamy's face, she tried to stifle the giggle that threatened to crawl up her throat. She despised both Creamy and Black, believing that they thought they were better than her.

They act like they're the only bitches born with pussy between their legs, she thought; lowkey jelly of her wife-in-laws.

"Yes, daddy?" she asked as she turned to Sauvé . He silently strolled over to the couch where Black sat, before he took a seat on the imported cushions and crossed his leg over the other. He contemplated a just punishment for Creamy, that would be a sufficient message to his other ladies.

"See, bitch, the thing about a slackin' hoe is her being a bad example to this pimpin'," he spoke lightly. The purring of his all white Persian cat caused his eyes to fall to the fluffy furball as it padded into the room and leaped into his lap. The only bitch I can trust, he thought as the feline curled up as he softly stroked her behind her ear.

Lifting his stare back to Creamy. "Pick up my trap, whore," he demanded, and without hesitation, the white girl bent over to do as she was told. "Naw—naww, hoe—" Sauvé chuckled menacingly and Creamy froze. "Not with your hands, bitch. Pick it up with your mouth. Each bill," he sneered with a crooked grin.

Embarrassment canvased her face, but Creamy knew better than to test his pimpin'. On hands and knees, she used her lips and teeth to capture each and every sweaty, nasty dollar before placing them in her hand and attempting to get up.

"Naw," Sauvé stopped her in her tracks. "Crawl over her on your hands and knees and give it to me," he growled as the cat purred softly in his lap.

Anger erupted in Black's eyes; she despised him. At that moment as her friend crawled like a dog, Messiah came into the room, and froze upon witnessing the act of Creamy's dignity being stripped away. His eyes lifted to Sauvé; man and child eye wrestled in a heated match of hate and curiosity.

Sauvé hated the boy for being Black's child, and wanted to rid him from the equation and push Black Diamond to her highest potential. He knew she'd be the best hoe to ever fuck for a buck if he could get rid of her brat. Messiah on the other hand, was more curious of the life than he was about the malice dancing in Sauvé's eyes.

"Messiah, get back in that room, baby. I'll come for you in a few minutes," Black told him, but Messiah was too enchanted with what his young eyes was capturing. "Messiah Dior Ridge, did you not hear what the hell I just—"

Smack!

The sound of Sauvé's hand against her face was dangerously loud.

"Whore, you don't know when to speak and when to close your dick suckas. This my domain!" Sauvé spat, before his dark eyes returned to Messiah. The dance of murder reflecting from the young wolf's stare caused Sauvé to chuckle.

"What's up, lil nigga? You got something to say?" he growled.

Messiah was so angry that he shook, and Black hurried to her feet and over to him.

97

"It's ok, baby. Mama's ok." She tried to assuage his temper, but little did she know, Messiah was the most dangerous person in that room.

"That's what I thought, young blood. You're just a big ole mama's boy," Sauvé taunted him while absently stroking the kitten's spine. And when his gaze fell to the still kneeling Creamy, he reached his manicured hand out with his palm up. After she placed the moist money in his hand, Sauvé sneered. "Now stick out your tongue, baby," He requested with a softness to his tone that didn't match the glare in his eyes.

Confusion tainted Creamy's pretty features, yet she complied. Sauvé took two of the bills, straightened them and one at a time, rubbed them down her tongue.

"I'm gonna use your tongue to clean each and every one of these bills, bitch. And after you've licked the filth from each one of 'em, you're gonna take your funky ass back out there on that track and get my money out your ass. This is your last freebie, whore!" he growled as he scrubbed another bill down her tongue.

Creamy gagged at the sweaty taste of the money, but she knew better than to pull her tongue back in no matter how foul the taste. Sauvé turned his eyes to Black.

"And Black Diamond, since your funky ass don't know when to be a mother and when to be a hoe, I'm gonna remind you, who you are no matter how long you carried that bustard child in your womb before you spat him out your pussy. Get over here and make daddy smile," he spat before stuffing a wad of bills so deep into Creamy's mouth, she choked.

Everyone present, save for Messiah, knew what "make daddy smile" entailed. Sasha giggled before a sharp look from Sauvé made her compose herself. Black's pleading eyes shot to him before turning to her son.

"Don't do this, Sauvé . Not in front of my—"

"Hoe, are you being disobedient?" He demanded with narrow eyes.

Messiah was confused as his eyes bounced back and forth from the man he despised and his mom's. Black dropped her head in shame as she gently squeezed Messiah's shoulder and lifted her chin. She held on to all the dignity a woman in her position could have as she made her way back to the couch.

With each step, she toyed with the idea of going for the razor she kept under her tongue, but her thoughts were too conflicted.

If I kill him, Creamy and the other girls would be free. Messiah—I see the way Sauvé looks at him, I've lost one child, I won't lose another. If I don't kill him, he may kill one of us. If I do kill him, who will take care of us? He's all we got, she thought as she took a seat beside him.

Blacked looked over at Messiah as she unbuckled Sauvé 's pants.

"Messiah, go outside, baby. I'll—"

"Whore, you got one more time to try me!" Sauvé spat in a deadly whisper. "Get to yo business, bitch, and I betta like it!" he spoke as his heartless eyes rose to find Messiah, before he leaned back with a smug smile. "Let the lil punk watch, he may learn the difference between a hoe and real mother!"

Sauvé laughed softly as Black freed his dick. Tears clouded her vision—God can't be real, she told herself. It finally dawned on Messiah what was about to transpire, and evil bled into his stare.

"Mama, you don't have to be scared of him. I'll take care of you!" he shouted.

Black was a wounded lioness as her wet eyes turned to him, and smiling a sad smile, she leaned down to "make daddy smile". Messiah flung the door open and before he bolted out into the sunshine that contradicted the darkness in his world, he left the pimp with a promise that couldn't be taken back.

"I'm gonna kill you, Sauvé ! I'm gonna kill you! I promise!"

***

"How you did that shit, lil homie? Show me how you did that shit again!" Juvenile asked excitedly. He was a big homie in the Beans, the natives dubbed the ran down apartments.

SunJay had just replayed the scene of him earning his first body. He looked up to the big homie, and wanted him to know he was 'bout that action.

"I told that nigga, 'this the Beans, nigga'!" he lied while forming a mock gun with his fingers and pretended to pull the trigger. "I shot the fool in his back, face, head, and both eyes!" he shouted, and Juvenile dapped him up as if the deed was the livest shit.

"Yea, lil one. You're gonna be the next to carry the torch round here." He laughed as another cat joined them. They were standing in the back of the Butta Beans by the dumpster when Bozo approached. A teenage kille, he loved his hood just as much as the project like complex loved him.

He locked B's with Juvenile and SunJay before taking a freshly rolled blunt from behind his ear, and after sparking it, Bozo took a deep pull from the sweet. He held the weed smoke as long as he could before that burn caused him to cough it up, and with tears in his eyes, he passed it to SunJay.

"That's that corn, lil bro. That west Dallas corn that'll help you grow," he said, laughing.

SunJay had never smoked in his life and wondered if the funny looking cigarette was like the stuff Blow had him and Messiah selling. He wanted to pass on the experience, but when he looked to Juvenile, he knew he was being tested.

Fuck it! he thought as he put the blunt to his lips. *"Just suck the smoke down your throat, lil dawg,"* Bozo encouraged him.

With one more glance at his mentor, SunJay pulled from the blunt as hard as he could. The cherry on the tip glowed bright and as the smoke entered his young lungs, his body instantly rejecting the foreign intruder. SunJay coughed so hard that he dropped the blunt, and laughing, Juvenile bent to retrieve it.

"You certified now, lil nigga. You thuggin' with the squad tonight," he spoke before hitting the blunt.

***

"Man, what you talm'bout? Franklin Roosevelt was a bad sum bitch!" Cotton shouted as he stared at his cards.

It was Friday and as usual, Pimpin Maxwell was hosting one of his famous card games in the back of his gambling shack. It was a house that had a shabby exterior, but the interior was a sight to behold, and was even furnished with imported comforts to appease the lions that frequented it.

Crap games, poker, and every other vice that entailed the possibility of leaving with a bag could be found in motion in either of the many rooms Pimpin Maxwell had turned into his vision of Vegas. Rooms of Lust was the handle the streets called them.

At that moment, Pimpin was engaged in a mean game of poker and the convo about politics was heated. The four men playing were successful at their crafts, and had no qualms with parting with a buck. Pimpin Maxwell scanned his cards; the hand of Texas Hold 'Em was tense. Depending on the fall of the cards, someone was gonna walk away with twenty-five bands.

"Yea, Franklin Roosevelt is the reason you old muhfuckas and ya mammies get social security," a short Puerto Rican

businessman added. Pimpin Maxwell snorted before chomping down on his cigar he loved so much.

"Yea, the muhfucka gave us social security, but he also upped the taxes on our black asses. For all the good he did, he sucka punched us by way of the government regulating our muhfuckin businesses. Now, every time a nigga with too much melanin in their skin starts a business, he has to hustle for his family and for big brother!" he said, snorting again.

The cigar juice was bittersweet in his mouth as he laid his cards down and looked up. "All I got is a measly two of a kind." He shook his head in disappointment. "Now, Reagan was a man after my own heart—a Klansman that respected niggers. The man was a gangsta at heart." He laughed as JoJo laid his cards down with a smirk on his face.

The man had a royal flush. The looks on the other men's faces were confirmation as the Trinidadian raked his money toward him.

"Well, gentlemen, looks like I'll be stuffin' a few more coins in Justice's piggy bank." He chuckled, after seeing that he couldn't be beat.

Pimpin fucked with JoJo, though he was as dangerous as a famished lion, JoJo was a good man. The two of them had been close ever since JoJo and his people had made the move to the states from the islands.

Pimpin Maxwell hated to see him leave, but knew that every man had their own journey to embark on. And as much of an asset as he was, JoJo wasn't any different.

"So, it's official; you're movin' on to greener pastures, huh?" Pimpin Maxwell asked as he leaned back in his seat.

Just as he turnt so Bear could light the cigar clenched between his teeth, JoJo paused the count of his earnings to look up at his old friend and smiled. It touched him to hear the hurt in the man. They'd come up in the trenches together, but their history wasn't enough to stop JoJo from getting his family back on track.

"Yea, my brotha Miko just came here from Trinidad and Leah wants to move to Houston to be closer to her family," he revealed.

Smoke clouded in front of Pimpin Maxwell as he nodded his understanding, knowing he'd never see the old man again. JoJo wasn't a fan of phones and neither was he. They were crocodiles and though crocodiles ate from the same swamp, they respected the laws of the murky waters.

"By the way, Roosevelt was the better president. He was more for the ghetto than those other chumps that played God up there in the oval office. The people liked him. That's why he was the first president to break the no third term tradition.

"That's bullshit! That's what that is," Pimpin Maxwell *chuckled, before leaning forward and dumping the ashes into an ashtray.* *"See, the man opened the doors for social security and even looked down at the slums every now and then, but muhfuckas were still broke!"* He laughed before *standing and placing both hands on the top of the table. Pimpin Maxwell made eye contact with each man before speaking his piece.*

"See, Ronald Reagan was a hustla. Reaganomics was some shit only a nigga with a bankroll mind could think of. The muhfucka was hustling and sellin' weapons to Iran for the freedom of them U.S. hostages that was being held in Lebanon. He was a slick muhfucka, but he was good for the economy." Pimpin picked up his glass of scotch and sniffed *the aroma.* *"Remember back in eighty-four when they had that big ole tax cut? Matter fact, Reagan forged the bipartisan coalition in Congress that year that lead to the enactment of those big ole tax cuts. Yea, Roosevelt blessed the old folks with social reform, but it was that Klansman Reagan that signed the reform bill that provided long term solvency to Roosevelt's system."*

JoJo laughed before standing; he was gonna miss the debates between him and his boy. *"Yuh lost yuh mind, boy. It wasn't a good thing the man signed the enactment. He—",*

"Pimpin?" Sticking his head through the door, Slim Jimmy interrupted his spiel. All eyes went to him. *"Ole Blue is outside the spot actin a fool, drunk again."*

Irritation blossomed over Pimpin's face before his gaze drifted to JoJo, and his old potna slipped his favorite thirty-eight special from his waist. They'd warned Blue about bringing heat to the establishment; one too many times.

With a nod of his head, Pimpin Maxwell bit down on the end of his cigar before heading for the door. All the while, he was praying that he didn't have to murder the old bastard. Hopefully, a simple old fashion ass kickin' will sober him up, he thought to himself.

***

"Imma kill that nigga! On my daddy's life, I'm gonna kill him!" Messiah swore.

He was in a heated daze as he walked the streets. He didn't know where he was headed, but he knew he had to get as far away from that house as possible. Ever since they'd been evicted from their home and was forced to live with that evil cat, Sauvé, Messiah had to face off with a reality that would one day take him under.

Black's lonely nights and crazy days were his new life, but he had a plan. Black didn't know he'd been stacking his chips, and all the bread he'd hustled off the packs he and SunJay had gotten off of Blow, he'd stashed in a secret spot.

"Muhfucka, you sons of bitches can't ban Ole Blue from the shack! After all the big cheese I done blew up in this sum bitch, y'all mean to tell me that I can't get up in the joint?"

His drunken rant captured Messiah's attention, and it was then that he spotted a group of men who seemed to be trying to calm a drunken man.

Scanning the men's torrent ganders, Messiah's young eyes paused when recognizing JoJo standing ti the side of the drunk. The OG's orbs were studious; quiet fires.

Messiah shivered at the coldness of his gander, recalling a time he'd gone over to Justice's house to see if she could play and JoJo answered the door. His cold stare seemed to shoot straight through to his soul and Messiah would never forget the evil he witnessed in the man's pupils.

"Now, Blue, I've warned you 'bout being loud and disrespectful at my place of business. I've known you since bell bottoms and butterfly collars, so I'll give ya this last pass free of charge. But if you don't quiet down and find ya way back home to ya wife Lula May, I'll be forced to disregard all those years of history between us," a soft voice carried on the midday breeze.

Messiah's eyes found the speaker and for the first time ever he was in awe. The man was a boot black, slightly muscular playa, and though he merely stood five-eleven, his aura made him seem seven foot tall. The sun caught the big diamonds on his left and right pinkies, but it was the man's attire that Messiah wanted a better look at.

Taking tentative steps close, he imagined himself dapper within the same garments. The tones complimenting the hue of his dark skin, Pimpin was in tuned with playerism, but the demon staring out from his hazel eyes, told a wicked tale!

"You threatening' me, Maxwell?" the drunkard spat.

Messiah hurried and took cover behind one of the many cars that lined the block and watched the dance of pride between the men. The man in the white suit stepped forward and smiled; pointer finger and thumb absently stroking his manicured goatee. Though his smile was disarming, the storm in his pupils contradicted his attempt at diplomacy.

"Blue Johnson, you're the second friend of mine that's accused ole Maxwell of threats." Pimpin Maxwell's eyes roved over Blue. "Now, when have you or anyone else ever known me to do somethin' so barbaric? I'm a gentleman at all times, pimp friend of mine."

With a quick glance at JoJo, Pimpin Maxwell seemed to have made a silent decision that disappointed the islander.

105

Strolling over to Blue, and placing his hands on his shoulders, Pimpin' stared him deep into the windows of his soul.

"Go home to your beautiful wife, Blue. You're drunk,"— He whispered, but with pride blindfolding him, Blue Johnson's drunken stupor wouldn't allow him to walk away.

"Get your filthy hands off me, snake muhfucka!" he spat before slapping Pimpin Maxwell's hands away.

The atmosphere grew tense as the goons surrounding the two men went for their heat, but Pimpin Maxwell's raised palms calmed the hail of bullets that were sure to rain down upon the stubborn man. Pride always blindfolds men from rationality, and more often than not, there's dire consequences for that weakness.

JoJo spat on the ground as the taste for blood swam through him. It fed the dark of his heart. He craved the recoil that followed the squeeze of the trigger. Pimpin Maxwell held his smile as he stepped backwards.

"Still the same ole Blue Johnson, you've never knew the difference between a crocodile and a lizard. Get on home, Blue, you'll thank me in the morning." He nodded before turning his back to his old friend. His squad followed suit.

Neither man saw him as a threat, but Messiah saw the flash of the big pistol as he slid it from under his shirt. He was bringing it up when Messiah shouted— "Watch out!" He surprised himself.

Life seemed to take on a slow-motion effect as the air became electrical. The group of men spun on their heels, but it was old man JoJo that saved Pimpin Maxwell from a bullet in his back. His hands were quick and like magic, his trusted thirty-eight appeared in his right mit, before it coughed a ball of fire that hit Blue Johnson between the eyes.

The crackle of the shot echoed throughout the day, followed by a stunned moment. The wind was soft as the look of surprise became forever frozen in time on Blue's face. The nickel plated .45 fell from his hand as his body tilted backwards, and landed crooked in the spot he'd just stood in.

Each man captured the execution from a different view, but being behind the man, it was a messiah who'd been cursed to see he exit of the bullet exploding from the back of Blue's noggin! All eyes had fallen to Blue's corpse, all but two sets. As Messiah vomited, Pimpin Maxwell and JoJo's gazes were fixated on the young boy. Neither were strangers to death, and expecting the kid to bolt in fear, they wondered if a child's innocent blood would have to be splashed against the cold streets of Dallas, Texas.

With a quick glance at his dead friend before turning his eyes back to Messiah, Maxwell was grateful for the youngin's outburst. He didn't know where the boy had come from, but he'd saved his life.

"You boys get this cleaned up—" he nodded to the body, before tapping JoJo's shoulder. Without a word, they headed in Messiah's direction, "come on, JoJo, let's see if the kid has a guardian angel."

***

Entry 4:
"Yes, I had fallen from grace, Messiah. I met the wrong man at the right time. At least it was the right time for him. He took advantage of my love, and though I'm not ashamed of loving him, I'm more in wonder of why I did.

I was so naïve back then. I believed him when he told me that fucking men for him would be the ultimate way to show him that I loved him. I believed him when he claimed it would prove how down I was.

I sold my body to whoever could pay the right price. I became a high-priced whore and to my credit—I was damned good at it. Before I knew it, I'd fallen so low that I became a full-fledged dope fiend. Yet, beyond it all, as I think of the man you've become, I realize that every sacrifice was worth your survival.

You are a prince, baby, and one day will be a king. I know you may disagree with my lifestyle, but one day you will see that love is more than the shit you see on TV. All that happily ever after shit only exists in Cinerama.

What people don't focus on is the "after" of that cliché. It stands for after all the bullshit you'll have to endure in order to obtain happiness. Fuck happiness, Messiah. When you get your bag up, you'll be able to buy dreams, happiness and a bad bitch!

Mama

Chapter 8

1987

"Whew, girl! It's hot as hell out here!" Creamy exclaimed. She'd just met up with Black by Lipsticks, a gentleman's club. They'd been out there humpin' for their wages and both women had earned their weight in gold. The two breadwinners felt the envy of the other hoes on the stroll and reveled in it, yet, Black was a numb vessel drifting upon foreign waters. She didn't know where the current was taking her, but she craved for her destination to be far away from the nightmare that had become her reality.

"Yeah, it is hot, ain't it?" she responded absently. Creamy caught the tone of her voice and with a glance, she could see the shine fading from Black's eyes. And knowing "the life" was a cancer that can't be medicated, Creamy shook her head in pity.

"Look, Black Diamond, I know this life ain't what you're used to, and anybody with eyes can see it's killin' you. Every bitch wasn't created to be whore, suga. You need to get out the life before it becomes so much a part of you that it steals more than merely your self-worth," she proposed, searching through her purse for "something" that seemed important to her.

They were on the stroll in North Dallas and the sky was grayer than it was blue. The sun would trade places with the moon soon, but the life of a whore had no sense of time.

"Girl, Sauvé would kill me!" Black laughed bitterly, Her eyes trailing to Creamy as she rummaged through her purse. "What about you, Creamy? Why won't you leave the life? You're way too beautiful not to have an escape plan," she inquired.

Creamy was truly a beautiful white woman. She was a thick six-foot amazon with strawberry blonde hair, and though her assets weren't as firm, her curves placed many in the mind set of Ice T's wife, Coco. When she walked, her ass and titties vibrated, and the goddess always added a little more umph to her strut.

Her lime green eyes held a sadness when she looked up at Black. With a half smile, Creamy pulled something from a slit in her purse that she'd cut to hide what she didn't want to be found.

"This life is all I know, Black. My mama was a whore and I'm gonna die a whore too, suga. I was born to fuck, Black Diamond," she replied, opening a Pandora's box of truth.

Black frowned at the admission, not feeling her philosophy. "But you don't "have" to live like this, Creamy. You choose—"

"Girl, please!" Creamy held up her palm to stop her. "I'm tellin you that I love to fuck and "enjoy the life!" I couldn't imagine living the life of a square bitch, I'm not the domestic type, suga."

She laughed before nodding toward the alley beside the club. Without waiting for a response, Creamy walked off, leaving Black with a pitying expression. Yet, after a moment, she shook her head before following the crazy white woman. Creamy sat her purse on the stained pavement and glanced around suspiciously to ensure they weren't being watched.

A big smile stretched across her face as she waved a metal pipe in the air as if it were a prized possession. Black watched as she stuffed something inside it before lighting the end of it, and sucking the smoke deep in her lungs. After holding it in for as long as she could, Creamy blew the funky taint into Black's face, causing her to scrunch her nose in disgust.

Black had smoked weed and even tried cocaine in her younger years, but she'd never smelt the foul odor from the shit Creamy was smoking. The expression on the white woman's face was a mixture of ecstasy and shame; a contradicting reality, yet a real one nonetheless. Creamy held the pipe out to Black and the woman's heart warned her to run as far away from the white girl and her form of escape as she could.

"Girl, it ain't gonna kill you, it's nothing like heroine or none of that addictive shit," Creamy enticed her, and skeptically, Black's orbs bounced from the blackened stem, and back to her friend.

"What's that shit, Creamy? I don't—"

"It'll take all that pain away—make you forget all that shit you hold in bottled up—" Creamy played on her psyche.

Black deliberated for but a moment before, with a trembling hand, made the biggest mistake she'd ever made! Reluctantly placing the pipe to her lips, she allowed Creamy to spark the flame.

"Suck the smoke down, suga. Let it take all your pain away," Creamy played devil's advocate.

Black's resolve shattered as she inhaled the thick smoke and as soon as the foreign taste filled her lungs, she knew she'd just sold her soul to something that wouldn't give it back. As her face went numb, her worries, all the self-pity— it all evaporated with the exhale of the clear smoke.

For the second time in her life, Black Diamond, birth name Ruth Ridge, was in love. This time around what she couldn't have known was the abuse her new lover would take her through. Her new lover was possessive and at times disrespectful. Yet, at all times, he would be ready to take her worries away.

Black's new husband was crack cocaine, and upon their first date, he pledged 'til death do them part. Black could *have never fathomed how slowly nor how deeply that pledge would run.*

***

Pimpin Maxwell maneuvered the big 1979 Deville through the city as his thoughts flipped through the city streets of his mind. When he and JoJo'd approached Messiah, they found him on his hands and knees up chucking his lunch. And expecting him to flee, Pimpin's old knees were ever so grateful when he'd emptied his stomach, before standing to face them. Wiping the back of his hand across his mouth, his eyes fearless!

Pimpin's eyes lifted from the puddle of bile at the boys feet, and bore into his gaze. Embarrassment was evident on Messiah's face, but Pimpin chuckled; vomit was a natural reaction for one who'd just witnessed something so savage. He commended the kid for that being his only reaction.

"I know yuh, boy. Ain't cha Cedric and Eddie Ruth's boy?" JoJo asked.

Messiah's young eyes bounced back and forth between the two men in an attempt to gauge their intent. Maxwell noticed the boy revered JoJo a lot more than he did him and JoJo's next words told the tale.

"Yuh come over to the house for my daughter, Justice," he confirmed, his eyes studious. Pimpin Maxwell laughed—

That's why the boy seems so tense; JoJo done scared the boy shitless over his baby girl, he thought.

Yet, Pimpin's second thought stole the mirth from the situation. His eyes roved over the kid, he'd heard that Messiah and his moms had fallen on hard times since Ced had been killed, and his heart went out to the lil souljah as he digested his appearance. The dirty clothes and busted XJ900's on his feet told the truth of how fucked up things had become.

Pimpin Maxwell had had a thing for Black back in the gap, and though she was his man's lady, lust was a stronger force than loyalty in many situations. Especially when the two people sharing it, is able to close their eyes and pretend that if the secrets can be kept, it justifies giving into what should never been considered.

And on a cold night in November, he and Black had done just that! Sinned, and vowed to keep the secret to protect everyone involved. In the end, Black had become distant and Pimpin Maxwell respected that. With that in mind, Pimpin's vision trailed to where Messiah sat, gazing out the window, and he vowed to himself that he'd make it his business to create better days for the boy and his moms.

"So, you're Ced's boy, huh?" he asked, trying to strike up a conversation, yet Messiah didn't respond.

He didn't know where they were headed but at that moment, as long as it was as far away from the fuck boy Sauvé as possible, it was good with him. He kept his eyes on the passing scenery where it seemed to be fiends and dope pushers on every street corner.

The lights were beginning to come on, and though Messiah knew his T-Jones would be worried, he just couldn't face her at that moment. He kept reflecting on how broken she'd looked as she sold her soul for that nigga Sauvé, and it set his soul aflame!

"You don't talk much, do you?" Pimpin was persistent. "Look, boy, you're rollin' wit' Pimpin Maxwell, so you gotta have more words than just 'yes' or 'no' in your vocab."

Still, Messiah said nothin'. He was wondering how he could make things better for his Queen, he'd watched her struggle and didn't like it. He wondered if the money he'd saved up was enough to buy her a house.

How much does a house cost?" he thought.

"How'd you know my pops?" he asked suddenly. Pimpin Maxwell worked the grain expertly as Earth, Wind, and Fire played softly in the background.

How does one explain to a child that his father was a rotten son of a bitch, but we were good friends? Wouldn't that mean that I'm a rotten son of a bitch as well? he wondered for only a moment before deciding to shoot straight.

Pimpin knew one couldn't begin a friendship with lies, for once that first piece of deceit was spoken, there could only be a "foundation" of deception to build upon.

"Me and your old man came up together back in the day, youngin, I also know ya T-lady and her brother Herman Earl," he revealed, and for the first time since he'd gotten in the car, Messiah's orbs trailed to him. He studied Pimpin Maxwell with curiosity dancing in his gaze.

"Then why haven't I ever seen you at the house?" Messiah asked, a hint of skepticism in his tone.

Pimpin Maxwell glanced over at him before returning his attention to the road. "You know what a pimp is, Messiah?" he inquired as he pulled into the entrance of his high-rise apartment building.

Messiah's eyes beheld it, and his jaw dropped in awe! It was the most beautiful place he'd ever seen.

"Yea, a pimp tells girls what to do and if she doesn't listen, he slaps her," he spat in disgust.

Pimpin Maxwell's head snapped to him. "Who the hell told you some shit like that, cat daddy?"

He laughed uneasily as he punched in the code to the iron gate that was supposed to protect the residence from the boogyman, but in all truthfulness, it was merely another decoration used to entice the upper class to pay the theee thousand-dollar deposit.

As the gate began to roll open, Messiah verbalized some shit that damn near caused Pimpin to drive the customized gold grill of his new Caddy into the iron bars.

"Nobody had to tell me that, that's just what Sauvé does to my mama and the other girls when they don't move fast enough for him."

Chapter 9

The Present - 2010

Pimpin Maxwell felt sick to his stomach as he eased the midnight blue Jag to the curb of Gigi's. It had been years since he'd been to the club, but that wasn't what caused his bones to ache and his stomach to burn. His soul cried for merely the taste of his friend that had kept him sane for the past few years.

But as his eyes captured the beauty of the luxury car he now owned, looking down at the Giorgio Armani suit he wore while he wiggled his toes in the soft skinned loafers, he was reminded of the promise he'd made to Messiah.

For the chance at reclaiming his glory, and for the sacrifice of trust that Messiah'd placed into the old pimp, Pimpin Maxwell vowed to never again place a pipe to his lips. It was a fool's promise, but regardless as to how far he'd fallen from his glory days, one thing everyone could place their bet on was ole Pimpin Maxwell's word.

Though he was Dapper Dan down and had a pocket full of money, Pimpin Maxwell felt self-conscious. He knew he would be the center of attention. The fiend that became a dream! He laughed at thought.

After seeing him slip from the Jag, the ladies reckless eye balled him, and though the dope had stolen a lot of his handsomeness, the ex pump still had his flare!

The doorman had spotted him and was shocked. "Maxwell!" he called out from the front of the long line.

Pimpin's vision scanned the crowd for the culprit, until he found him beckoning him to the front of the line. Pimpin Maxwell chuckled, it was, Cotton, a fella that once worked for him back in his heyday.

Damn! Cotton always been a big cat, but the man looks like a burnt version of the hulk now! Pimpin Maxwell thought as he made his way toward the front of the line.

He could hear the murmurs and agitation of the of the unlucky folk that had been waiting in line for hours, only to get passed up by the new and improved him.

"Hey! Bitch, ain't that that dope fiend ass nigga that's always in front of HiHo!" a short red bone probed in surprise.

Pimpin cracked a smile, giving them a twinkle of the gold grill Messiah'd taken him to cop from Big "T" plaza. And tho it was cheap, it had its desired effect.

"Bitch, please!" Red bones home girl sassed as her and Pimpin's eyes locked within a battle of something that only two freaks could understand. "That nigga right there is money, girl. The smell is all over him," she added as an afterthought.

Pimpin Maxwell digested their attire and mannerisms, and knew they had to be the foundation that placed his pimpin' back into perspective. "I knew that was you, old playa. Look at you, Pimpin, I—I thought..." Cotton stuttered, lost for words.

They both knew what he was trying to say, and Pimpin Maxwell flashed him a four hundred dollar smile and nodded. "Yea, baby, I fell, but now everything's swell. What you know good, Cotton?" He embraced the big man.

Cotton was stunned; he could've sworn not even two days ago, he'd saw Pimpin Maxwell at his lowest point in life, but there he stood. Pimpin was back on his ism.

Ain't no way this nigga done went from a fiend to a king in one day? he thought as Pimpin dug into his pocket and pulled out a bankroll.

116

Cotton's eyes widened. Oh, hell naw! This nigga done robbed somebody! His mind screamed as Pimpin Maxwell peeled two fresh hundreds from the roll.

"I'm bringin' those two young prospects wit' me, Cotton," Maxwell said, nodding toward the two women who'd spoken on him when he passed them by in the line.

Chuckling, Cotton's vision trailed to the ladies, regulars at the club, both were gold diggers who'd stiff-armed his advances. Cotton beckoned them forward with a nod, and they sashayed their half-dressed asses over to them.

Thirsty ass bitches! Cotton thought.

"What's up, Cotton? Who's your friend?" Shica, the red bone inquired. Cotton chuckled to himself, the fake ass bitches wouldn't have given him the time of day if they hadn't witnessed the camaraderie between him and his old partner.

"This my boy Maxwell and he's paid so y'all can slide through with him," he replied, purposely leaving the "Pimpin" part off the name. The thicker and more aggressive of the two's name was Tammy.

"Heeeyyy!" she sang as she stepped forward and interlocked her arm with Shica. It was something familiar about the slim cat with the foreign swag. His vibe was different from the men of that era, but somehow more attractive. Pimpin Maxwell waved them forward, but before he could follow, Cotton grabbed his arm.

"Let me spit something slick in ya ear before you dash, ole playa," he whispered before nodding to his boy to hold the door down for a moment.

He and Pimpin stepped out of earshot before Cotton turned to him with a serious mug on his face.

"Look, Pimpin Maxwell. I know muhfuckas turned their backs on you when you hit the dirt, but you know you've always been my main man. Dig, you know I've never liked that snake muhfucka Bear, and as soon as you hit rock bottom, the reptile ass nigga traded teams. Watch out for the sucka, Pimpin. Not too long after you fell from grace, the jive

clown instantly came up. It's crazy. I wouldn't be surprised if he'd been stealin' that entire time," he professed.

Pimpin Maxwell studied his old friend. He knew there were two sides to every coin, and what wasn't being said is the part that he should be concerned about. Pimpin wondered why Cotton was telling him about the snakes at his feet.

What's his aim? Every muhfucka that pisses between two legs has ulterior motives, and Cotton ain't no different. Pimpin Maxwell's thoughts were sharp.

Cotton saw it in his stare; the trust was tainted and he couldn't blame the man. He and everybody else Pimpin Maxwell had once shown his heart to had left him to rot when he began his dance with the pipe. With a knowing smirk, Pimpin Maxwell turned and made his way into the club.

***

SunJay was in a dark place in his mind. He'd locked himself in one of many rooms in his house, and allowed his thoughts to run astray. That was his undoing as he slouched in his recliner.

 Fuck, how did shit get so twisted? he wondered as he reached down and took the bottle of Ciroc he'd been murdering off the floor.

Twisting the cap off, SunJay took the bottle to the head, and with each gulp of the liquid fire, he fell deeper into the murky darkness of his mind. Without much thought, he suddenly flung the bottle at the nearest wall, watching it shatter into a thousand pieces, before the clear liquid cascade down the wall.

SunJay stumbled to his feet, wobbling in place before steadying his equilibrium, and making his way over to the in-house bar he'd had built. A full-length mirror lined the wall behind it, but that's not what had his attention. On the bar rested a brick of raw cocaine and his FN.

The gun held a full clip and as the liquid demon swam through his veins, sinister thoughts played within the darkest parts of his mental. Before he knew what he was doing, SunJay dug his fingers into the plastic wrap of the compressed brick and tried to tear it open.

When that didn't work, he went for the knife he kept at the bar to cut his limes for his drinks, and cut into it, the compressed block crumbled into chunks.

Without much thought, he separated a chunk from the rest, and crushed it against the bar with the butt of the pistol. The chunk turned into a fine crystalline powder, and transfixed, SunJay stared at it for a moment of forever.

If I do this shit, there's no turnin' back, mane! he told himself, yet the pain in his soul was poisonous.

He leaned forward and snorted the raw powder straight from the small mountain, and as soon as the cocaine hit the back of his nose, it wasted no time makin' love to his senses.

"Ahhh!" he growled from the burn.

His vision blurred, that monster coupled with the liquor was all it took to transform his thoughts into a panoramic nightmare! And as if driven by a dark force, SunJay snatched the tool up and jacked a slug into its head. Finding his reflection in the mirror, his mind began playing evil tricks on him as he began to see his life play on the big screen of his thoughts.

"Fuck Messiah! Fuck that sick bitch Kiesha and her bitch ass daddy! And fuck you too, God!" he screamed. "I made this shit shake, Messiah, now you wanna see me dead? Huh, nigga?" His pain ran deep. "Damn, fam. I fucked up." he admitted as his eyes overflowed.

He cried for his dawg. He cried for Justice, and then he cried for himself. He'd betrayed the ones he loved, and with a cold heart, he stared. His mind was black. Before he could tame the urge, the animal in him had the gun trained against his temple, and with one last glance at his reflection, SunJay closed his eyelids and pulled the trigger.

***

The club was packed as Pimpin Maxwell made his way through the mass of people in high pursuit of the prostitutes he'd sponsored to get in the club, but decided to cut his losses. Making his way to the VIP, Pimpin noticed he was the only one in the spot wearing his Sunday's best.

He'd been so out of touch with the trends of the generation that he wasn't hip to which designer was hot. But what he was sure of was the fact that he wouldn't be caught dead in those tight ass pants he saw some of the younger cats wearing.

Before he realized that it was merely the fashion of the era, Pimpin Maxwell thought he'd somehow mistakenly wandered into one of those funny clubs where the women were more man than the men, and the men more feminine than the women.

"Hey, sexy. I know your sexy ass ain't here alone, but just in case," the bottle girl began before giving him a hot gaze that spoke of a voyage to heaven. "I take you for a cognac man— not Hennessy though. Maybe," the lady said as she placed her painted nail between her teeth, giving him a thoughtful appraisement.

After a brief moment, Ms. Lady smiled. "You're more of a 1738 Remy Martin type. Am I correct?"

She held her smile as she gazed at him from under lowered lashes. Pimpin had noticed her at the bar as he passed earlier, and after taking his seat, he'd appraised her as she did her thing. He could see the freak in her, but as soon as his eyes fell to her feet, he knew she'd be a lazy slut; it was all in the shoes she wore.

Flats! If the hoe can't stand the pain of being on her feet in a pair of heels for a few measly hours, she'd believe she was the poster child for cruel and unusual punishment by the

120

time she was through workin' my regimen, he thought before giving her his most charming smile.

"Am I that transparent?" He chuckled before reaching into his pocket and pulling out a few bills. "Bring me the bottle, mama, and keep the change."

Lady winked before sashaying away, and feeling Pimpin's eyes stalking her, she added some extra spazz to that ass before disappearing into the crowd. Pimpin chuckled, and was smoothing the wrinkles from his seersucker suit, when a boisterous laugh captured his attention.

"Polar Bear! You that nigga, boy!" someone shouted. Pimpin Maxwell's blood pressure shot through the top of his head when he saw numerous men and women fawning over a big, country fed cat.

His old do boy Bear was draped in a wolf gray fur in spite of the heat in the club. The bubble-framed Versace shades covering his eyelids matched the gaudy jewelry he wore. Pimpin's mind instantly replayed Cotton's warning.

Watch out for that nigga, Pimpin Maxwell. Not too long after you fell from grace, the jive nigga instantly came up! The words festered in his mind as he watched groupies hang on to the man's every word.

As Pimpin observed how much shit had changed, his vision collided with the gaze of a light skinned diva that had the eyes of a famished lioness! Sitting pretty besides Bear's fronting ass, lady eyed him hungrily. And while ole Bear entertained the masses, the beauty took up her glass and ran her tongue around the rim of it.

Pimpin Maxwell's nature rose, it had been years since he'd ran his dick up into something fly, jazzy, and cool. He mentally patted himself on the back when the gorgeous creature excused herself from the center of attention and headed in his direction.

"Here you go, daddy. Make sure you get at me if you need anything."

The bottle girl had suddenly appeared, smiling as she sat a chilled bottle and glass before him. They shared a knowing glance before the buxom lady brushed her breast against his shoulder. Her face was inches from his ear when the moment was interrupted by perfect imperfection.

Pimpin's gaze lifted to behold the interruption, and noted lady had the type of sex appeal to make a man instantly see the whore in her. She ran her tongue over her full lips before brushing past the bottle girl and taking a seat without invitation. The club's employee glared at the bold woman, her expression sour as she analyzed the lady whom had unintentionally saved her from a life of prostitution. And giving Pimpin a final gander, she walked away with the last bit of dignity she had left.

Maxwell watched her leave before leaning toward Cat eyes and whispering, "I can smell a whore from ship to shore, hoe, and you got the fragrance."

The pretty girl flinched, surprised to had stumbled into the den of a lion. Attempting to rise from her seat, Pimpin gently grabbed her arm, and lady's sharp eyes narrowed. She was on the verge of warning him of who her pimp was when Pimpin Maxwell reached into his pocket and came out with them racks.

"Money flows like water in my world, Beauty. Let ole Maxwell see how swell you suck for a buck," he jazzed but knew she'd never see a dime of his bankroll.

***

SunJay's eyes slowly opened, and his reflection terrified him as he stared at the muzzle of the burna he held to his temple. He could still feel the pressure he'd just applied to the trigger, still feel the racing of his heart as he squeezed it over and over.

"What the fuck is wrong with me," he hissed as he tossed the FN across the room as if it were repulsive.

122

The safety being in was his only savior, and shaking his head in disbelief, he buried his face in his hands. Rage blossomed and without much thought, he slapped the opened kilo off the bar. White powder clouded the air as he fell back in his seat.

"SunJay, SunJay! You alright, baby? What's all that noise?" a feminine voice carried through the door as someone tried to open it. "Nigga open this mothafuckin door! Open this—" she demanded while banging on the door. Sunjay snatched it open, and Dream took a step back in shock of the madness in his eyes.

"Bitch, fuck you bangin' on my muhfuckin door for?" he steamed.

His eyes were blood shot, and the stink of liquor made Dream scrunch her nose, but it was the white residue on his nose that caused her blood pressure to shoot up. SunJay had never been a fan of nose candy and that fact alone told the tale for her.

She knew he'd been under a lot of pressure lately, and it had to be those growing pains that lead him to defile his morale. They'd been thuggin' for years and he knew if it was one thing she despised more than anything, it was a black man that lacked self-control. Without warning, Dream stepped forward and slapped the dog shit out of him.

"Weak ass nigga! You won't turn into a dope fiend on my watch!" she hissed as tears welled up in her eyes.

She was steaming. The five foot three, paper bag colored, gangstress was a product of East Dallas projects and SunJay held the keys to her soul. She'd thugged with him through the sugar and shit, and before she'd allow him to fail, Dream would kill him herself.

"Bitch, I'm bout to—" Blam! – Dream cut him short with a jab to the eye, and before he could recover, with determination in her glare as she fired a shot to his moving lips. They began to tear that bitch up.

***

I should walk over there and snatch his frontin' ass up! Pimpin Maxwell thought as he watched his old friend pop bottles and turn up with his team. As he entertained the thought, cat eyes nibbled his ear as she stroked him underneath the table.

"Damn, daddy, you're tense," she whispered seductively.

Cat eyes felt Pimpin Maxwell's length harden and without much thought, she ducked her head beneath the table. Pimpin Maxwell laid back a little to give her comfort to work for the compensation she'd never receive, but just as he began to relax and enjoy the moment, a beautiful creature stepped into his view.

He became lost in her beauty as Cat eyes pleasured him, but confusion interrupted his lustful stare when his name slipped from her mouth.

"Maxwell, you ain't changed one bit," she smiled. Pimpin Maxwell's eyes roved over the petite, vanilla-skinned queen. She resembled a lighter version of Tony Braxton, but with more pronounced curves.

Her short curly hair was unruly, but sassily made up. Yet, it was the fire red maxi dress she wore that brought her personality to life. It had perfectly placed tears in it and as it hugged her body in all the right places, Pimpin Maxwell wondered what it would be like to tear it from her flesh, sucking her pussy until her soul separated from her body.

Cat eyes rose from her position to see who was interrupting her flow, and to her surprise, it was Doll Face, Bear's first lady.

"Cat, excuse yourself, baby, this one's a friend of the family," she spoke without taking her eyes off Pimpin Maxwell.

Cat eyes frowned. She'd planned to have Pimpin's entire bankroll in her mits before the end of that night, but here was

Doll Face, the bosses' bottom bitch, tellin' her that she'd just given a freebie!

"So, I did all that suckin' for free? Polar Bear ain't gonna like this, Doll," she sassed.

Doll Face was stunned she'd just been questioned by a lesser bitch. Without much thought, she reached across the table and slapped spit from the young girl's mouth.

"I tried being polite! Now this is a boss bitch call. Get ya trick ass up and leave!" she demanded.

Fire bled into cat eyes' stare, and for a moment, Doll Face thought she'd have to mop the floor with her. But Cat checked herself before sliding from the booth and storming off.

"And clean your face! Don't nobody want no woman with another man's cum on her lips!" Doll Face shouted as cat eyes passed her.

Pimpin Maxwell studied, trying to remember where he knew her from, but he was as lost as a child that wandered too far from home. He couldn't recall where he'd met the lady and he was sure he never forgot a face. She saw his confusion and slid into the booth next to him.

"Maybe this will cure you of your amnesia," she smiled wryly before reaching behind her neck to unclasped the gold necklace that she'd worn since the day he'd given it to her. Doll Face slid it from around her neck as she and Pimpin made eye contact.

"Open your hand, Maxwell, this yours," she spoke softy. Pimpin Maxwell chuckled, assuming she was playing a game.

"Look, baby. Why don't you just tell me who you are, we're too old for—"

"Just open your hand, Pimpin Maxwell!" she demanded, cutting him off with persistence.

With a skeptical look, Pimpin obliged, and she placed the jewelry in his palm. Doll Face allowed her hand to linger, allowing her fingertips to graze his palm.

*"Um um umph. Boy, I still get chills whenever we touch,"
she said as she smiled, but Pimpin was perplexed!*

*"Is this lady some type of nut case? Hell, she talm'bout,
I don't even know her, he thought before his eyes lifted to
her— "May I?" he asked in reference to her still stroking his
palm.*

*Doll Face smiled in embarrassment before giggling and
pulling her hand back.*

"Oh, I'm sorry!"

*She couldn't tame her heartbeat as his eyes left her to
study the trinket. Pimpin Maxwell stared at the pendant
before his eyes returned to her. The heart-shaped pendant
had been in his family for years before it was given to his
mother, who died. As Pimpin Maxwell toyed with the
diamond encrusted jewel, it all rushed back to him. The
night, the reason he'd given it to her, and finally, the girl. His
stare was deep.*

*"Catrina?" he whispered. Doll Face smiled. "The last I
saw you, you were..." He couldn't formulate the words to
reveal what their last encounter was like. She nodded her
understanding as tears filled her pretty eyes as she studied
him.*

*"It's okay, Maxwell, you can say it." She used her palms
to prevent the storm from falling. The clouds were there, yet
she smiled. "Yea, I was a dopefiend, Pimpin, and I sold my
pussy for fifty dollars a dick, but you know what, baby?"*

*Pimpin Maxwell didn't respond, knowing she needed to
relinquish her sins. "I'm better now, Pimpin Maxwell. I
haven't seen a street corner in three years," she admitted.*

*At that moment, something odd happened. Pimpin
Maxwell seemed surprise at how powerful the feeling felt.
His hand went to his chest, cause after years of thinking it
had eighty-sixed on him, he could feel his heart!*

*"I just came over here to see if my heart still beats outside
my chest whenever I'm in your presence," Doll Face
confirmed with a nod. Pimpin casually leaned back in his*

seat before taking the bottle and breaking the seal, before taking the Remy to the head, wincing after he was satisfied.

"So, does it?" He asked, curiosity strong. Doll Face slid from her seat with a smile on her face, her heartbeat running a race as she gazed down at him.

"It's nice seeing you back on your game, daddy, enjoy your night. And Pimpin?" Her eyes fell to the floor before recapturing him. "Forgive me"— she smiled sadly before turning, and allowing her heels to carry her away. Pimpin watched the sway of her hips as his mental wrapped around why she'd asked for his forgiveness.

"You've grown up, Catrina, and I gotta forgive self before I can forgive you." He whispered. Pimpin sat and enjoyed the scene for ten more minutes, but soon grew tired of the club as a whole. He turned the bottle up once more before standing to make his exit.

"Excuse me, sir. That lady over there in the far corner asked me to give you this," a short chubby waitress with an excessive amount of make up on her face said.

Pimpin Maxwell's eyes followed her outstretched finger to find Doll Face at a back table with two other women. He took the folded napkin from her and unfolded it.

No, it doesn't beat outside my chest anymore. It now stops completely! The words were inscribed in big bold letters she'd created with her lipstick.

Pimpin returned his eyes to her just in time to see someone obscure his view, and from the strange color of the fur coat, Pimpin Maxwell knew it was Bear.

I know this hoe ain't stoop that low! he thought, but the passionate kiss they shared gave him confirmation. He knew the kiss was a message for him and so, with a smile, Pimpin Maxwell grabbed his bottle and saluted the crowd. As he gave the two a final glance, the craziest thing transpired.

Pimpin blinked a few times to convince himself that his eyes weren't deceiving him, but there was no mistaking it,

Bear had just reached back as far as he could and slapped the shit out of Doll Face.

***

"Oh my God, SunJay!" Dream mumbled around a mouthful of dick. She moaned deeply, holding him in her throat as she suckled his flesh. As she slowly held him, she had him so deep within her oral, that her lips touched his pelvis. They were on the couch in the sixty nine as SunJay used his fingers to spread Dream's flower.

Sucking her clit, slurping sounds filled the room as her toes curled, and inspite of his busted lip, and the many scratches canvassing his face, her juices were ointment to their sting.

Knowing her body, he reached around and spread her right cheek, allowing his tongue to roll over her exit. He used his tongue and lips to freak her. The ecstasy was feverish as they lost themselves in a race to see who would bust first. Dream hummed as she bobbed her head up and down like a suction cup. She sucked, pulled, and worked his muscle until easing her lips up around his head. She sucked it, licked it.

"Uh, my muhthafu—fuckin' God!" she cried in pleasure before returning her vulgar tongue kisses. SunJay slipped his thumb in her asshole. "Eat this pussy, nigga. Eat it!" She tensed up, while making love to the head of his nature with her tongue.

She saw his toes curl as rain overflowed from her fountain. SunJay bucked his hips as his power shot to the back of her throat, and like a big girl, Dream swallowed every drop.

"I'm the only drug you need, SunJay"—she mumbled before planting a wet kiss on his mushroom.

Chapter 10

Her tears had dried on her face. There was no more left to cry as she tried to clear her mind. Justice's wrists were raw from the friction of her many attempts at freeing them from the thick rope they'd used to bind her to the chair. Naked, blindfolded, and cold, Justice didn't know where she was, nor where they'd taken her daughter, but she knew that if she didn't free herself, she and Karma were dead!

She tried to think, but all she had were her visions of the past and partial ones of what was to come. Those alone confused her more than gave her clarity, and Justice cursed God. She cursed Messiah for allowing the streets to spill into their home but mostly, she cursed herself for being so naïve.

I need to find Karma! With that thought, she fought with all her might to free her wrists, but the material that binded her only cut deeper into her flesh. Yet, she ignored the pain. She ignored the blood that dripped from the abrasions on her wrist from her fight to get free. Her ambition came from her love for Karma.

"Messiah, save us! You promised!" she cried. At that moment, a gentle breeze caused her to stiffen. Someone— him—or one of the others, had returned. She could feel their presence, feel someone studying her nakedness, their eyes pausing on what should have been forbidden for them to see. Justice felt violated.

"Why though? Why would you cross us?" she asked, feeling their presence hovering above her. "You're supposed to be family!"

***

After leaving the hospital, Messiah rode through the city, his head full. *You must start with your circle, Messiah. It's never the people we expect that sins against us, but always the ones you was good to that slices your throat.* His mother's words replayed in his mind, and before he knew it, he'd eased the car to the gate of Gator's estate.

It was a big ugly gate that separated the big house from the rest of the world, as as he awaited the gatekeeper's presence , his mental ran wild—to see him on the many cameras. *Someone close had done the unthinkable!* He thought.

They have to call, they want something form me. If they didn't, they'd have left Justice and Karma lying face down wit' Mrs. Rosa— He concluded.

The animal in him had awakened, and reaching over and taking the black book off the passenger's seat, he replayed Pimpin Maxwell's words. *"You must quiet your agony, Messiah. Pain and anger blindfolds a man to what was in their face the entire time. I think the answers to your problem is in that there black book of yours.*

With that thought, Messiah rubbed his hand over the covering before opening the book and searching for answers within a world of smoke and mirrors.

***

1987

"Who is this handsome young playa, Pimpin?" Foxy, Pimpin Maxwell's bottom bitch, asked as she smiled down at Messiah.

Pimpin Maxwell had taken him up to his penthouse, and that was Messiah's first introduction to the fruits of macking. The wall-to-wall red carpet, the marble and wood furnishings, coupled with the four half naked women, were enough to steal the self-control from the average man, but for an eleven-year old boy, the experience was wonderous.

"Don't just stand there like a geek freak, young blood. The woman wants to know who you are."

Pimpin Maxwell chuckled as Holly, his Swedish girl, slid his suit jacket off his shoulders while another exotic freak untied his gators. Messiah watched in fascination as they undressed him, and was mesmerized at how the women catered to the pimp. And when Pimpin retreated to the back room, the ladies set their affections on Messiah.

"Girl! Look at him! He's so cute!" Holly cooed.

Her naked breast stood tall, holding Messiah's attention as she pinched his cheek. And though he lusted, "something" inside him compelled him to smack her hand away—

"Babies are cute and I ain't no baby!" he spat.

Shock registered on her face as Pimpin Maxwell reentered the room, chuckling with a confirming nod. He'd been thinking about it since they'd been in the car, and now he was sure he'd have a sit down with Black Diamond about taking the boy in and teaching him how to be a man. He felt he owed the boy's father at least that much.

"That's right, playboy, never allow a woman to treat you like a child 'cause then she'll try to play you like one," Pimpin pulled his coattail.

***

Messiah looked from Holly to him, his young eyes studious as he slowly made his way over to Pimpin Maxwell.

"Will you teach me how to be like you?" he inquired, and Pimpin smiled before squatting down to his level. Eye to eye, he studied the depths of Messiah's dark eyes. Pimpin

Maxwell knew "the life" wasn't created for a certain type of person, and didn't want to taint it, nor the boy any further with his decision. He stared deep into the youngin's eyes and there hidden just beyond the surface was a wilderness that only a muhfucka that had seen too much could possess. Pimpin nodded his confirmation.

"First, we gotta get you home before Ruth tears the city up lookin' for you, but first thing Friday morning, I'll be there to get you," he confirmed before looking to Holly. "Take lil one home."

***

12:08 p.m.

"Boy, why you have that boy in here? You wrong for that, Juvenile," Mesha fumed with a roll of her eyes. Standing around the dining room table with four other young women cutting and bagging work, she watched as SunJay's eleven-year-old gaze captured every detail—the bagging of each stone, the weighing of each ounce and more intriguing, the naked women.

He couldn't understand "why" they'd discarded their clothes no more than he could take his lustful stare away from their different sized breasts. As he observed, a strange smell wafted from the kitchen, and a moment of déjà vu struck him. With one last glance at the women, SunJay turned and headed for the kitchen.

"That's too much cut, lil buddy. We ain't tryin to whip them boys, this that scutta butta, fam. We'll shut the market down with his shit, but if you keep adding water and baking soda, it's gonna be more water whip than dope," Juvenile schooled Bozo before taking the Pyrex bowl and swirling it in a circular motion.

He watched the baking soda and cocaine mixture swirl before dropping the glass container into the boiling pot that was bubbling on the stove. In seconds, the beige liquid began to percolate. Juvenile used a fork to whip the work in a counterclockwise motion.

SunJay stared in amazement as the foreign aroma became etched into his senses. He watched as the older men cooked ounce after ounce before resting each one on a paper towel so the paper could soak up the excess water.

"Someday soon, lil homie, I'm gonna teach you how to work this stove." Juvenile said, before turning to him with a knowing smirk on his face. He had just pulled the Pyrex out the boiling water when Mesha rushed into the kitchen

"Juvie, we have to get out of here. The feds is—" she was in the midst of saying when the lights went off in the apartment.

Juvenile hastily tossed the glass valve and went into action. He grabbed SunJay roughly by his arm and pulled him along as he took off to the back room. He made it to the closet just as he heard the front and back doors crash open.

"FBI! FBI! Everybody down. Nobody moves!" a chorus of voices sounded in union.

Juvenile flung the closet door open and shoved SunJay inside. The boy was shivering as Juvenile closed the door just before shit turned bad.

"Say, Bleed. Y'all ain't no muhuckin feds. You niggas work for—"

Boom!

The explosion silenced Bozo forever more.

Chapter 11

It was late when Holly dropped him off.

"Be safe, baby, see you Friday." She waved before pulling off. The night had a slight chill as Messiah stood on the curb staring at the house that was now home to him and his mother. He resented it just as strongly as he did the people inside.

His gaze turned to the street, and knowing Justice's house was only around the corner, he gave one last glance toward the house before his feet carried him away from the reality that resided on the other side of that door.

I wonder what SunJay is doing, he thought as the wind swept over him with a softness that contradicted how hard the night could be for a young nigga in the ghetto.

Messiah buried his hands in his pockets as he turned onto Justice's street, never knowing he was about to learn another harsh lesson in life—there's no sunshine when she's gone.

***

Juvenile got straight to the business as he rushed to the mattress and tossed it away from the box spring. The street sweepa was dark against the pale surface and the seventy-five round drum rested neatly beside it was beautiful. Juvenile quickly snatched the powerful rifle up and snapped the drum into its rightful place.

It was a triggerless creation that fired when pumped, and as soon as the sound of the bedroom door creaked open, he spun towards the it, and jacking the pump action back with force, he bared witness to the power of the big tool.

That bitch roared as he jerked it as if he was jacking off. And whether or not the intruder was truly a federal informant or a jack boy that came for his head, Juvenile wasn't gonna let Bozo's death go unpunished. Even over the roar of the gauge, he could hear distant gun shots and terrified screams coming from the front room.

The buckshots tore a massive hole through the door, and through it, Juvenile's murderous eyes witnessed a light-skinned cat fly into the hallway wall from the impact. Even though the jacket he wore had the acronym "FBI" on the front of it, Juvie knew the FBI didn't come to slaughter everything in a residence. And that's exactly what was transpiring in the front of the house.

The room was dark as SunJay stared out from the slightly cracked closet door. While Juvenile was letting his enemy have it, SunJay was able to capture the demonic expressions on his mentor's face in the brief flashes of fire. Silence was profound in that moment, and feeling his gaze, Juvenile's eyes flickered to the closet. He placed a finger to his lips when he noticed SunJay witnessing the reaper at work.

With an artificial smile of reassurance, he began to tip toe towards the bedroom door, but before he could take another step, hell penetrated the wall in a hail of hot lead. SunJay saw the momentary surprise on Juvenile's face before his scalp parted like the Red Sea, and before his body hit the floor, it was as if the angel of death wanted to make a statement and caused Juvenile's body to jerk maniacally before crumbling to the floor. Vomit rushed up SunJay's throat, but he forced it back down as he reached underneath his shirt and took the dirty .22 from his waist.

As soon as he had the steel in his small hand, all his fears evaporated, but his naivety blindfolded him to the fact of his small weapon being useless in comparison to those of the op. They had the type of heat that made the small tool he held seem like a dagger in a sword fight. The destroyed door creaked open, and a masked shooter with a FBI vest on, slowly slipped into the room. His masked face was evil beneath the pale moon that spilt through the cracked blinds covering a window.

"You niggas hurry the fuck up. We ain't got much time before the laws or this dude's people start comin' out-chea!" he shouted over his shoulder.

SunJay's blood froze, not only because the masked man's eyes traveled to the cracked closet door, but because he'd recognized the voice.

***

The soft tapping noise caused Justice's eyes to shoot open in confusion. She didn't know if she was imagining it or if someone was truly knocking on her window, but she knew whatever the sound was had just saved her from a nightmare. She rolled onto her side, and as soon as her face felt the moist spot on her pillow, she was reminded of why tears were slowly drying on its surface.

A few hours before, JoJo and her mother had told her that they were moving, and Justice's young heart was shattered. The first thought was Messiah! She'd begged them not to; she'd even begged to stay with Porsha and her family, but her parents weren't hearing any of that. In the end, Justice had cried herself to sleep.

Tap, tap.

There was that sound again, and Justice's eyes shot to her curtained window. It was only one person that would be bold enough to tempt JoJo's wrath and that someone was in the form of an eleven-year old boy. Justice rushed to the window and threw the curtains open to find Messiah smiling at her. She glanced back at her opened bedroom door before looking back to him and holding up a finger.

She tip toed to the door and silently pushed it closed. Justice hurried into a pair of sweats before pulling her long t-shirt over her head and pulling on her top. All the while, something kept telling her to look up, and when she did, she found Messiah staring at her.

She blushed, realizing he'd just watched her change, and with a final glance to her door, she hurried over to her window. After pushing it open, Messiah helped her out before giving her a mannish smirk.

"Girl, yo' booty getting fat," — He laughed, and blushing, Justice slapped his arm.

"Boy, shut up!" she whispered before pulling him in for a hug. "What's wrong, Messiah? Yah can't sleep?" she asked as her eyes studied him after they separated.

Messiah was ashamed to admit that he was searching for an escape from his reality, so he did what was instinctive; he lied.

"Naw, I just missed you." He looked away when the words left his mouth.

Justice was touched, but she could always tell when he was lying. As she studied him, her very own reality caused her to look up at the pale moon. The sky was a dusky purple, a starless night that blew its chilled breath against her skin.

"I—I missed you too, Siah," she said before her gaze fell to him.

Messiah could feel her spirit, something fucked up was about to happen, and his young heart betrayed him in spite of him not knowing why they were becoming enemies.

"Messiah, I got something to tell you. I don't want to, but my—"

"It's cool, Justice, you want to break up," he interrupted her with his assumptions. Justice's eyes watered.

"Yuh dottish, boy, I don't want to break up. Yuh put words in my mouth,"—she spat, her Trinidadian accent was thick. Embarrassment splashed across his face as Messiah studied her.

"My bad, Justice, I just don't want to—"

"Listen!" she fussed, cutting him off. "Messiah, we're moving to Houston." Her words rushed out in a jumble, and Messiah froze. His stare was powerful as he digested the revelation.

Moving? he thought as he stuffed his hands into his pockets. Houston? Where the hell is Houston at? He wondered as betrayal suddenly blossomed in the spirit of his young mind,

Justice was doing exactly what his father done, the same shit everyone he'd ever gave a damn about did. He felt that Justice was leaving him. He turned without responding and began walking away.

Fuck, everybody! I'll never let nobody get close to my heart again! He vowed to himself.

His pain bled into his eyes as Justice grabbed his arm to stop him, but he jerked away from her.

"Don't touch me, fam. You're just like everybody else," he spat through clenched teeth. Justice was fearless as she jumped in front of him.

"I love you, Messiah, I promise I'll come back," she vowed.

***

SunJay held his breath as the killer aimed an AR 15 at the closet as he crept up on it. Just send something hot through the door, nigga! His mind urged.

"Brah we got the work and the loot, them folks on the way! Lets burn!" someone yelled and rushed to the bedroom door.

Sirens could be heard faintly and both men were felons. Luck is on your side tonight, he thought with one last look at the closet, before nodding and following his mans away from the cemetery they'd created. SunJay exhaled as he lowered the small gun he gripped so tightly his hands hurt. His heartbeat was still wild as he waited and listened, and only after he was sure the coast was clear did he slip from his place of safety and hesitantly move toward his fallen soldier. Juvenile was a bloody mess as he rested in a pool of his own blood, staring absently from eyes vacant of life.

For reasons unknown to even him, SunJay squatted down and forced his hands into his mentors' bloody pockets, and he liberated rolls of money from each one before he retched from the smell of Juvenile's loosening bowels. SunJay climbed to his feet as the sounds of sirens grew more pronounced.

Turning and rushing to the window, he risked one last glance at his big homie before the squeaking of tires encouraged him to hurriedly push the window open. SunJay slipped into the night with revenge in his heart and the image of death immortalized in his mind.

***

Messiah paused mid-stride— "What you just say?" he studied Justice's face for signs of bullshit, but all he found was the water that baptized her stare. At the stage of life where they were blinded to life's twists and turns, he and Justice believed that the profession of love was the most sacred thing.

"Messiah, I tried to stay, I don't "want" to go, but my dad..." She became choked up as her eyes overflowed. "He says I have to go. I—I told him I love you, but he—he..."–

Messiah pulled her into his arms as she broke down into sobs. He had to tame his emotions. Pimpin Maxwell's game played in his head as he rubbed her back. Pimpin wouldn't cry. He fought the urge. Justice looked up at him.

"He said I don't know what love is, but I do, Messiah. We're love. Ain't this love?" she cried.

Messiah released her and stepped back, his mind and heart wrestling as he pondered her question. Is this love? Mama said love ain't real.

His thoughts were his enemy. Justice read the confusion on his face before it melted into something resolute, and Messiah allowed the only truth he knew to slip from his mouth.

"I don't know if love is real, Justice, but I want it to be." He looked up to the heavens before returning his gaze to her. He extended his hand with his pinkie finger extended. "Promise that you'll come back, Justice. If love is real, pinkie promise me that you'll wait for me—that you'll be mine forever!" he pleaded.

Justice nodded "yes" before slowly lifting her pinkie finger to seal the deal with an adolescent promise that temptation was surely to test.

Chapter 12

1991

Four Years Later

"You've been losin a lot of weight, hoe"— studying her, Sauvé considered his assessments before nodding. "As a matter of fact, both you "and" Creamy look a bit "thin"!" He glared from the doorway of her room. Black had just gotten dressed, and the skin tight mini dress she wore fit like a glove. Yet, nervous under his glaring scrutiny, she wondered if he was on to their secret vice, but his next words eased her anxiety.

"That's just a good sign that my pimpin' is in another dimension." He chuckled as he leaned against the doorframe of Black's room.

Sauvé smiled to himself when reflecting on the man that had blessed him with the gift of white slavery. If the ole man could see me now, he thought as he lusted for what he knew he could have on demand.

And when he strolled into her room and took a seat on the edge of the bed, Black suspiciously glanced at him out the corner of her eyes. She knew when he was on his freak shit. She'd studied his moods, and whenever he sweated on the nose or whenever he seemed to be a tamed storm, Black knew he wanted some pussy.

"I'm ready, suga! Let's go get his money!" Creamy shouted as she entered the room and plopped down next to him on the bed.

141

Her eyes were mischievous as she winked at Black before reaching into her bra and coming out with something. Sauvé's dark eyes turned to slits at the sight of the pre-rolled joint.

He'd forbidden his girls from using any kind of drugs but he knew that even the most level-minded person craved an escape from the harsh reality of the gutta. He allowed a joint or two, but that was all the escape he'd allow. Frowning, Sauvé glared at her.

"Bitch, time waits for no pimp nor nan hoe, and you're on the clock 'til you walk a hole in your sock," he spat with a scowl on his face. Creamy poked her lips out in a cute pout.

"Damn, daddy. I just wanna make daddy happy before we get out there and get our pussy funky," she seductively responded as she too noticed the sweat that shined on the bridge of his nose. "Ain't that what's on your mind, daddy? This pussy?"

She inched her mini dress up a little so he'd have a teasing view of her treasure. Without waiting for a response, Creamy lit the joint and took a deep drag before leaning until her lipstick painted lips were an inch from his nostrils, and exhaling a stream of tainted smoke, she massaged his length through his trousers.

The smoke caused him to frown, but he still accepted the joint that Creamy placed between his lips. His dick swelled as he inhaled. Black watched in shock as Creamy undid his pants and did what she did best. Yet, the moment of satisfaction given isn't what froze her in place.

It was the aroma of the joint that held her still. It was more of the hardened cocaine that wafted around the room and the knowledge of why Sauvé's eyes were now buck, that cause her to back pedal toward the door. Sauvé's eyes landed on her at the same time a strange expression eased into his features. He smacked his lips as if tasting the smoke.

"Bitch, this shit taste funny," he growled as Creamy's head bobbed up and down faster.

Pleasure always does it to weak muhfuckas, and Sauvé took another deep pull from the deeply rooted evil that resided inside the perfectly wrapped joint. His nut was rushing through him as the euphoria of the crack and weed mixture took him on an erotic odyssey.

He'd never felt the way he felt at that moment, and he never would again, no matter how hard he chased that moment of bliss. The boogeyman had now become his down fall, and the height he was falling from now would cause him to land onto a reality thats stolen the soul from thousands of niggas far greater than he!

"Sauvé, baby? Are you okay?" The beckon pulled him back from the memory of two years prior, and blinking, Sauvé stated in contempt at the present. Smoke hovered on the air in the room, and his eyes trailed around the almost empty living room, he shook his head in disgust! All the imported furnishings and amenities were now gone to the dope man, and the realization only fed his hate for women. He couldn't believe he'd allowed a slut to outwit his pimpin!

"I'm stronger than this shit!" he told himself before tossing the metal stem to the ground, before his eyes shot up at the sound of someone knocking at his front door.

"Don't answer it, baby, they'll go away in a minute," Sasha offered as she reached down and retrieved the pipe off the floor.

She studied it to see if there was even a particle of dope left within its gut. Sauvé glared at her in disgust, the drug had raped her of her model's frame, leaving her merely a skeletal shell of her former self. Sauvé licked his dry lips before storming off. "Junky Bitch!" he mumbled.

***

It was 1991 and Messiah had grown into a sho nuff playa. Pimpin taking him in was a godsend for the young wolf, and though it killed him to leave Black in the hands of the sadistic pimp, he knew it was nothing he could do. It crushed Messiah to see what the streets had done to her, but vowed he'd rescue her as soon as his numbers were right.

"Messiah, I really do love you, boy. What you mean you don't believe in love?" Liberty asked and stared at him perplexed from the passenger's seat.

Liberty was a seventeen-year-old feline Messiah had been rockin' with for the past year, and though love was a fickle thing in his young heart, he had fallen head over heels for shawty. He truly G'd for lady, but held that truth close to his chest because he wanted to see the family's reaction to her.

He wanted them to see that all women weren't the same. "You don't love me, Ms. Lady, you just digging the moments we share," he shot, while easing the Navigator to the gate of the high rise he shared with his extended family.

As he punched in the security code, he could feel Liberty's eyes burning holes into the side of his head.

"Enjoyin' the what! Diggin' the moments? Nigga, what you think I am? Some type of hoe or something?" she spazzed with a snake of her neck, rolling her eyes as the gate rolled open.

Messiah glanced over at her with a smirk on his face; little did she know, his entire world consisted of money, hoes, and bloodshed. This was the first time he'd allowed Liberty that close to his comfort zone cause Pimpin Maxwell had schooled him well—

"Dig this here, Mack buddy. Your game is the only hoe you ever trust. Your mama taught you all you need to know if you can look beyond what you think of as a horror story, and find the jewels"— He had told him.

Messiah eased the SUV into his personal parking spot as he reflected. "Never show a muhfucka where you rest your head unless you trust 'em wit' your life, and it ain't that much trust in all the world, Pimp! For the right price, the one you think loves you the most will put your brains on your pillow," Pimpin had pulled his coattail.

"Messiah? Messiah, do you not hear me?" Liberty asked, her frustration snapping him back to the present. He turned his eyes to her while pulling the keys from the ignition.

"Huh? What you say?" He asked, and Liberty rolled her slanted eyes and smacked her lips. Messiah laughed. Lil one makes a nigga wanna run dick in her every time she makes that face! he thought.

The Ethiopian and French bloodline gave Liberty the "bad bitch" award, and as Messiah unlocked the doors, he knew he'd give her his virginity. He felt like a lame, still not knowing what pussy felt like. But Pimpin had made him promise to keep his dick in his pants until his fifteenth birthday.

"Come on now, ma. What's wit' all this fresh shit you kickin'? I bring you into my galaxy and here you are actin up." He paused before pushing his door open. "You can't go in front of the ladies acting all stuck up and shit 'cause they'll read you your rights quicker than the police."

He laughed before exiting the big body and waiting on Liberty to follow suit. She did, but just as he activated the alarm, she asked the question he'd expected.

"The ladies?"

***

"Who are you, sweet thang?" Sauvé asked as he assessed the thick girl with lust in his gander, and Foxy smiled at him with a hint of promise in her gaze.

"I'm looking for, Sauvé?" She smiled sweetly, and Sauvé straightened his posture while patting his matted hair. He attempted to muster a bit of dignity as his old pimpin' resurfaced.

"Well, look no more, pretty baby I'm Sauvé, one of the livest niggas to ever had placed his gators on a hardwood floor." He splayed his arms wide with a stained smile. Foxy was repulsed behind her fictitious smile.

"May I come in?" she proposed, while holding up a gold bottle with a red ribbon tied around its neck.

***

"She's jazzy, Messiah. Where'd you find this one!"

Holly gushed as her fingers ran through Liberty's long black hair. Liberty didn't know how to react to the four half dressed women that seemed to cater to Messiah and Pimpin's every beck and call. Yet, the studious gaze that Pimpin Maxwell glared at her with made her feel naked.

"Holly, you and the girls go and fix us some drinks," he spoke before placing his infamous cigar between his teeth, and allowing his eyes to return to Liberty. "Take Ms. Jazzy with you."

Holly smiled at Liberty before taking her hand. "Come on, baby. Let us show you around our humble abode."

Pimpin Maxwell and Messiah watched them laugh at some type of joke Holly'd whispered, before they disappeared around the corner.

"So, that's the young woman that's got your nose open?" He smirked, as Messiah took a seat. And reclining on the soft leather couch, his vision drifted to the soft carpet as he thought of something fly to say. He wanted his mentor to be proud of his choice in the girl.

"Yea, Pimpin. She's cool as a breeze and the bitch loves me," he replied.

Pimpin Maxwell chuckled to himself before lighting the tip of his cigar. He puffed on it before looking over at his protégé; Messiah had grown into his own, and Pimpin had vowed to himself he wouldn't attempt to influence the boy.

"Love?" he whispered so low that Messiah looked up and stared at him through the cloud of smoke. "Do you love her too?" Pimpin asked.

He'd observed the young girl's posture—her mannerisms, and he'd saw something in her eyes! Something he'd become familiar with as much as he was familiar with his own dick! He studied Messiah as he exhaled the woody tasting smoke.

"You said love is a fool's game, but I do have strong feelings for her," Messiah acknowledged, and Pimpin nodded his understanding. He figured as much since she was the first girl Messiah had brought home, so he leaned forward before pulling the cigar from between his teeth, and asked the million dollar question.

"Do you believe her?"

***

"As I was saying, I know when choosing up, I need my choosing fee. I was just trying to make sure you were everything the streets made you out to be," Foxy confirmed while filling three glasses with the expensive champagne.

"So, where's my trap? Whore, I'm Sauvé, the grandest pimp on this side of the hemisphere!" he jazzed, and Foxy opened her purse before reaching down into it. She could feel their eyes on her as she pulled out the roll of money and tossed it to him. Sauvé eyes lit up with excitement; It had been months since he held so much money and even longer since he'd copped a new hoe since he'd blew the others.

"Let's toast to the real pimps and hoes of this era." Foxy lifted her glass and held it high before giving Sasha a faux smile. She'd recognized jealousy anywhere, and the girl was as jelly as a "P and B" sandwich! She felt threatened by Foxy's glamor, and as Sauvé joined her in toast, Foxy didn't miss the smack of the white woman's lips!

"I can toast to that—" he began before his eyes shot to Sasha. "Hoe, have some manners," he growled.

She rolled her eyes before following suit. "To the real hoes," she jazzed with a smirk before downing her glass.

Sauvé smiled before doing the same, and Foxy demurely sat her glass on the floor before standing and retrieving her purse. Sasha noticed the move, but Sauvé was thinking about all the dope he was about to go and buy with the money. Sasha's eyes narrowed.

"What, you're too good to drink with us?" she asked as sweat began to break out on her face, and suspicion began to ease into her features. "It's hot in here," she mumbled as she scrutinized Foxy.

Horrified, she suddenly snatched the bottle from the table, causing a bit to spill over the top. Sauvé's glare shot to her at the same time his vision began to blur—"That's the strongest champagne I've ever tasted!" He thought as Sasha shot to her feet, the bottle slipping from her grip.

"That—that's not champ—" she tried to say before her lungs closed and her hands shot to her throat. Without warning, Sasha fell face first into the cheap glass coffee table. Glass shot everywhere as Sauvé shot to his feet.

What the fuck! he thought as he felt his blood racing through his veins. His breathing became labored as he shot to Foxy, who'd collected the champagne bottle and was stuffing it inside her purse.

"What I think she was saying was that's not champagne," she giggled as contempt bled into her eyes.

As she retrieved her glass and poured its contents into the stabiles carpet, she watched as Sauvé battled to breathe. Frantic gasping sounds filled the air as he fell to his knees, and Foxy stared transfixed at the brutality.

"Messiah said to tell you he kept his promise."—she smiled, and with that, Foxy turned on her heels and headed for the door. Sauvé choked on his own tongue as Messiah's last words to him played in his head.

"I'm gonna kill you, Sauvé, I'm gonna kill you – I promise!"

Chapter 13

Five Days Later

Messiah eased the Benz into the lot of faces, a strip club in the gutta of East Dallas. Pimpin had allowed him to whip the gold hued 600 Benz for his birthday, and as soon as he parked, he was assaulted by the monstrous bass vibrating from the tricked out Lincoln town car beside him. Painted burnt orange, and squatting on twenty-four inch Lorenzos, the whip was freaky! The driver's side door was ajar, and it's occupant reclined with his fresh Filas kicked up on the window sill. Messiah's jaw dropped!

With a fresh "triple D" styled tapered shag haircut, Sunjay bobbed his head to Mr. Pookie and Mr. Lucci as he took a blunt of exotic to the face.

Cracking a golden smile, he laughed when Messiah took a double take at the sight of the twelve new golden slugs in his mouth, and easing the volume down on the car system, SunJay tossed up the four-nine kings gang set. The gang was a force in the Cliff, and Sunjay had recently became official!

"What's brackin, Blood, I see you in the foreign," — He acknowledged with a nod to the Benz. "Come fuck wit ya boy real quick." He waved Messiah over.

As Messiah exited the Benz, and headed to the passenger side of the Lincoln, his mind was in overdrive. He wondered how SunJay had come up so hard when they both hustled for Blow and Gator.

Sliding into the passenger's seat, he tilted his head to the right with a questioning stare on his face, and SunJay laughed. He loved his ace and knew his mind like he knew his own.

Chuckling, he reached under his seat, and retrieved a brown paper bag before tossing it into Messiah's lap. Messiah stared at the bag before returning his gaze to his day one.

"Damn, nigga, just open the muhfuckin sack!" SunJay urged, and laughed before reclining his seat and putting the dro stick back to his lips.

Messiah opened the bag and was stunned to see all the dead faces staring back at him, and his vision shot back to SunJay suspiciously.

"Fam, what's this?" he asked perplexed. SunJay exhaled a thick cloud of smoke, and his gaze never diverted from the windshield.

"You really wanna know, dawg?" he said, his words low.

Messiah looked at him as if he'd just asked the dumbest question ever, but as he studied his best friend, he noted something dark lurking behind his stare. SunJay extended the blunt to Messiah, and even though he didn't smoke, he made an exception for his b-day.

Accepting it, he placed it to his lips before pulling deep, and as soon as the potent smoke hit his lungs, they rejected it. Snot and spittle flew from his nose and mouth as he coughed it back up, and SunJay burst into laughter before reaching over and slapping his back.

"Be easy, daddy. That's that Hercules," he warned.

After Messiah regained his composure, he felt as if he'd just stepped into another galaxy, and hated he'd taken so long to allow Mary Jane to make love to his nerves.

"You remember back in eighty-seven when them niggas murked Juvie and nem? Remember I told you I was there?" SunJay asked as he accepted the blunt back.

Messiah was lifted as he recalled how SunJay had come to him and laced him to the events of that night, and nodding in acknowledgement, he wondered where his fam was going with his tale.

"Yea, I remember, but what that gotta do with this?" he asked and pointed at the bag of money.

"Chill, Bleed. Let me take it from the jump, but just know I kept you in the blind for your own good, and not for no selfish shit." SunJay took a deep pull from the half a blunt before passing it back to Messiah. "Bleed, I never told you that after they knocked brah's shit back, that shit did something fucked up to me, Messiah. It rottened my heart, fam, and at the time, I didn't know what to do, so I did the first thing that came to mind."

As the words slipped from his lips, SunJay reached underneath his shirt, and pulled a black cannon off his waist. The Glock 17 looked plastic, but the extend hanging from the grip of it, gave reality to its authenticity. Messiah took a cautious pull from the dope as he watched SunJay slide the heat underneath the seat, they both knew Blow's "no gun" rule.

SunJay turned his lowered gaze to his dude. "The ole man still don't know you hustle?" He asked, the question came out of leftfield, but Messiah shook his head.

"Naw, fam and that's my business, not his. But stop stallin', nigga, and tell me the B-I." His patience had ran thin, but as soon as SunJay allowed the words into the atmosphere, Messiah wished he'd still been naïve to how fucked up life could be.

"Shid, I went into Juvie's pockets and took the bread he had, and the shit had fam's blood all over it. I used half to re-up and stashed the other half until now," he admitted.

Messiah nodded his understanding recalling how the few times they'd came to re-up, SunJay had "insisted" that he had the ticket. "That's eighteen Bandos, pimp, half of that blood money." He laughed as he cut the car off and pulled the keys from the ignition. "It was twenty in homie's pockets. "That's" half, plus some of what I stacked off our flips," he said as he pushed his door open.

The sun was out, but the day was cool. The red Karl Kani pants he wore hung from his waist as he stared around the parking lot for any sign of danger.

"So," Messiah began as he pushed his door open and tossed the blunt clip to the pavement. And slipping out the car, and gazing over its roof at his man's, he knew it was something fucked up 'bout to be said, but he also knew his ace needed to release that demon. "You feelin' some kinda way for takin' from a dead man?" he asked.

SunJay's laugh was dark when he met homie's stare, he wanted—needed Messiah to understand his next words.

"Naw, Bleed. That's just it. I don't feel shit!" SunJay revealed as his eyes strayed to the club. "Messiah, when I saw your ole man lyin' on that floor losin' his life, and then witnessing niggas whack Juvenile nem, homie, I lost that good shit in me that gave me a conscience." SunJay watched as strippers exited the gentlemen's club, and waved at them.

"Hey, SunJay. What's up Messiah!" They greeted, and both men nodded as they headed for the club in silence, before SunJay stopped and tapped Messiah's arm.

"When you look at that bread, you'll see that some of those bills still got my nigga's blood on them, but the shit that may fuck with you even more, is what I'm 'bout to drop on you now." SunJay turned to face the homie.

His eyes seemed to conceal murky waters of buried secrets as he not only stunned Messiah but also gave birth to a desire of revenge that would eventually lead to a river of blood.

"Messiah, that night them cats ran up in the spot, I was never 'pose to make it up out that bitch."

SunJay allowed a group of hyped men to pass them before he opened a Pandora's box that housed a secret that caused the blood to boil under his skin. "I know the niggas that took Juvenile under and I'm gonna kill all them boys."

***

2010 – The Present

Keisha opened the door with a big smile on her face, and Messiah noted the cream-colored Givenchy dress, that highlighted the brightness of her red dreadlocks. The garment hugged her body like a lost lover finally reuniting with their significant other, and made love to every curve as Messiah's thoughts became a slave to her seductions.

She's a slut and knows how make this shit look good! He thought as his eyes took him on a journey of her every slope. Yet, it was the deep, plunging neckline of the dress that teased the animal within him. Whoever the doctor was that had enhanced her breasts had sculpted them perfectly. And as they saluted him, Keisha witnessed the lust in his eyes speak to his dickhead.

With ravine of the assemble splitting until her navel, Messiah anticipated her titties spilling from the thin material, and when his vision fell to her feet, Kiesha smirked seductively. She knew how observant he was, and her pedicured toes were pretty, while on display inside the six hundred dollar pair of Tod peep toes. When Messiah's gaze ventured back up top, Keisha's fierce gaze was wild—

"Jah look tired, Messiah but still handsome," she spoke with a sweetness that contradicted how rotten her heart truly was. Kiesha was Gator and his deceased wife's only child and being the plug's daughter was more of a curse for her than a blessing. Gator was overprotective and even though he'd raised her to be a killa, he still went over the top to ensure her wellbeing.

Yet, no matter the measures he took, nothing seemed to quiet the call of her pussy whenever she was in Messiah's presence. He didn't waiver from the showdown of the eyes, and though he'd often toyed with the idea of taking her down, he tamed his nature. Allowing pleasure to taint the water of business would be a fool's move and Messiah was no fool.

Wonder how daddy would feel knowing his princess takes dick in every orifice of the female's anatomy? He smiled at the thought of her pretty lips wrapping around his masculinity. "Where's the old man?" he asked as he skipped the formalities.

Kiesha had become accustomed to his cold demeanor and wasn't fazed as she held his stare. She stepped into his space with a seductive grin on her lips, and lifting a manicured hand to the side of his face, her eyes told him what her body craved. She stepped a little closer, pushing her breast against him.

Kiesha knew Messiah could feel how hard her nipples were as she allowed her soft hand to trail down his face. "Jah just need some of dis sweet pussy and him will sleep like a baby that has just been breast fed," she whispered. Then, allowing her sharp nails to scrap down his chest and over his abs, she paused at his dick print. "I see de fire in your eyes when Jah look at me. Jah picture your dick sliding in and out my kitty, so why not?"

"Whag won, star? I know ya not trying for de boss's baby girl's poonanni, huh, rude boi?" A deep Rastafarian voice interrupted the moment, and Kiesha's pretty face melted into a frown. She rolled her eyes in agitation before turning to face him. JonJa was a towering Jamaican from the slums of Kingston and he was Gator's new underboss since Blow was sent up the river to do a six-year bid.

JonJa stood in the doorway, clutching a Draco with a banana clip that resembled a boomerang. He was a six-four Adonis with long blonde dreads that were accentuated by inky black tips, and it was no secret that he lusted for the plug's daughter just as it wasn't a secret that Gator encouraged the union.

Yet, the wild woman wanted what she wanted, and what she wanted was the boss from the slums of Dallas, Texas. Turning, she strolled over to the towering dread head with a hypnotizing sway to her hips, before sweeping a stray dread from her face. Glancing up at JonJa with a gaze that touched his soul, Kiesha allowed her stare to make love to his imagination as her hand stroked his chest.

"Or maybe it's you dat craves de poonanni, JonJa? Maybe it's you dat craves de forbidden, hmm?" she said, giggling.

JonJa recognized the promise in her tone as he studied her but kept his scarred face expressionless. "De thing is, Jah will never even smell de pussy, JonJa. So, miss me wid de interferences!" she spat before storming past him and into the house.

Messiah silently observed their exchange, and JonJa's eyes were flames when they found him analyzing him. He felt there was something going on between Messiah and Kiesha, and as soon as he had proof, he vowed to himself that he'd take the blade to the American's neck.

"Don show up here unannounced again, mon," he hissed. Messiah merely smirked before attempting to pass, but JonJa wasn't finished. "And stay away from Kiesha, star. She's spoken for." His words were dangerous, deadly.

Messiah allowed his eyes to speak of his gangsterisms, he lust at the thought of upping his burna and pushing dude's scalp back, he knew an army of dreadheads that were wild wild like a western manned Gator's fortress.

He'd be dead before he made it off the estate, so Messiah tamed the urge and moved to step into the house, but JonJa's hand shot up to stop him. His palm was in the center of Messiah's chest as he gave him the screw face.

"In my country, I whack de bumba clot and feed him to de wild dogs." He smiled wickedly, and Messiah looked down at the huge hand before slapping it away. He looked JonJa up and down in challenge.

"If that's your bitch, playboy, let me give you some game for a lame. "Check the hoe, never the nigga!" If yo' hoe can't tame her pussy, no matter how many niggas you trip with over her, you'll never be able to domesticate it." He jeweled the Jamaican before laughing at the fire that ignited in his eyes.

JonJa wanted to shed blood but knew Gator had too much money invested in Messiah. Messiah took three steps past him before pausing and looking back.

"JonJa," he called to the Jamaican, and JonJa's icy eyes found him from underneath a cascade of loose blonde dreads that swung freely. "If you ever put your hands on me again, I'm gonna knock your brains along wit' those pretty dreadlocks all over that wall," he vowed, while forming a gun with his fingers and mockingly pulling the trigger. "This the Triple D, where President Kennedy got whacked, and Bonnie and Clyde from! We don't give a fuck 'bout what y'all do in Jamaica!" he spat.

***

"Say, Bleed, we just pulled up in your section, what the B-I is?" SunJay asked as he spoke into the bluetooth.

He and a few of his partners had slid down to H-Town to rock with his relative, Head, and staring out the tinted windows at the murderous stares they received from the natives of Jailhouse apartments, he chuckled. Hood to hood, shit never changes, everyone is a warrior of the house!

"That's what's poppin', bitch. Pull round to the back, me and the gang-gang out here thuggin'," Head excitedly replied.

Head was a young savage known to go get his mans for the right price, and chuckling, Sunjay disconnected the call before tapping the headrest of the driver's seat.

"Slide to the back of the complex." SunJay ordered before shaking his head at the number of young niggas that

patrolled the land. Their faces were hardened from the ruthlessness of the gutta and SunJay could relate.

The slums breed killas younger and younger everyday. He thought, while absently caressing the dick that jutted from the bottom of the P.89 in his lap. The extended clip housed thirty rounds of fire that would give him thirty chances at bed timing his target. Murda sat beside him and noticing the tension in his boy, he passed SunJay the blunt of gas he'd just lit.

"What you thinkin', dawg? You think these H-Town niggas gonna pull some fuck shit?"

SunJay accepted the blunt as he stared out at the ruins of the concrete jungle. Just like every other section of the gutta, a dark cloud seemed to hang over Jailhouse. SunJay watched a young diamond of the ghetto as she argued with who he assumed was her baby's father. The little boy she held on her hip cried as his soggy pamper hung low off him.

SunJay shook his head before taking a deep pull from the stick, and watching the cherry glow bright as he sucked the soul from it, he didn't ease up until his lungs warred against the onslaught. And exhaling, he repeated the process before passing the stick back tot his mans.

"Naw, my G, I fuck wit' these early boys and Head is my Blood. He official." SunJay's words were low as his fingers stroked the extended clip as if he could feel each bullet enclosed beyond its surface. "I'm thinking 'bout this shit with Messiah. Damu, on gang, something ain't right, blood!" He shook his head in confusion. "This whole situation is ugly and before its all said and done, I bet blood its gonna get—"

"Mane, fuck that boy Messiah!" Murda spat, his aggression paramount as he hit the dope. "When I get my shot at that boy, Ima burn 'em, on Fo Nine Kings!" he declared over a lungful of smoke.

Dark clouds converged in SunJay's pupils as his fingers impulsively wrapped around the handle of the burna. And before he could tame it, the beast in him overrode his humanity. SunJay aimed the dark hole of the tool at Murda's temple.

"I fucks wit' you, Murda and I know you and bro got blood in your eyes for each other." His words trailed off as he contemplated his actions. "But you can't forget he's my brotha, fam, no matter the issue I have wit' him," SunJay said, his gangsta speaking volumes.

Murda put the blunt to his lips and filled his lungs with smoke, and SunJay studied him, wondering if he'd have to put his road dawg's brains all over the interior of the truck.

"That's the point, homie, he's your brotha. Not mine! Me and Messiah gonna sign it in blood, on some real cowboy shit, and if you fucked up 'bout that" —Murda's words faded as the Yukon eased to a stop.

SunJay hesitantly tucked the tool as he turned to see what the business was. They'd arrived at their destination and that's where they'd found Head, M-Low, Huncho and Lil Papa. All four men were with it as they sat around the green electrical box, SunJay assessed their get down.

Head was shirtless, clad in fitted pair of designer pants that was held up by a Christian Dior belt. The twin Heckler and Kochs tucked into his denims complemented the look. SunJay's eyes fell to the two pipes that rested on the stained pavement; both assault rifles held drums that housed a hundred rounds of 7.62s that were guaranteed to rip shit up.

SunJay pushed the door open and allowed the sunrays to kiss his drip, but before he could place a foot on the concrete, Murda touched his arm. SunJay glanced back at him curiously.

"That boy not only ran us out the city for dem dread heads, but the fuck boy whacked my brotha!" he spat before pushing his own door open. Murda tossed the blunt clip to the ground before leaving SunJay with something to consider.

"When its time for me to put my gangsta down wit' your brotha, Jesus Christ won't be strong enough to stop the convo of that stick talk."

***

"Jah know what I mean, Dada?" Kiesha please her case to her father.

Gator sat silently behind a big oak desk in his study. Kiesha had just come to him about her frustrations with JonJa and even though he understood her argument, he also understood JonJa's persistence. Gator knew how stubborn his only child could be and smiled at her pouting.

"JonJa's actions aren't to harm ya, the man just likes you, Princess. Why don ya give de mon a chance, Kiesha?" he probed, while leaning back in his seat.

Gator was a fifty-year old thinker that had come to the states to make a way for his family, but mostly help expanded his father's drug empire. When he first came to Dallas back in the early nineties, a war between the Jamaicans and the natives of the city threatened his goals, yet Gator was a smart man.

Rather than go to war, the young ambitious man offered the city the type of numbers of uncut cocaine that simmered the bloodshed. Kiesha was his world and as she leaned against the edge of his desk, he admired how beautiful she'd grown to be.

"DaDa, I love you wid all my heart, but Jah will not choose de mon for me. If ya don't tame your watch dog, I will give him death. I swear it by de blood of my mother," she vowed.

Gator's eyes darkened as he swept the graying dreads from his face. *"Don't ever swear by your mother's name again. Let my wife rest in peace, Kiesha Goldsmith!"* he shot at the same time JonJa escorted Messiah into the room.

Gator could sense the boiling tension between the two wolves, and chuckled, already privy to the silent beef between them and respected it. He was also aware that it stemmed from his daughter's promiscuity. Gator stood to his feet and smiled at Messiah, he genuinely liked the ambitious youngster. The old man turned his sharp eyes to his daughter with a stare that said, we'll continue this conversation later.

"Leave us," he demanded before his orbs trailed to JonJa. "Both of you." He ordered, and the big Jamaican tensed, not trusting Messiah, and it showed in his hesitancy.

He felt slighted that Gator was attempting to dismiss him, and noticing his hesitancy, Gator's gaze trailed from his daughter to behold him.

The boss in the elder man's stare dared the younger dread to tempt his authority, not missing JonJa's grip tightening on the mini AK. His fierce eyes held Messiah as he nodded.

"I'll be right outside de door, waiting!" He put emphasis on the last word.

Everyone in the room caught the double meaning, and Kiesha giggled as the big Jamaican stormed out of the room, mumbling words of murder in his native tongue.

"Keisha?" Gator barely rose his voice, but the way he said her name demanded respect.

Keisha allowed her fierce gaze to touch Messiah before she sashayed over to her father and planted a soft kiss on his cheek. "Ok, Dada. Don't have a heart attack on me. I have things to do anyway," she spoke sweetly.

Kiesha embraced her father, and as she did, she flickered her tongue like a snake over his shoulders where only Messiah could see.

Just like the serpent she is! he thought. Kiesha turned to leave and just as she was passing Messiah, she paused. "Jah have my number, star. I'm a big girl and Jah don have to fear my—"

"Kiesha!" Gator demanded, his voice was as sharp as a sword. Kiesha's amused laughter followed her out the room as Gator extended his scarred hand to Messiah.

"My apologies, son. Respect these days is as scarce as finding a good woman," he spoke with a smile as Messiah shook his hand with a firm shake. He and the old man had developed a strong respect for one another ever since Blow had introduced them.

"No need for apologies, OG," he responded before taking a seat in one of the two chairs that were positioned in front of the desk.

"Respect is a demand and sometimes you have to become disrespectful in order to obtain it." He chuckled.

Gator sat in his seat and leaned forward, resting his elbows on the desk. Being in the game so long had gifted him the ability to read the aura of people, and steepling his fingers, he studied his young associate. He could see there was something bothering him by the red tinge of his eyelids, the rugged shadow of his beard, and the black alleyways of his eyes, that revealed a melody only a true gangsta could dance in the rain to. Gator had had his days where he'd experienced the stab wounds of life, so he recognized the internal bleeding of Messiah's heart.

"Something dark has happened in your world, young Messiah. I know de look of a man that's staring Lucifer in de eyes and Jah have it. Tell me, boy. What's happened?" he asked as he opened the doors of concern.

Gator's words were like an unexpected hug at a time when one feels against all odds, and Messiah dropped his head and when his eyes rose again, they reflected inky black waters.

"My family—someone snatched my wife and daughter, and shit is all fucked up right now." He gritted his teeth against the revelation. Gator was stunned to hear of the storm that was brewing right beneath his nose, and

exploding from his seat, he slammed a fists against the polished oak desk.

"I will murder de bumba clots that had a hand in de deed!" His words were a deadly whisper as he turned to face the wall behind his desk.

Gator had grown to love Justice and Karma as if they were his own family, and it burned him to know something so disrespectful had transpired so close to him. He slowly made his way to the wall and studied the many different shaped knives that decorated the surface. After a moment's contemplation, he chose a long black casing.

"You know, Messiah," he begun as he took the black sheath down from its mantle.

At that moment, JonJa rushed into the room with a menacing glare on his face. He'd heard the sound of Gator's hand making contact with the desk and the silence that followed troubled him.

"Wha de problem?" he inquired with the barrel of the gun trained on Messiah.

Gator ignored him as he turned to face them before pulling the machete from its case. The gleaming blade reflected his bright eyes as he admired it.

"In my country, Messiah, we murder for nothin'! A mon's family is sacred, mon, and der should be dire consequences for de violator dat trespasses." His Patios dialect was thick as he stepped around his desk and stood before Messiah. "Yet, before I shed blood for you, Messiah, I must know…" Gator's words trailed as his stare connected with the younger man's.

Messiah waited for the question that he'd been anticipating since the day Gator ordered Messiah to either kill SunJay or exile him from Dallas/Fort Worth. With life and death swimming in his stare, Gator asked the question that had plagued him for the last few years.

"Messiah, did you have a hand in SunJay stealing my diamonds?"

***

The room fogged with weed smoke as they thugged in the small apartment. The group of men sat around passing blunts of "that good" around as they were entertained by the few freaks Jailhouse Head had invited over.

Huncho and Murda battled each other on the PS3 as Papa, M-Low, and the gang tried to coax the ladies into fuckin' the clique. Head nodded for SunJay to follow him as he headed towards the back room, and as soon as they were out of earshot, SunJay posed a question that he'd been dying to know the answer to. "You think that shit solid they sayin' 'bout Monk?"

They entered the room, but Head didn't answer the question. Monk was a savage! He and Head had spanked a few niggas together, and Head didn't want to believe his bro would eat the cheese and wouldn't condemn him on hearsay. When he stepped into the bedroom closet, Sunjay's curiosity was piqued, but he didn't move to investigate until his mans beckoned him.

Head was pushing the last of the clothes that hung on hangers to the side. SunJay watched as he ran his hand down the corner of the wall, and after a few seconds, there was a sound of air decompressing, and before his eyes, the wall rolled in on its self. SunJay stared awestruck at the vast arsenal arranged on the shelves built into the cache.

There were M4's, Mac's, M16's, and numerous other calibers of weaponry in the assemblage, and with a cocky smirk, Head glanced back at his Blood.

"Fam, Monk too wicked to eat the cheese, and Brodie gonna burn somethin!" He spoke his piece before eyeing the cache of guns. "As for you, I don't know who you're trying to spark, but we got dem sticks on deck." He smiled as he nodded to an array of AK 47's. SunJay nodded too, his mind was heavy with what he planned on doing.

"That's what it is, Damu, 'cause what I'm bout to do, me and my niggas gonna need something wit' foreva drums," he spoke his heart. Head looked at him curiously as SunJay reached over and picked up a grenade launcher, and placed the weapon on his shoulder; surprised at how light it was.

"You gotta show me how to use this bitch!" He was excited as he peeped through the sight. Head studied him before glancing to the machinery.

"That's gonna bring some heat your way," he said. SunJay laughed.

"Fam, heat is the last thang a nigga worried 'bout when he goin' to war wit' God." His eyes traveled to Head. "Especially when Heaven or Hell is the conclusion."

***

The Black Widow
Part 2

Entry 5:
Once upon a time in the dangerous Congo, a prince spider crawled through the lush vegetation of the jungle. His fur shined brightly as his long legs moved fluidly. He was a proud spider and knew he'd be king one day.

His beady eyes were alert as he took his daily stroll; the day was a hot one and the sounds of the jungle were alive with the numerous predators that inhabited the land. With a glance, the prince recognized the languid sway of the poisonous black snake that hunted in the weeds.

He felt the hungry stare of the lioness that crouched low in the high grass as she patiently stalked her prey, and yet the prince spider whistled as he found shade under the branches of a poisonous evergreen.

He wanted to rest and watch the wildlife. His long legs were poised as he observed the lands, and just as he was setting his vision on the snake that had just captured its food, a piercing scream captured his attention.

His quick eyes moved in all directions until he found a beautiful, Black widow crying by the trunk of the tree. Her oiled, black body glistened under the sun. But it was the red markings in the shape of an hourglass that gave birth to the lust within the prince.

Hurriedly, the prince spider made his way over to her, he didn't know what had caused her to cry out in distress, but he vowed to slay whomever it was that had brought harm to her.

"What troubles you, beautiful Black widow? Tell me and I'll slay the object of your affliction," he vowed. The shapely Black Widow spun at the sound of his voice.

"Ouch"—she winced before stumbling, and that's when he noticed her nursing her two front legs. They looked disfigured as she placed most of her weight on her hind ones. "Who—who are you?" she asked.

She studied him suspiciously. The prince was awestruck by her beauty, he'd never laid eyes on one as enchanting as the Black Widow.

"Why, I'm the prince of the spiders and I heard your cry. Come, I'll take you home and nurse you back to health. You'll rest on the web spun of the finest filaments of my body. I'll love you with all I have and we'll birth our children in the most beautiful of meadows." He waved his long legs in a wide arch to emphasize his point.

That day began the first of many for the prince spider and the black widow. The prince held true to his word and loved her with his life, but for some strange reason, the black widow refused to allow him to enter her.

Every time he broached the subject of sex or attempted to seduce her, she'd cry and tell a tale of being used for pussy. She'd then dry her eyes after he'd reassure her that he was nothin' like the other guys.

"I'm sorry, my prince. It's just that sometimes my insecurities, the sins of my past lovers gets the best of me. But I vow to you that my pussy "is to die for!" Just have patience love," she'd vow as they cuddled.

Weeks passed and after a long day of exploring the land and expanding their webbed castle, the prince returned to this beautiful black widow. He'd missed her, and as he stepped onto their webbed floor, the aroma of roasted grasshopper greeted him. Yet, it was the trail of soft red rose pedals that caught him by utter surprise.

He followed it, he followed it until his eyes led him to his personal garden of Eden. What he found was a promise of an erotic odyssey, for there lying upon their soft, silky, webbed bed, was his goddess; naked and ready.

"Come, my prince. Tonight I fulfill my vow to you." She smiled seductively as she waved her mended legs.

With haste, the prince hurried over and mounted her before they lost themselves within a passionate kiss. The black widow spread her many arms and legs for him, enticing his arousal as she embraced him. Ecstasy smiled as that black widow purred, and thrusting her pelvis upward, impaled herself onto his harden nature.

They fucked with a dire intensity that carried them somewhere between heaven and hell, pleasure intermingling with the perfect amount of pain. The black widow felt his explosion as he erupted inside her, and she allowed him to drain himself before releasing him and switching positions. She crawled low onto the bed until her face was inches from his dick.

"A promise is a promise," she whispered before placing his hardness in her mouth.

As she pleased him, his eyes drifted closed, and he moaned in pleasure. Her fellatio was sloppy—wet! And as she swallowed him the strangest feeling made his eyes shoot open in alarm. Pain was instant, and though he was stronger than her—it was too late! The black widow was swallowing him—"Literally!" Yet, before he was devoured, he heard the silent cries of pleasure.

"I told you, lover. My pussy is to die for."

Chapter 14

Three days later
2:31 a.m.

The consistent ringing of the doorbell caused his eyes to snap open in confusion, but it was the screeching of fleeing tires that brought him completely out of his liquor induced slumber. Messiah snatched the black and gray .40 off his lap, before stumbling to his feet.

Now alert, he searched for the threat, but all he found was peace. It took him a moment to capture a coherent thought, and as his vision swept the newness of the house, it all flooded back to him. I'm at the spot on Sanger! He smirked.

Weeks earlier, he'd approached the former owners with a proposition of buying it, but the old man declined. At least he did until Messiah flashed him a Louis Vuitton duffle, stuffed with two hundred and fifty dead men.

Now, as he stood, allowing his eyes to take in the renovations he'd had done to the home he'd grown up in before shit went sour, he felt a sense of accomplishment. His mother was gonna love it! Glancing back at the recliner he'd just risen up from, he recalled the night before. Sitting before the picture window, he'd gone head up with a bottle of Remy XO, and lost! With each swallow he baptized his pain, along with the shame that came with his failure to protect his family.

With every thought of his beautiful wife and daughter, he'd guzzled more and more from that bottle until the cognac won. *Now, standing gazing out the window, he noticed he'd slept a full day away. The sun had sunken and the pale moon hung so low it appeared as if he could touch it.*

As he admired the starless sky, Messiah suddenly remembered the screeching tires, and cursed himself for not being on point. That could have been for the fam, and I was asleep! he whispered. That's when it dawned on him that perhaps they had left a message!

Messiah rushed over and unlocked the door, praying that whatever message he might find outside wouldn't include the body parts of his loved ones.

God, I know I ain't fucked with You in a minute, but if you're really up there somewhere this is your chance to prove it.

Inhaling deeply, he snatched open the door, and what he found, made him drop his gun and fall to his knees, uttering a much different prayer.

***

Ms. Pretty Pussy
Lil mama keep it hot and gushy
Ms. Pretty Pussy
I like the way you put it on me
You got the prettiest set of pussy lips I've ever seen
If I wanna eat ya, I can eat ya cause ya pussy clean
Thought it was all hair, the way that pussy sits up in them jeans
Now that I got you naked
I can see how that pussy hang

Plies' "Ms. Pretty Pussy" blared from the club's huge speakers. The club lights were dimmed to almost darkness, save for the strobe lights that pulsated. The flashing gave momentary glimpses of the glistening bodies of strippers that did what they had to do to make ends meet.

Peeping Toms gentlemen's club was packed with electric energy, and as SunJay played the wall, he smirked at how turnt his squad was. Yet, anyone with eyes could tell he himself was on high alert.

The strobe light flickered with the beat, but draped in Purple Label, everything black, he blended with the darkness perfectly. His drip was official, but his most treasured asset that night, was the gray M&P .45, equipped with a see through thirty.

The streets had been silent since he and Murda's return, but he'd bet blood on it, that he'd need every slug in the transparent clip pretty soon. His eyes roved the crowd as he sipped his drink, while blowing his brains out with a blunt of Cali's finest, and exhaling a mushroom of smoke, his orbs drifted beside him where his mans stood.

As dollar bills fluttered through the air, Murda stood seemingly in a trance as a thick Latina dancer showed that work for him. And excitingly tapping Sunjay's shoulder, he jabbed a finger down towards lady's percolating ass cheeks. Bent forward, with her hands on her knees, she looked back at it as if her own flesh turnt her on. As senorita made her ass cheeks give them a round of applause, the rapid flickering of the strobe lights gave the scene a matrix like appearance, and rolling her hips, queen knew the erotic massage her backside gave his dick print would encourage him to become rain man. And that he did!

Murda made it rain a thousand ones on that ass, and as the fresh bills made their descent, SunJay chuckled before popping a Percocet. Turning the double Styrofoams up to his lips, he allowed the cold splash of codeine to wash it down; the crushed ice was cold against his lips as his thoughts got the best of him.

What the fuck am I doin here? Shit ain't sweet, mane, and these niggas turnt up as if murder aint in the air! His thoughts were troubled waters as he used the back of his hand to wipe his mouth.

I need to snap out this shit or
I'm gonna do the wrong thang
I wanna fuck you, that pussy lock is everything
Plies' lyrics enhanced the atmosphere, and SunJay could feel the drugs working on his system as Murda excitedly slapped lady's ass with stacks of ones.

"Mane, look at this hoe! She might get the B-I tonight!" he leaned toward SunJay and shouted. SunJay nodded without looking his way, the young wolf was alert as his phone vibrated on his hip. Unclipping it before glancing down at the screen, he took another sip from his cup as he read the text.

I miss you, papi. This pussy does, too.

SunJay smiled as another text came in, this time a video, and his dick instantly rose at the sight of Dream playing with her clit. The short video ended wit' a vow to cum on his strength whenever he made it home to her. As soon as he placed the phone back in place, the lights in the club went out completely.

Fuck? He thought, and when the music stopped, Sunjay's paranoia lead him to ease the metal of his side. Chatter filled the room as curiosities mounted, and his clutch tightened on the guns rubber grip, Sunjay prepared for the smoke. Holding the M&P down by his leg, his impulses were homicidal, but just as he slowly lifted the tool, Lil John's classic began to play.

Ouuu nah nah nah nah
I'm so horny, and I want you to fuck me
I'm tired of masturbatin'
got my body shakin'
No organism fakin' wit' me
A green spotlight blared on the center stage, and was the only source of light in the room as a goddess appeared on the stage. SunJay watched as she expertly pivoted until her back was to the crowd, and with all eyes on her ass, she bent at the knees, and began rolling her hips to the beat. SunJay

was captivated by her stature and build. He stared as she worked her ass feverishly.

Wearing a navy blue quarter mink, enhanced by the navy blue bandanna covering the bottom portion of her face, lady stirred an air of mystery. The diamond encrusted slave color around her neck was connected to a golden leash that fell down her back, and descended until it became lost between her chocolate ass cheeks. Sunjay peeped her as she spread her feet shoulder length, and dropped low before tooting that ass up—Beautiful! He thought.

Her left buttock had a detailed, roaring lions head tattooed over the entirety of its chocolate surface, and the right side depicted the image of a giant black widow. The dancer shook her assets while winding her hips before pausing to look back at it. And without warning, she reached back and spread her cheeks, spell bounding her audience as they got a peek at her darker side!

At the apex of her act, the room was set ablaze when a gleaming escaped from between her feminine lips. The spectators went into a frenzy as the sharp blade slowly eased lower, and Sunjay's mind was blown.

Frozen with his cup midway to his lips—I wonder how much control it takes for shawty to push that shit out like that? I bet that pussy got a lock like a vice grip! He gripped his dick head at the vulgar thought.

His eyes were trained on her pouting lower lips, and as the room hooted and whistled, he allowed his eyes to transgress the woman's anatomy. She was a femme fatale that was slim thick with flawless skin, and her ass was fatter than firm. Sunjay was twisted at how her hips jutted from her body in a beautiful curve.

"Man, you seein' this shit, fam!" Murda was hype as he nodded towards the stage. Yet it was the man playing in the background of the club that had stolen SunJay's attention.

It was something about his build that was familiar, and it made him uneasy. SunJay returned his eyes to the goddess just as she squatted until her ass cheeks met the back of her calves, and placing her hands on the back of her neck, she began to make her ass jiggle. With her vibrations, the blade slipped further out until it dangled from her essence.

Her pussy lips held its prey for dear life as chocolate paused, leaned forward, and placed her hands on the stage. And gazing out at the crowd from between her legs, she concluded her interlude!

The blade fell from heaven, clattering against the stage before the spotlight blinked to blood red. And as the dark skinned diva spun on her heels to face the crowd, SunJay caught a peak of her trimmed garden before the red tint dimmed into a soft darkness.

The club went wild as dollar bills fluttered in the air, and though SunJay'd enjoyed the show of eroticism, the laws of the jungle were embedded in his bloodstream. He was one with the danger that lurked just beyond his lust.

He watched the goddess drop to her hands and knees, and on all fours, she glared at him through a pair of blood red, glow in the dark contacts. Her stare was hungry as her fingers wrapped around the handle of the sticky knife. SunJay hit the blunt one last time before tossing it to the ground as he stared into the glowing eyes that were fixated on him.

Chuckling at their blunder, he played the part to perfection as he reflected on their only mistake. The hair! He thought as he remembered the first time he'd met the plug's daughter. The way her red dreads had contrasted with dark skin was majestic to him.

SunJay cursed himself for allowing Murda to talk him into comin' to the club, fuck! He thought before acting as if the drugs were wreaking havoc on his equilibrium, and theatrically stumbling into Murda.

"Damn, nigga that oil got you sloppy!"

"Shut the fuck up, nigga, and listen!" SunJay hissed.

"That's Kiesha up there on that stage and that fuck boy JonJa 'bout ten foot to our left," he whispered in Murda's ear.

Confusion enveloped Murda as his eyes shot to the stage. Instinctively pushing the Latina dancer away, his eyes shot to Sunjay—

"Kiesha? Kiesha who? The plug's daughter?" He asked skeptically. The Latina shot up from her position on her knees where she used the darkness as camouflage as she ate Murda's nature, and placed a hand on her hip.

"Un um, nigga, run me my bread! I ain't did all that suck—" Thsts as far as she made it before the blade cut through the air, tumbling twice before punching blood from her throat. A soft wetness tainted the atmosphere, causing SunJay to blink against the spray of blood.

Blinking rapidly , he cleared his eyes just in time to see the Latina clutching at her throat where the dagger was embedded. Blood poured over her hand as she stumbled , and unaware, a passing bottle girl collided with her. With something slick on the tip of her tongue, the woman was on the verge of spazzing, but by the time the girl looked up, it was too late.

As soon as her glare beheld the blood pouring from in between the Latina's fingers, she dropped the bucket of ice that chilled the bottle of Ace of Spade, and a scream clawed its way up her throat as the bottle shattered against the floor. Her scream, however, was overshadowed by a cry of rage.

"Kill dem bumba clots! Get he fun boy! Dead, mon!" Kiesha screamed as the DJ killed the music in surprise.

With the M&P already drawn, cocked, and locked, SunJay was ready to act up! He raised the powerful gun and sent fire toward the stage, pushing the club into a house of hysteria. Club-goers and strippers ran for their lives as SunJay turnt his devil up...

There's no innocence in war! he told himself as his fire cut down a group of civilians in an attempt to eradicate the' enemy. Shouts of agony told the tale of innocent blood, but self-preservation was a deeper reality than stolen life.

SunJay dropped low as he pulled Murda down with him, and saved his man's life as a spray of hollows pierced the wall where he'd just stood. Murda looked to the heavens as he made a cross over his chest in appreciation. SunJay learned that he wasn't the only one speaking that pipe talk as a volley of bullets flipped a stripper over the table they took cover behind.

The woman's eyes blinked as she stared at them with a plea in her gaze, and all the two men could do was watch as the reaper stole her soul.

"Whag won, SunJay? Don't be pussy, boy, huh. Come dance wid de devil!" JonJa shouted over the chaos, before sending a spray of bullets through the crowd merely to clear a path.

"We gotta get the fuck out of here, Bleed. These Rasta muhfuckas wit' it!" Murda shouted over the melee of the crowd. SunJay nodded as his eyes searched for their exit.

"I'll cover you until you get to safety and you do the same for me," he spoke as a strange look blossomed on Murda's face. The look confused him until his boy spoke words he'd never expect to part from Murda's lips.

"I left my strap in the car, dawg."

***

Confusion was his companion as he tried to wrap his mind around what he was seeing. There was a package tied at the wrists and ankles, and thrashing as the plastic bag over her head deprived her of oxygen.

Karma! Messiah's heart cracked, as he rushed over and snatched the bag away from his daughter's head. Tears stained her pretty face as she wheezed, and Karma's five-year old lungs contracted before accepting the fresh air she needed to survive.

Messiah scooped her into his arms and rushed her into their home, before resting her on the couch, and rushing to the kitchen. He was desperate as he ran over to the drawer Justice kept their silverware, and he yanked it open with so much force that it came completely out of its cradle.

Silverware clattered against the floor as he tossed the drawer to the side and snatched up one of the sharp butcher knives. Karma's cries spoke to his spirit as he rushed back to her.

"Daddyyy!" she cried, and Messiah studied the binding before slicing through the ones on her wrists.

"Daddy's here, baby. Just give me a second," He soothed her, and as soon as her arms were free, Karma shot up from the couch and wrapped her arms around his neck.

"It hurts, daddy—my arms!" she cried hysterically as Messiah held her close.

"It's okay, Queen! It's ok!" It killed him to do it, but he pried her arms from around him. "Baby, I need to get your ankles free. Give me just a second."

Tears blinded him as he held her at arm's length. Karma nodded, and the fear in his daughter's eyes woke the evil within him. He quickly freed her ankles and tossed the knife away. Messiah could feel her weakness as he pulled her into his arms and stood up with her— "Are you okay, baby, where've you been? Where's your mother?" He cried as he held her.

"Young blood?" Pimpin Maxwell's voice carried through the open door. "You in there? Say something slick so I know it ain't no trick."

He was cautious as his eyes fell to the discarded gun that lay next to a folded piece of paper on the porch.

"I'm in here, ole head, in the living room," Messiah responded, and Pimpin retrieved both the gun and the paper before rushing into the house.

"Hell going on, cat daddy? I found—" His words faltered once his eyes captured Messiah and the curly haired girl.

176

"Holy god of all pimps!" he whispered as his eyes analyzed. "What's going on, son? Where did Karma— I—" Noticing the knife and cut rope, his mind automatically reminded him of the gun and note.

The note! he thought as it dawned on him what must have happen. "Youngblood, I found this on the porch. I think it's for you—" He tucked the burner before hurriedly unfolding the paper. Messiah frowned in confusion.

How did I miss that? he wondered as Pimpin Maxwell began to read aloud.

"You said that betrayal was suicide, but you betrayed me without a second thought. Your daughter is too precious to die for your sins, but your wife will be sufficient.

If you love her, I want the diamonds you and SunJay stole from that Jamaican and five hundred thousand of untraceable hundred-dollar bills. You have two weeks to deliver my demands or your wife will return to you in the same condition that your heart is currently in—in pieces!

Sincerely yours,
Betrayed

***

Entry 6:

My prince, I've watched you evolve into a sho nuff playa, and I now know that allowing Pimpin Maxwell to take you under his wing was one of the best decisions I've ever made. By now, you're hip to the differences between a bonafide mack and a sho nuff pimp. Two different realities trapped within the same crafts.

I've witnessed you choose your lane and carry the mack title with pride, yet, I'm not under any illusions. I'm old enough to know that your heart will eventually be captured by one of these little hoes out here in this cold world. I say hoes because no matter how classy a woman may appear in the publics eye, somewhere beyond all those mannerism and self-respect resides a hoe, baby.

Rather that hoeish nature is exclusively for her man or it's untamed and on display for all to see, every woman has that freak in her. There are three types of hoes in this world, Messiah, and you must recognize them all.

There's the woman that's merely a freak and enjoys fucking her man. She's merely a woman that's in tune with not only her sexuality, but also how to keep her man satisfied. In the end, she treasures her pussy and won't share it with anyone outside of her man.

Then you have the hoes that don't give a fuck of who know she's morally liberated. This woman sells herself for money, diamonds, and pearls. At times, she'll trade her essence for merely the attention of the right man. She could care less about how many men bragged about her pussy as long as she got paid for it.

The last whore is the most dangerous of the three—the sneak! This bitch appears to be unbothered by a man's money, looks, or swag, but behind closed doors, she's fucking three or four different men. She's the most dangerous because she acts as if she's a good girl.

Messiah, my job isn't to deter you from finding your rib, but to give you the game on how to recognize a boss bitch. See, a boss bitch is defined by her ability to listen to the jewels you bestow upon her and apply them to "y'all's" benefit. She's also defined by her ability at wearing three faces.

The first being the face she must project to the masses, the image of a lady. Her walk must exude sex appeal, and when she sways her hips, she'll hypnotize a square—take a sucka fast and make a lesser bitch insecure. All the while, her stance is respectful of you.

The second face is the image of a hoe! Now a woman should never allow the next man to partake of what's only reserved for daddy. This face is the addictive portion of her nature that will keep you lost within her seductions.

The fact that she can be a slut for you will keep you captivated. A boss bitch thrives on eating her man's dick, fucking him to sleep, and introducing him to the essence of what's taboo, Messiah.

The third and most important face is the hardest to master in this day and age. It's the face of a woman! Everything about a real woman is authentic. She knows her limits as well as the value of her pussy. A real woman will never be swayed by good game or fall for the words of a fallacious man. She'll fuck with you no matter where you're at in life! Hell, the cell or if you're on your dick in those trenches. She truly exists, baby. The problem is finding her.

Mama

Chapter 15

Next Day
2010

"She'll be fine, Mr. Ridge. She incurred a few scratches and seems a bit disoriented, but nothing internal or detrimental to her overall well-being. There's a small laceration on her right wrist that we had to medicate, but as I said, she'll be fine." Dr. Stevens advised, soothing Messiah's anxiety.

Messiah had been at the hospital all night and he wore a hole in the floor with his pacing. His thoughts were a jagged puzzle of a million pieces as the words in the ransom letter played in his mind.

You said that betrayal was suicide, but you betrayed me without a second thought. Messiah tried to see beyond his confusion, but there were so many crooked roads in his mental, he could only stand at a crossroad of indecision.

"Mr. Ridge?" the physician's voice seeped as it crept into the fog of his reflection. Messiah crawled from the depths of his thoughts to find the man scrutinizing him. *"That was quite a fall she took. The abrasions on her wrists, and—"*

"What you implying, Dr. Stevens?" Messiah took a step into the doctor's space. *"You're attempting to say something diabolical happened to my daughter?"* he challenged him.

The lanky man was at a loss for words until Coffe eased the tension. She stepped between the two men before looking to Messiah.

180

"Of course not, Mr. Ridge. I think what the doctor is trying to say is that even though it's not uncommon for kids to play a bit roughly—" she glanced at the doctor to ensure she wasn't overstepping her boundaries. Dr. Stevens nodded his consent, mentally thanking her for intervening. Coffe smiled as she ran her fingers through her hair, "Karma was a bit disoriented as we tended to her injuries, and spoke of bad men, guns, and something strange about her mother. I think she—"

"Doctor Stevens! Code blue! You're needed upstairs in room 288B."

She was interrupted by the hospital intercom's system, and Messiah and Coffe's eyes met in a collision of panic as the doctor headed for the elevators without so much as an acknowledgement. Messiah heart pounded like a conga drum.

288B was his mother's room; Black was dying slowly.

***

Rain pelted the streets in a heavy down pour, bathing the city of Dallas in dark waters as lighting struck across the heavens. Messiah was at the end of his count as he bundled the last of the two hundred bands he owed Gator for his next shipment. Luther Vandross played softly in the background.

I'd rather have bad times with you
Than good times with someone else
I'd rather be beside you in a storm
Than safe and warm, and by myself

Messiah kicked himself in the ass for being so reckless; he and Justice had a big fall out earlier. She'd went through his phone while he was sleep and stumbled across some explicit texts from a freak he wanted to bring into his stable.

Consequently, Justice and Karma had stormed out to spend the night with her cousin Kim. The soft knocking at the door jarred Messiah from his thoughts, and his eyes automatically wandered to the clock on the wall. The click of the money machine finishing its count sounded as he slid the Tech .22 off the dining room table.

Only the devil or his friends shows up to a man's spot at two in the morning, he thought as his eyes fell to the scattered dead faces that surrounded the bundled stacks of money. There was nowhere to hide such a large sum of currency so quickly.

Fuck it! His mind whispered as he checked the magazine on the tool, before retrieving the remote to the seventy-two-inch plasma he had built into the wall. Clicking on it, every angle of his property appeared on the thin screen. His eyes digested every inch of her voluptuous frame.

It was so dark that only when lighting flashed, was he able to capture anything beyond her curvaceous silhouette. Yet, with each flash, he caught a glimpse of Porsha's pigeon-toed stance. Her wet and wavy hair dripped from the heavy rain, and as she tilted her head to the side, she wrung her long tresses.

Messiah wondered why she was there; he was sure Justice had schooled her to her whereabouts. He rested the burna back in its place before pouring himself another shot of the aged cognac, and downing it, a thought dawned on him!

Justice sent her to fish! He thought with a chuckle, before pouring himself another shot before heading for the door. His head was fuzzy from the brandy and kush smoke he had indulged himself with earlier, and opening the door, what he found caused him to question himself.

Fuck? Is it the liquor or is this bitch under dressed for this type of weather? He thought as his eyes devoured Porsha's lack of clothing.

"Hey, Messiah, where my girl at?" She smiled, and Messiah could have sworn it was seductive. The smoke gray raincoat barely reached mid-thigh, and if Messiah allowed his imagination to run wild, from the skin she showed, that's

"all" she wore, save for the ostrich skinned, gray thigh-high boots on her feet. Her gaze was half-mast as she studied him.

"Justice ain't here, Porsha. She's at Kim's," Messiah replied.

Porsha's lips formed a pout as she crossed her arms over her C-cups. "That damn girl could've texted or something!" She rolled her eyes before glancing back at the raging storm. Resolution played in her eyes when they recaptured Messiah, "Well, nigga, I ain't goin' back out in this rain right now."

She stared at him while bouncing her leg impatiently. Messiah took a soft sip from his glass before stepping to the side, and as she passed him, her Christian Dior Miss perfume made love to his senses.

***

"What the hell am I doing here?" Black questioned as they stabilized her. She'd had a panic attack and tried to leave the hospital. The doctor gave her a mild shot of haloperidol and it calmed her enough to get her into the bed, as Messiah stood back and let them do their jobs, his mind twisted—

She's gonna die here. My Queen ain't gonna make it. His thoughts were a tropical storm that raged within his internal.

"Mr. Ridge – can you hear me?" a concerned voice swam into his pain.

Messiah fought to find his focus and found the worried expression on both Coffe's and Dr. Sung's faces. The Asian doctor had been paged immediately after Black had lost her grip with reality.

"My fault. I—I was just thinking," he sputtered. After a brief assessment, Dr. Sung nodded his understanding.

"It happens," he acknowledged. "Listen, your mother has been under a lot of pressure, and in these types of cases, its not uncommon for the patient to slip back into a comatose state." His words were low as he glanced over at Black. "She

doesn't recognize me, Mr. Ridge. Somehow her conditions are worsening and—"

"What I'm trying to understand is why the fuck can't y'all fix it!" Messiah cut him off.

Anger was a festering disease within him, and as his eyes bounced back and forth between the doctor and nurse, his thoughts were homicidal.

If Queen flatlines, I'm gonna whack both these mufuckas!

"That's not how this works, sir, but I assure you that we're doing—"

"Not enough! That's what y'all doing, homie. Not enough," Messiah said, cutting the doctor off as he left them by the door and walked over to his mother. She looked as if she'd aged ten years since he'd last saw her.

"Coffe, can you go get that black book out the waiting room and bring my daughter?" he asked without looking their way.

***

"Shid, you damn near live here, so I ain't gotta say make yourself at home," he said as he sat his glass on the table and headed for the stairs. "I gotta piss and I'm gonna find you something warmer to put on, playgirl." Messiah chuckled while climbing the stairs. "You hit queen and let her know you're here," he said as he disappeared onto the second floor.

Porsha glanced around, her eyes spotting the stacks of money on the table, before she strolled over to it and glanced up at the stairs. The money stunned her, but that wasn't what had brought her to the table, hurriedly, she reached down into her pocket and pulled out a small capsule.

Porsha risked another glance at the stairs before twisting it open and pouring the Molly into Messiah's discarded drink, and using her finger, she stirred it. With mischief in her intent, she hoped against hope that the liquor dissolved the substance.

She hurried back to the window and cracked the blinds, and as a flash of lightning reflected in her eyes, Messiah made his way down the stairs with a pair of his wife's sweats in his hand.

"You get at Justice and let her know you're here?" he asked as he tossed her the sweats and headed to retrieve his drink. His eyes scanned the table to ensure that everything was as he'd left it.

"What? You think I stole some of your money?" Porsha teased him as she joined Messiah at the table.

She reached past him and grabbed the bottle of brandy, her eyes finding Messiah's as she tilted the magnum to her lips and took a deep drink. She frowned as the heat burned a smooth trail down her throat, and Messiah laughed before tilting his glass to his lips.

"This shit ain't made for the inexperienced." He nodded before downing his drink. His eyes studied her, then asked, "What you doin' here, ma? It's two in the A.M., and ain't nobody out at this time of night except creeps and freaks."

Porsha smiled a seductive smile before taking the glass from Messiah's hand. She filled it halfway with Brandy and took a lady-like sip from it. "Well, I'm surely not a creep," she sassed with a promiscuous giggle. Messiah's eyes grew big in curiosity, but just when the silence became thick, the lights went out.

***

Black had fallen into a dreamless slumber, and for that, Messiah was grateful. He reclined in the chair by the bed, with Karma curled up in his lap.

"Daddy, are you mad at mami?" she asked, while looking up at him. Messiah smiled down at his beautiful daughter. She had his eyes and nose but her mother's hair, facial

structure, and skin tone. He played with one of her many curls.

"And why would I be mad at mami, baby?" He laughed in spite of the internal chaos that he wrestled with. Karma glanced down as she played with a button on his shirt.

"For being mean to me—"

Her words confused him. Messiah studied her curiously before giving her a soft smile. "Sometimes mama is mean to you because she loves you, Karma. And no, I'm not mad at her. When she gets home, we're going somewhere safe."

His words were a truth he prayed came to past, and Karma's eyes were as big as an owl.

"Are we going to Disney World, Daddy?" she cried out exuberantly. Messiah laughed to keep from crying. He could see Justice in the details. He missed her. A river welled up in his eyes. "Daddy, why are you crying?" Karma asked as her eyes mirrored his.

Messiah allowed a lone tear to baptize his face, and with the descent of the next droplet, a reflection of his wife stared out from the water.

***

Shadows played over the room as Messiah lit one of the big candles that Justice used to decorate the living room. He perspired slightly, not understanding why his body seemed to be on fire, and sensitive to every shift of movement. The flickering flame tangoed on top of the candle as his stare found Porsha standing by the window, gazing out at the storm.

"Power outage," he acknowledged, before making his way to the table and taking a seat in one of the straight back chairs. And chuckling to himself—

I ain't ever been this lit off no drank! he thought, and Porsha turned to him, knowing the drugs was working its magic.

"What's so funny, boy? That liquor on yo' ass!" She giggled before strutting over, and pausing before him. His eyes captured the texture of her boots, the softness of her creamy thighs, and once their eyes met, his dick rose.

Porsha's finger traced the face on one of the bills on the table, her eyes falling to the sash, allowing the coat to flutter open, before lifting to find Messiah staring at her. The dancing flame played in his pupils as she pulled the end of the sash. The coat fell open and just as he'd thought, Porsha was as bare as Eve in the garden.

"Porsha, what you doing, my nigga? You know this foul."

His words were uncertain as his nature called to him. Porsha was a bad bitch. Her titties sat up without help and her manicured pussy was pretty and wet. The earring in her navel glistened as she stepped forward and straddled him, and when she spoke, Messiah smelt the liquor on her breath.

"This pussy is callin' to you, daddy. Ain't nobody gotta know bout this shit," she moaned as she grinded against his weakness.

Porsha wrapped her arms around his neck as she allowed that freak in her to stare out from her eyes. The natural smell her pussy gave off, intermingled with the insanity of the moment clouded Messiah's judgment. When lust and liquor is in the midst of a snake bitch and an unthinking man, the only conclusion is treason.

That's exactly what Messiah tainted his vows with as he palmed Porsha's soft ass cheeks and sucked her protruding nipples into his warm mouth.

"Yea, suck that muhfucka, nigga! Do that shit!" she cried out.

***

Hours Later

Messiah thanked Coffe when she tucked Karma into the bed next to this mother, and Coffe smiled as her eyes trailed to the black book in his hands.

"I see you're an avid bible reader. I wouldn't have taken you—"

"Its not a bible, Coffe"— he cut her off. Coffe took in his rugged handsomeness.

"Oh, so what is it?" she inquired as she walked over to him, as Messiah placed the book onto his lap and opened it.

"It's my mother's diary, she recorded our life," he revealed, and surprise blossomed over Coffe's face as she made her way to the seat beside him.

"Oh my God! It's her memories on paper!" she exclaimed in an excited whisper, and Messiah nodded his confirmation.

"Can I listen? I promise not to ask a bunch of questions," she vowed with a "please" expression on her cute face. Messiah laughed at her silliness.

"It's peace, mama, but be warned, this shit is Rated R! He admitted before he begun to read.

*** *

Messiah was naked from the waist down as she rode him with a fierceness, holding Porsha's cheeks spread as she gave it to him, impaling herself on his rigidness.

"I'm gonna cum—cum! Oh shit!" she cried as she tossed her head back in ecstasy.

Porsha's back arched as her climax mounted, and Messiah could feel himself reaching the apex of his own journey as she talked that freaky shit to him.

"Suck my titties, Messiah. This—this pussy 'bout to cry for you, Daddy. You ready? You—you—shiiitttt!" she cried as her essence closed tightly around him and saturated his dick with her honey.

Porsha rocked her hips back and forth as she attempted to baptize his nature with every drip of her waters. Messiah swelled inside of her, and as soon as his volcano erupted, he lifted her up off of him. Porsha wanted to argue, but instead, dropped to her knees and swallowed his lava. What neither one anticipated was Justice witnessing the entire sin!"

***

"Arrugh!" Justice screamed as her eyes popped open. She perspired as she sat up in the queen-sized bed. The room was illuminated by a night lamp, and outside of the bare essentials, it was the only other piece of furniture she'd been gifted in the prison her kidnapper held her captive in. It was locked from the outside and windowless, and Justice cried; not only because of her predicament, but mostly because of the nightmare she'd just had. Not because she felt it would come true, but because it already had.

Chapter 16

1991

Messiah eased the big Benz off the loop as his pager went off for the fifth time. He chuckled, knowing it was Pimpin, cause he'd been doing so for the last past hour.

I wonder what the old man has planned for my fifteenth birthday, he wondered.

He figured it would be another surprise party, but as he pulled into the lot of the huge glass structure, Messiah realized he'd never been to a hotel before. And sliding out the spacious vehicle and gazing up at the towering structure of The Renaissance, he was in awe.

"Excuse me, sir. May I get your keys?" the valet asked, surprising him. Messiah stared at him in confusion, he didn't understand why dude in the funny looking outfit was asking him for his keys.

"My keys?" He asked skeptically, and studying him, something dawned on the uniformed Italian man.

"Oh, it's your first time to a Renaissance!" The young attendant was surprised. Or any other upscale establishment; that's for sure! he thought as he explained how things went.

Messiah felt stupid as he hesitantly handed him the keys, and not knowing the man stood, waiting for a tip…Messiah strolled toward the entrance without a second thought.

Five and a half bands for half a book ain't bad, I'll put my wrist to that thang and bring back thirty-two's. Let them hoes go for six apiece and I'll still kill em! His thoughts were a hurricane as he did the numbers on the half of kilo he'd just copped from Gator.

He smiled at the numbers he'd turned as he bopped into the reception area of the grand hotel. Messiah was in awe of the vaulted ceiling that depicted images of the classical painting, *The Return of Judith to Betula* by Botticelli. The brilliancy of the crystal embellished chandeliers held him captive as his young mind digested the beauty that took him fast.

"'Bout time you made it. I was just 'bout to call in a missing person's report," Pimpin Maxwell said, his voice stealing his attention.

The debonair playa was on deck in a pair of soft pink slacks that were complemented by an off-white silk dress shirt, and the eggshell white gators that covered his feet looked as if someone had just taken the reptile out of its murky waters. Pimpin smiled at the dapper Dan Karl Kani unit his protégé wore.

Messiah's hair was cut into the bob trend and highlighted by a double edge up. Pimpin Maxwell draped an arm across his shoulders. "Today, you get your wings into the life, Messiah. I got a surprise for you that you'll never forget!"

***

SunJay heard knocking at his door and glanced around the efficiency apartment his G-Lady had signed off on. The forest green leather sectional was littered with discarded clothes, and there was an empty pizza box on the scarred coffee table, but other than that, there wasn't much to see.

SunJay took his shirt from the pile and tossed it over the other half of the brick he and Messiah went half on, and upping the tool from his waist, he made his way to the door.

"Who it is?" he called, while sliding to the side of the door. He could hear someone exhale a long whoosh of breath.

"SunJay, quit playin' and open the door!" she whined. SunJay laughed before retucking the gun, and opening the door. Tamika was a twenty- three year old freak who stayed down the hall from him. She'd put the pussy on him off rip, and blown his young mind. Tamika was a short thick freak from the best for less section of the cliff, and outside of some good pussy and fire head, she didn't have much to give a man that aspired to be more than merely a street nigga.

Yet, when a man's dick was hard, he'd disregard all morals and sense of attraction. SunJay flashed her a golden smile as he fantasized about how vicious her sex game was.

"What's the business, lil baby?" he asked.

Tamika placed a hand on her hip before rolling her eyes. "Nigga, don't be getting all fresh like you ain't see all those pages a bitch sent you. Dude, you know what?" she asked and paused to pat her head.

SunJay glanced at the scarf, fighting back his laughter. I bet her dome hot as a muhfucka underneath that shit! he thought.

"Fuck you, SunJay!" she spat as if she could read his mind.

Tamika turned and tried to walk away but SunJay caught her around the waist. Pulling her into the apartment, he kissed her on the back of the neck.

"Hold up, lil mama. What's wit' all this otha shit you on, fam?" he whispered, while kicking the door closed.

Tamika pretended to be feeling some type of way as she scrunched her nose and feebly attempted to push his arm away, but as he spoke to the wilderness in her, her rose and her body betrayed her.

"Quit, boy, you makin' me wet!" she moaned in a seductive, pleading voice, while grinding her ass against his nature, and leaning her head back against his shoulder.

Freak bitch did all that fakin' and shakin' just so the boy would take her down, SunJay thought as he kissed her ear.

"You gonna let me put this muhfucka down your throat or what?" he whispered.

Tamika slipped his arms from around her and turned to face him with a seductive smirk that made her appear cuter than she actually was. As she unbuckled his Levi's, she leaned in for a kiss, but SunJay's hand shot up to block her lips. He nodded toward his dick.

"You know I ain't wit 'all that kissin' shit, ma, but you can kiss him!" he jazzed with a nod toward her hand.

Tamika rolled her eyes before dropping to her hunches, and freeing his dick, she stroked it. She gazed up at SunJay while planting a wet kiss on the head.

Ummm! she moaned as she ran her tongue over her top lip.

SunJay's eyes drifted closed as she stroked him faster, while bathing his nature in her saliva. Little did the young goon know, evil was slipping through his front door at the same time pleasure surged through his veins.

***

"Young blood, when ya ole lady tells you how much she loves you, you never told me if you believe her." Pimpin was nonchalant as they rode the elevator up to the suite he'd rented for the night.

The fuck? Messiah thought as he looked at his mentor with a peculiar expression on his face. Where that shit come from? he wondered.

Rubbing his hand over his hair, Messiah chose his words wisely. "Yea, Pimpin. The lady says she lovin' on me and shit."

Pimpin Maxwell studied the young boy before glancing down at his presidential. " But do you believe her when she tell you she loves you?" he probed.

Messiah was used to the older man's teachings, so he knew Pimpin Maxwell used clichés and hypotheticals to drop jewels on him. His mind was con's away from the game, he was thinking of the best reaction to feign his surprise when everyone jumped out and yelled, Surprise!

He silently posed before responding, "Yea, Pimpin Maxwell, I do. Liberty is a good girl from DeSoto. She's not like these other hoes out here," he professed, and at that moment, he realized that he hadn't heard from his gal all that day. He frowned. Odd! His mind screamed, before a smirk appeared on his lips.

She's here at the surprise party! He concluded. He smiled up at Pimpin Maxwell, but the chuckle the old man gave him was sinister as if he doubted his profession of Liberty's fidelity.

Messiah gave him a questioning gaze, and Pimpin reached down into his pocket and pulled out a velvet box. "Messiah," he smiled, before extending the small box to him. "Have you ever heard the cliché a person's eyes never lies?" he asked as Messiah studied it, wondering why Pimpin was giving him a ring box.

"Well—" Pimpin was persistent as he nodded to the gift. "You gonna open it or stare at it as if it's the plague?" He urged.

Messiah laughed before opening the box, but the contents caused him to look up at Pimpin Maxwell in confusion. Pimpin smiled. The three-carat diamond pinkie ring was yellow gold and depicted a cracked heart. The clarity of the stones was symmetrical. Beautiful!

Messiah's eyes revealed his confusion at the gesture, his mind bouncing back to the same inquiry. Why a heart? Pimpin Maxwell chuckled as he read the youngster's mind, and reaching into his pocket he came out with a silver cigar case, just as the elevator dinged open on the fifth floor. He freed one of the imported cigars and placed it between his teeth.

"It's a token of the game you'll receive; a remembrance of this day that will always remind you of your first true

introduction into the life," he acknowledged before taking the imported tobacco from between his teeth.

"It's a three-carat diamond that will remind you where your heart belongs at all times, youngin', and as long as you don't break it, it will always be intact and in its rightful place," Pimpin Maxwell spoke and nodded before taking the trinket from Messiah and pulling it from its confines.

Pimpin Maxwell placed the diamond on Messiah's left pinkie. "You're married to the game now, playboy, and this is the vow I ask you to make this night. Cause your game can't start until you've made this pledge," he proposed.

I knew it! It's a surprise party! Messiah thought as he glanced down at his finger. "Sup, ole man, why you being all mysterious and shit? You actin' like we getting married!" he burst into laughter.

Pimpin Maxwell leaned against the wall as a couple passed them, and the woman chanced a glance at the two well-dressed men, her eyes telling Pimpin that he could get it if circumstances were in their favor.

Once they were out of earshot, he returned his vision to Messiah, before twirling the cigar around his fingers—"I need you to promise me that no matter what you see tonight, no matter what, you'll hold your silence. You'll keep your composure and stand tall like a true playa."

Pimpin stepped away from the wall and stared Messiah deep in his orbs. "You can't make a sound. If you want to cry, you do that silently!"

His eyes were dark as he placed his cigar back between his lips. Messiah had a confused expression on his face as he studied the older man, but after a brief moment, he sealed the deal.

"That's a bet, Pimpin. I promise."

***

Her head game was sloppy as his dick hit the back of her throat, causing SunJay's toes to curl as the demon surged from his nuts.

"Fuuuck!" he growled as his seed shot from his nature.
Whack!

Something sharp made contact with the back of his head, and he fell to his knees in agony. Tamika seemed confused as she stared up bewilderedly, and as soon as her vision captured the monster standing before her, a horrified scream slipped from her lips. The guns eyes were filled with malice as he glared down at her, and she looked up into the eyes of a masked gunman.

The sawed-off pump he'd clobbered SunJay in the head with had a small film of the boy's hair and scalp on the bottom of it, and as he took aim at the back of SunJay's noggin, an evil smile stretched across his face.

"You know what it is, lil daddy, where that work at? Don't play us like no lames or I'm gonna put ya noodles all ova this bitch!" he spat as another man entered the equation.

He too was ski'd up, but rather than a gauge, he brandished an Uzi with a long clip. His eyes fell to Tamika and murderous intent bled into his stare when spotting the drying jism on her face. The sight of SunJay's pants being down around his ankles was a clear indication that his baby's mama had done more than he'd instructed her to. SunJay was dizzy as his hand went to the back of his head.

"Fuck you niggas, dawg. Roach ass fools gonna have to show that action. I ain't tellin' y'all shit!" he vowed.

The first gunslinger struck him again, and SunJay blacked out, falling face forward into the pile of clothes on his couch. Tamika noticed her baby daddy's intent when he raised the Uzi, and she dove across SunJay's sleeping body.

"Nooooo, Stebo! You said we was gonna take his shit! Don't kill the boy, baby!" she cried.

Stebo had been plotting on SunJay ever since he'd spotted him stuntin' in the Lincoln squatting on twenty-four inch big heads. The young boy was just hard to touch due to his recklessness with the burna, and that's when he decided to bring Tamika into play.

Stebo reached down and grab a handful of her hair from underneath the silk scarf.

"Bitch, get your trick ass up!" he growled, and she screamed as she scrambled to her feet.

Feigning unconscious, SunJay'd heard it all! His thoughts were a tornado, but it was one thought that held prominence within the twist of his mental storm— I gotta get to my burna!

***

When Pimpin and Messiah entered the suite, Pimpin placed a finger to his lips to remind him of his vow of silence. A melody of pleasure serenaded the air, feminine moans drifting from the back room brought a peculiar frown to Messiah's face. Glancing to Pimpin, his young mind ran wild with wonder—

I know this nigga ain't bring me to no orgy! he thought with a mischievous smirk spreading across his face as he followed Pimpin through the suite.

Pimpin headed for the bathroom where the sweet melody was coming from, and as Messiah followed, he glanced down at the diamond pinky ring.

"I need you to promise me that no matter what you see, you'll keep your composure like a boss and enjoy the show. You can't make a sound! If you want to cry, you do that shit silently." Pimpin Maxwell had reminded him just before they'd entered the room.

He knew the old man had a surprise for him and as he admired the shine of the strange ring, Messiah noticed Pimpin stop abruptly. He almost ran into the man, but stopped midstride, to find Pimpin standing in the doorway of the open bathroom. A thick trail of steam wafted from the room as Messiah wondered what was so intriguing.

"Oh, oh wooo!" The song of a familiar voice talked to his gut. Something told him to turn and run, but curiosity was an apple to curious Eve and just as she had, Messiah partook of its knowledge.

Stepping around Pimpin Maxwell to get a better look, Messiah's eyes captured the eroticism that unfolded before his young eyes; within the fog of steam, a dark-skinned cat had a creamy-skinned, shapely woman bent over in the hot tub and he was pounding her treasure with deep vicious strokes.

Messiah glanced back at Pimpin Maxwell in utter confusion before returning his vision to the scene, and it was at that moment, reality and fiction battled one another as he tried to figure out if what he was seeing was real or some type of trick of the eyes.

"Fuck me! Give me this dick, boy!" "Liberty" moaned in ecstasy.

Messiah's heart fell to his feet as Pimpin walked up beside him and place a hand on his shoulder. "See, pimp friend of mine, the thing 'bout the eyes is they don't have a conscience. A muhfucka will look you in the eyes and lie to you"—At the sound of Pimpin's voice, Liberty's head shot up.

"Oh my God! Messiah!" she screamed before pushing playboy out of his moment of heaven.

"He raped me, baby!" she screamed in desperation, but Messiah couldn't hear her, cause heartbroken, he'd turnt and bolted from the room, just as Lil Woo busted on her ass cheeks. Pimpin Maxwell laughed as the young girl stumbled from the tub, going after Messiah.

***

Blood was everywhere, the substance leaking from the wound on his head as he army crawled toward the door his *assaulters had left open. "I gotta get help, or I'm bout to die!" he thought as he collapsed.*

He'd made it to the door, but couldn't see through his swollen eyes.

"Help!" he whispered. SunJay'd thugged it out as long as he could until their torture got the best of him. In the end; he was merely a fifteen-year old boy entering a reality where even the predators were food the jungle needed to feed upon.

"Please," he moaned, and God must've taken a moment to glimpse towards the gutta, because a loud scream interrupted the silence. A young girl was passing by his apartment when she saw the bloodied boy, and rushing in, she knelt down beside him.

"Hey, can you hear me?" she screamed, and SunJay had to force his swollen eyes open a little.

"Need help," was all he could formulate before the darkness enveloped him.

Chapter 17

Four Days Later

"How is he?" Black asked as she entered the suite, and Pimpin closed the door behind her. He took her coat before shrugging his shoulders.

"The boy will bounce back, it was just too much pressure at one time," he admitted.

Pimpin studied her. He'd heard stories of her addiction, and though her cheeks were slightly sunken, the women's physique was still enticing to him. He knew she'd been one of Sauvé's girls, and after the man was mysteriously poisoned, Black and the other girls had been on renegade hoeing time.

Pimpin Maxwell heard that Black Diamond drew in a pretty penny, and it saddened him to know that she'd eventually end up in the hands of an undeserving stable. Yet, that was the life.

I can't save every hoe, he thought, knowing he'd never disrespect Messiah or the memory of his father like that.

"Where is he?" Black interrupted his thoughts as her sharp eyes canvassed the beauty of the penthouse, nodding her head in admiration. Good to see he's well taken care of, she thought.

"Foxy!" Pimpin demanded, and Black looked at him curiously as Foxy emerged from the back room carrying a food tray stacked with fruits and food.

"He's still not eating—" she reported as her eyes met those of Black. Pimpin Maxwell made a face before waving a dismissive hand.

"Let the boy alone. He'll come around when he's ready," he said as his vision recaptured Black, "This shit was more your idea than it was mine. Go get your boy and smack some sense into his head," he proposed. Black nodded before lifting an eyebrow to Foxy.

The younger woman smiled a tight smile, hip to Pimpin having a soft spot for the dark-skinned woman and she didn't like it. Foxy set the tray down on the dining room table, and without looking back, walked toward Messiah's room.

"Follow me," she shot over her shoulder, and Black giggled at the younger woman's insecurity. Pimpin Maxwell took a sliced strawberry from the tray of food.

"Yea, that kind of shit!" he said and laughed.

***

"Biiitch, Messiah and SunJay getting a check!" Porsha sang into the phone.

Laughing at the extra in her girl's voice, Justice twirled the phone cord around her fingers as her thoughts became a whirlwind.

I wonder if Messiah ever thinks of me? Has he found another girlfriend? she wondered. Justice had become a cinnamon-skinned diva, and at five foot even, the Trinidadian's titties and ass were juicy. Her curly hair had grown into a wavy mane that flowed down her back, and at 15, she was mature.

"Porsha, I don't care about all that mess, I'm so over that boy," she lied. Porsha laughed, knowing her girl was fronting, but rather than calling her out on it, she chose to take a different route.

"K, so what's up with this new nigga you've been kickin' it with since you've been down there in the H? Ummm, what's *his name again?" She fished, while getting comfortable on the couch.*

Justice smiled at the thought of her boo, LaMont was a few years older than her and he was said to be a prospect for the number one draft into the league.

"Just because you're my girl don't mean you can be all in my tea, Porsha!" she giggled while contemplating. Justice paused as she described the feeling she had. "He's so fine, Porsha. His name is Lamont and he's that nigga around here." Justice lay back on the bed and stretched her legs straight up into the air, admiring her small feet.

"Have y'all fucked?" Porsha asked, and Justice's nose crinkled at the question.

"Ugh! Nosey much!" She laughed, while rolling her eyes. She reflected on how many times her and LaMont had come close to doing the deed, and her temperature rose.

She'd vowed to her father that she'd wait until she was done with high school, but at that age, her body spoke to her in ways that threatened the pledge.

"Maybe," she teased Porsha. "Maybe not." Her words were playful, and Porsha burst into laughter. She knew Justice's ass hadn't given up the goodies. Yet, she also knew how her friend didn't back down from anyone.

"Justice, your scary ass ain't let that boy between your legs!" she mocked her, and Justice hated it when people doubted her, and slipping from her bed, she made her way over to the mirrored dresser. Cradling the phone between her head and shoulder, Justice poked her mature breast out and cupped them.

"Bitch, you don't know that, you're just—"

"Save it, Justice—" Porsha cut her off.

"Excuse me?" she replied defensively. "How you gonna cut—"

"Truth or dare?" Porsha challenged, and Justice paused, her mind a force field.

Turning to study her butt, she allowed herself to fall victim to the moment.

"Dare!" she took the challenge just as Porsha'd anticipated. She could hear Porsha smiling from the other end of the phone just before her next words stunned her.

"Bet!" Porsha exclaimed.

Justice was confused, yet, more curious of if her backside had grown any since the last time she checked.

"Bet? What's the dare?" she inquired.

Porsha paused before giggling, and Justice wasn't prepared for her challenge.

"I dare you to fuck that nigga!" she spoke with that "yea, bitch" tone to her voice.

Justice's eyes grew wide as she contemplated her next move, but reluctantly accepted the dare. Figuring there was no way that Porsha would know if she'd carried out her end of the bargain, Justice committed her treasure to a moment in time.

"And Justice?" Porsha called to her. "Summer break is in three weeks, and I'll be there for the special day," she said and laughed before disconnecting the call.

***

Messiah heard the knock at his bedroom door, but didn't want to be bothered. He ignored the persistent knocking until his visitor tossed politeness out the window, and invited herself in. Black closed the door behind her and shook her head at the sight of Messiah in bed with a pillow over his head.

"Get out of my room, mane!" His muffled voice was irritated.

Without notice, Black stormed over to the bed and snatched the blanket away from him. Messiah popped up in bed with something sharp on the tip of his tongue, but the sight of his Queen quieted that beast in him.

"Damn, mama! Why you playin' so much!" he demanded, and Black glared at her boy. Messiah had grown to be a handsome young man; his dark skin was smooth and his big eyes gave him a sleepy look, and she could see her late husband in the details.

"You better get yo black ass out this bed, Messiah Ridge!" she yelled as she addressed him by his government.

Messiah's left eyebrow rose as he studied her, and though her beauty was still intact, he could see the life that monster was robbing her of. He loved her no less and as he slid from the bed, Messiah laughed.

"Mama, I ain't no kid no more," he spoke over his shoulder as he slipped into a pair of sweats.

"I know Pimpin sent you in here to try and talk me out my feelings, but I'm straight, Queen. I'm just—"

"Actin' like a lil bitch. That's what you're doing, Messiah." She gave it to him uncut, -no Chaser.

Messiah's pride clouded his irises, and Black smirked at his anger; she knew her child. He was mama's baby. She walked over to the bed and took a seat on its edge, before patting the spot beside her.

"Come vibe with me, Messiah, let me tell you something." Messiah was in his feelings from the jab she took at him and stood in place. *"Messiah!"* Black demanded, and they stared at each other, lioness versus her cub.

Though Messiah considered himself grown, his respect for her won over. He strolled over and he sat next to her. *"Mama, you know I'll never disrespect you, baby, but watch how you handle me. I'm a man now."*

He stuck his bird chest out with pride, and Black laughed before slapping him upside the head. *"Boy you'll always be my baby—"* she found humor in him rubbing the back of his head as if she'd hit him harder than she'd actually had. Black composed herself and studied her son—

He's going to be a success, she thought as Messiah called her assessment.

"What?" he asked with a perplexed look. Black rubbed her hand over his wavy hair—"You liked ole girl, huh?" she touched a soft spot.

Messiah flinched, embarrassed that his Queen heard of how he'd been played.

"So, you've heard?" He dropped his head.

"Heard!" she retorted before bursting into laughter. Messiah was confused, offended that she laughed at his plight. Then she dropped a bomb he could've never anticipated. "Heard? Nigga, I'm the bitch that followed the girl around Dallas until I found the dirt on that prissy bitches facade!" Black admitted before crossing her legs at the knee.

"As soon as Pimpin told me about how smitten you were of her, I was on that bitch. I pulled Pimpin Maxwell's coattail, and he approached that young boy, and the rest is history—" she pulled the wool from over his eyes.

His first reaction was frustration, but before he could speak, Black jeweled him with the type of diamonds that would one day make him one of the most successful playas in the game. She reached under his chin and turned his face to her.

"See, baby, the mistake in your game wasn't in loving lil mama, it was more in you loving her until it made no sense rather than loving her until it made "no more cents!"

Black smiled a sad smile. "Messiah, that hoe's love was built from the security you provided, but her loyalty was never invested."

She jeweled before standing and smoothing the wrinkles out of her dress. Reaching down, she took Messiah's hand and led him to the window, before parting the curtains and pointing down to the city lights that were twenty floors down.

"It's a big world out there, baby, millions of women, boss bitches! See, you fell in love with what Liberty did "to" you rather than what she could do "for" you, and the mere

thought of her fucking or sucking the next dick tested your sanity."

Black turned to face him, and Messiah's orb's trailed to her—"You was smitten with the freak in her rather than recognizing the hoe in her. Your dick blindfolded you, Messiah, and it always will if you don't learn to fuck a bitch with your mind rather than one of the weakest portions of your nature."

Black paused before digging down into her bra, and Messiah frowned when she pulled out a roll of money. Without breaking eye contact, Black—Messiah's moms, handed him the bankroll.

"That's three grand, baby, "my" choosing fee." She studied him for a reaction, but all she witnessed was confusion. The night was about to get more complex for the young cat as Black pushed him into a world of solicitation and compensation.

"You had a hand in killing my pimp, Messiah, so now you'll take his place. You're the successor and have inherited me, Creamy, and Candy. I suggest you make amends with that tender thing, Liberty, and make her "pay" for sinning against your game," Black proposed before turning him to face the city life once more.

Messiah stared out at the city of Dallas before allowing his eyes and mind to see beyond it's Horizon.

"The world is his the world is yours, baby, pimp hard!" she whispered.

Chapter 18

2010-The Present

"Oh my God!" Coffe whispered once Messiah closed the book and looked up at her.

"Did that really happen? I mean—" She was at a loss for words.

Messiah merely smiled as his eyes trailed to his sleeping mother. Her beauty was still evident, but he knew the monster had won the war, and he wondered why people sold their souls for the kind of shit that could never compensate them for the exchange. His dark eyes traveled to his daughter, but his words were for Coffe.

"Will she survive this?" Coffe's facial expression was uncertain as her eyes went to Black.

"She's a fighter, Messiah. She—"

"She's a fighter striving for a Pyrrhic victory. A warrior with a dying heart," he interrupted her.

His eyes were a hint of fire that set her aflame as he captured her within them. "Don't play me like a sucka, Ms. Lady. Especially now. Not with everything that's close to my heart being sentenced to the guillotine." His words were a whisper as Coffe studied him.

"If your mother doesn't receive a suitable donor soon..." She said before her words trailed off, allowing the silence to reveal the conclusion to the story.

Messiah was nodding his understanding when his phone stained the silence. He pulled it off his hip and glanced at the screen:

Unknown— it read, and Messiah knew it was the call he'd been waiting on. He swiped the green icon before placing the phone to his ear.

"Peace?" He answered, but there was a merely a thick silence on the line before a soft whimper could be heard.

"Hello?" Messiah probed.

"Siah—Messiah?" she cried, and his heartbeat accelerated. Justice! His mind had trouble wrapping around the concept, and he exploded from his seat.

"Justice, bae? Where are you at, ma! Tell me and I'll set that bitch on fire!" he declared, that gangster shit spitting from his heart.

Justice sniveled, having to compose herself before she could speak. "I'm, I'm," she started to say, but paused. "I don't know, baby. But forget me! Fuck them! This nigga—" Her words were cut off as the sounds of tussling ensued.

Fire surged through Messiah's veins as the distinctive sound of someone being struck sounded and a distorted voice came over the line. "Mr. Messiah? Nice to—" -

"Who the fuck is this? Let's get to the show down, pussy. Stop all this cloak and dagger shit and let's—"

"Silence!" the voice shouted through the voice animator. "Tomorrow night at nine thirty p.m., there's gonna be an extravaganza—a playa's ball, so to speak. You're to wear a tux, so forfeit any weapons, Mr. Ridge." Messiah's anger overflowed as he paced the floor.

"If you hurt her, I'm gonna—"

"One more thing," the voice said, cutting him off nonchalantly. "You're to come alone with at least half my bread. No gimmicks, playboy, or I'll put a bullet in this bitch's head. If you notify the authorities—well, I'm sure you won't do that, will you, playa?" The caller said.

Messiah looked up to find Coffe's shocked eyes on him. "Well, until tomorrow, relax, playboy, and Messiah?" the voice taunted. "This is a masquerade event. No one will know one person from the other." The call disconnected, but seconds later the address came in.

***

Paradise was awakened by the sound of her phone vibrating on her dresser. The man sharing her bed held her as if she was his bitch, and for the past few weeks, she had been. Paradise had been fucking JonJa since Messiah ordered it, and oblivious to her snakishness, the Jamaican stirred when she attempted to get up.

"Let it ring, mon. Dey don't want nothing."   He grumbled, and Paradise rolled her eyes before slipping from his embrace.

"It may be my daddy, he's known for his late night calls," she said and yawned. Paradise could feel his lust as she walked away.

'Bout time this nigga snuck from underneath that bitch! she thought heatedly.

Messiah had vowed to Justice that he would leave the game alone, and in spite of all four of his women willingly being ready for him, Messiah tended to them from a distance. Paradise swayed her hips all the way to her phone, knowing the Jamaican was enjoying the bounce of her creamy backside. She took the phone from the dresser and opened the text.

Get the girls ready. Daddy wants to see y'all at the old house. He misses y'all.

A soft smile eased onto her lips. 'Bout time, nigga! Damn! she screamed in her mind.

"Who is it?" JonJa snuck up behind her, and she jumped in surprise.

209

"Boy, you scared me!" Paradise laughed before placing a hand to her chest, and turning to him with a pout on her face. *"You don't trust me, huh, JonJa?"*

The Islander merely smiled a rhetorical smile before gently pulling the phone from her small hand. As he read the encrypted message, Paradise dropped to her hunches and liberated his limp dick.

She held it in her warm hand, while gazing up at him through mischievous eyes, she kissed his dick head while stroking him to an erection.

"My daddy wants to see me and my sisters today, so I may not be able to get away with you, bae. But I'm gonna leave you with something nasty to think about while I'm gone," she whispered before lifting his muscle and sucking his nuts into her mouth.

***

"You think Messiah knows we snatched up his bitch?" Murda asked over a lung full of smoke. And after exhaling the long stream of tainted fog, he followed with a slow pull from the Black & Mild. The atrocious smell of the formaldehyde permeated the air as he took the wet stick to the face. The smell of the embalming fluid caused SunJay to frown as he finished wrapping the last pound of exotic.

He stared at the neatly stacked pounds of kush he'd lined up against the wall; five hundred vacuum sealed bo's of the high-grade ganja that were ready to be flipped. Irritation was evident when his eyes traveled to Murda.

"Dawg, this shit loud enough without you adding to it with that bullshit right dere!" He spat, nodding to the dip cigar.

SunJay waited on his boy's response, but to avail; Murder was as still as a statue—stuck with a distinct look in his eyes. SunJay shook his head in dismay before stepping to his people, and taking the sherm stick from between his fingers.

"Messiah's a smart cat, he'll figure it out sooner or later. I just hope this bitch means something to him, 'cause if not, my bro gonna skip the formalities," he spoke more to himself than to his orbited friend.

SunJay assessed Murda with disappointment in his eyes, the drug had taken him under. "When the time comes for the showdown, I hope God is present and is more omnipotent than the devil." He murmured before smashing the cigar against the wall. "If not, shid, life and death gonna be a gamble," he said as he spoke over his shoulder, before exiting the room, leaving Murda to drift on his own wave.

***

Next day
Paradise, Lucy, and Creamy were comfy in baby tees, and boy shorts as they worked their stations. Paradise, with a scarf wrapped around her thick mane of hair, stood over a long table with a sheet of plexiglass laid across it. She was extra careful as she laid five and ten dollar bills lengthwise in rows of ten. Each bill was faced up in four rows as she took the first can of Easy Off oven cleaner, and sprayed each bill until they were saturated with foam. She had to use five cans before she got the desired effect, and after she flipped each bill, Paradise repeated the process on the opposite side.

She placed the kush-filled cigarillo to her full lips, and sucked the potent smoke into her lungs.

Call me
When you need someone to talk to - someone to fuck you
Call me
Satisfaction guaranteed- I'll give you what you need
Too Short's and Lil Kim's classic hit "Call Me" was the next song on the MP4 player.

"Ouuu, bitch! This my shit!" Juicy leaped from her seat and swirled her waist, and lifting her hands above her head, and gyrated her hips to the music.

They laughed as she dropped to the floor and made her ass clap, and their laughter brought Messiah from the back room where he was getting his wardrobe together for the night. He paused after spotting his young girl shakin' her ass.

He studied the thick redbone; she was a five foot three college student whose pussy was stronger than her desire for an education. Lucy was a born freak that had a body like the pornstar Pinky, but with a fatter ass and a juicier set of titties.

Though she wanted to quit school and whore full time, Messiah saw the bigger picture and made her stick with it, his eyes diverted to Paradise, whose yellow skin flushed when she noticed him standing there in a black hoodie with the hood pulled over his bald head.

"Is the bidness tended to or are you hoes celebrating my wife's kidnapping?" he questioned, before strolling into the room and over to the table of wet money.

As he awaited their answer, Messiah began peeling the bills away from the plexiglass, before depositing them into a bucket of water and acetone. Afterwards, he used a long metal rod to stir the liquid, watching as it turnt a grayish green from the ink being stripped from the currency.

"I have ten hours to have a quarter M—" His eyes lifted and bounced from each girl before returning to the bucket. "I taught you how to wash and print the shit to add to our hustles, but all you hoes want to do is shake your ass—" His eyes trailed to Lucy. "For free!" he spat before pulling a bill from the murky water.

Studying it as he used his fingertips to rest it upon a clean sheet of plexiglass, he could still see the outlines of the Treasury Departments seals as well as the president's face.

Messiah focused the hot lamp on the bill to help it dry, before his vision lifted to Paradise.

"Last I checked, I had four hoes in my stable, so why's only three present? Where's Diamond?" he inquired.

Paradise looked at Creamy before responding. "I don't know where wife-in law-at." A confused expression eased onto her face. "I've called her three times, but she ain't hit back."

At that moment, Creamy walked over to Messiah and dropped a black duffel bag at his feet, before giving him a smug expression as his eyes fell to the bag before traveling back to her.

Without a word, he squatted and opened it, to reveal stack upon stacks of artificial Grants and Franklins staring back at him. A faint smile eased onto his lips as he looked up at his girls.

"That's a buck and we'll have fifty bands ready for you in a few, daddy! You know we got you!"

Lucy purred, before crawling on hands and knees until she was at Messiah's feet, and lowering her head, she kissed his Dior shoes before glancing back up to him. Messiah chuckled. He knew her play was an effort for him to dismiss her free dance.

"Hoe, all that honey you drippin', you can save it for the bears and the bees, cause next time I catch you shaking yo' ass for another hoe or simp, you better have me some compensation for the demonstration, dig me?" He'd tapped into his pimpin. Lucy nodded her head in acknowledgement, but Messiah felt disrespected. "Bitch, a verbal question deserves a verbal answer—" he shot.

Lucy's pussy moistened to that boss shit; it was her achilles heel. "Yes, Daddy. I dig you," she confirmed before climbing to her feet.

Messiah patted her ass before making his way over to Paradise, where she sat at a table using a scanner to scan authentic hundred and fifty dollar bills before handing the images to Creamy. Creamy used the color printer that was filled with magnetic ink so the bills would look authentic.

"You think it will work?" Paradise asked.

Messiah watched as Creamy centered one of the washed bills before copying the imprint of a hundred dollar bill onto it. He knew the new hundreds were said to come out in 2011, and were supposed to feature a number of new security and anti-counterfeiting features.

"This shit looks the part and after I mix it in with the authentic hundred G's, it's going to be official." His eyes turned to her. "I'm just glad the new bills ain't out yet or we'd be preparing for my wife's funeral and not her ransom."

Chapter 19

2010

Deep in the country, three acres deep on a 9-acre property, a Mediterranean and Tuscan design structure was aglow from hundreds of garden lights. The house was 7,244 square foot of opulence, and as soon as Messiah was waved through the limestone flank gate, he knew the people he was facing off with were monarchs in terms of preeminence.

He followed the ground lights to the entrance of the magnificent estate, and stared in awe at the huge statue that jutted from the center of a cascading water fountain. It was a stone monument of Queen Nefertiti bathing in the azure waters. Messiah watched as guests milled about, sipping glasses of their pleasures.

The strangest thing about the scene was the masks covering their faces. Some were more elaborate than others. Some were multicolored, and still, all were worth a million words. A knock at the driver's side window drew Messiah's attention to a man that was clad in a white and black tuxedo, complemented by an all white phantom mask. Messiah eased the window down.

"Name and password?" the man asked. Messiah noticed the bulge of the burna as the man looked down at a clipboard, and he chuckled. This some real Hollywood shit, fam! he thought to himself.

"Zulu ninety-seven," he responded and watched the man's finger scroll down the page.

He paused midway before taking a walkie-talkie from his coat pocket. "Zulu ninety-seven has arrived and is coming your way, accommodate him with his identity," he spoke into the radio before urging him forward. "Drive until you reach the next attendant," he spoke to the confused expression on Messiahs face.

Messiah eased the car forward until he pulled next to a tall, slim woman in a sparkling red cocktail dress. He could only see half of her face, but the sharp features set flame to his imagination.

Her bone structure was pronounced, and as her succulent lips parted for a smile, Messiah marveled at how straight and white her teeth were. Her mask was a colorful scheme of feathers as sharp eyes took him in.

"Hello, Zulu Ninety-Seven. It's a pleasure to meet your acquaintance." Her voice was sultry as she handed him a gold bag with code name stitched into the fabric in fancy cursive letters.

Messiah's eyes rolled over her tall, slim figure. The queen's skin was as dark as a midnight sky and just as smooth. He nodded his admiration before opening the bag to find an all black masquerade mask with an evil frown on its face. A bright red ruby was centered in the middle of its forehead, and as Messiah studied it, he wondered what it represented.

"You have to put the mask and necklace on before you exit the car," she informed him, and when skepticism played over Messiah's face, she gave him a knowing look. "I think it's in your best interest to follow all instructions. You never know what awaits you at the end of the yellow brick road," she said with a smile that contradicted the words she conveyed.

That was all the motivation he needed, Messiah slipped the mask on. It felt like a second skin as he studied the strange necklace, and that's when the dark-skinned women opened his door.

"Step out and allow me the pleasure of putting it on for you," she offered, placing emphasis on the word pleasure. Messiah slid from the car, allowing the aroma of his Givenchy cologne to envelope her as her vision digested his attire.

Messiah's drip consisted of a red velvet Balmain dinner jacket, over a black silk shirt with matching pants, and the blood red bowtie complimented the Now-n-Later red, Mauri gators on his feet.

The feline's eyes paused on the center of his tailored black trousers, and she smiled at the imprint of his nature before using a manicured finger to indicate for him to turn around.

Messiah obliged and let her place the necklace around his neck. "Tonight, your identity is Midnight, the god of the night!" she whispered dramatically as she clasped the necklace around his neck.

Beyond it being snug, the weirdest thing happened. A beeping sound ensued as the jewel around the necklace began to glow, and when lady leaned to whisper, her lips brushed against his ear—

"It's a jewel explosive device that will detonate if you attempt to remove it before instructed. The explosive element ignites within a millimeter of a second, so play nice."

Her words were sweet as she reached around him and grabbed a handful of his dick.

***

Slim's white Jag was backed in beside SunJay's candy red Delta 88, and they stood in a super Walmart parking lot, and got to the business.

"You got the stuff?" Slim asked, before looking around suspiciously.

The stuff? SunJay thought as he studied dude, he'd never met Slim before that night, and only fucked with him because Murda vouched for him. SunJay's eyes traveled to his partner. *"Where you say you know this boy from again?"* he asked skeptically, and the look on Murda's face set off alarms in SunJay's gut.

"My nigga, the cats bread good. He—"

"Fam, I don't give a damn 'bout homies cash flow! I'm talm'bout your history with him? Where my dawg knows him from?" SunJay cut him off with heat in his eyes. Without waiting on a response, he turned to Slim. *"Say, fam. What's your name again?"*

Slim's face balled up with irritation as he huffed and puffed, but SunJay didn't give a fuck. Dude tossed his hands up to Murda. *"Homeboy, you know I'm solid. What's up with your boy?"* he asked before looking at SunJay. *"Man, you got the pounds of weed or not? I ain't got time for—"*

"Weed! Pounds?" SunJay gave him a peculiar look, before his heart began to race in his chest, and his glare found Murda.

The killer's eyes were just as wide as SunJay's as he began to regret introducing dude to his people; Slim had approached Murda weeks ago at the club. He and Murda both were making it rain, and afterwards, they both winded up at the Denny's down the street from the spot.

Murder didn't think too much about it when Slim approached him on some big boy business; all he saw were the jewels and the whip dude pushed and considered that as his credence to the street.

"Weed? Pounds?" SunJay repeated. *"Say, brah..."* His words trailed as he looked around with a keen eye.

The hundred Bo's in the trunk of the whip was a fleeting thought as his eyes took in a blue floral van about six car spaces down. The white man that stood beside it, smoking a cigarette appeared normal, but SunJay's instincts were in overdrive as his vision returned to Slim.

"Naw, playboy, I don't know what you talm'bout," he spoke cautiously. Murda felt the vibe and was on the verge of saying as much until SunJay surprised everybody!

"It's them alphabet boys, dawg!" he shouted before bolting between two cars.

***

The room was a wide expanse of Roman architecture, heightened by a massive chandelier that hung form the center of the room. Swarovski crystals hung from the ornament as the lights danced off the laser cut glass, and Messiah felt as if he was trapped within a beautiful nightmare. A live band was set up at the front of the room, and the trumpeter's rendition of one of Louis Armstrong's masterful pieces was as beautiful as if Satchmo was playing his trumpet himself.

The room was abuzz with masked couples dancing, drinking, and enjoying the hors d'oeuvres, but a contrast to the festive vibe, Messiah stood by a table that advertised aged bottles of wine from four different countries. He studied the labels as his mind took him fast—

I may not make it up out this bitch! How'd I let these people put a damn bomb around my neck? he wondered.

"You know what the beautiful thing about the story of the Beauty and the Beast was?" Her voice caught him off guard, and Messiah looked up into the most beautiful strangeness he'd ever laid his eyes on. She was a caramel brown, doe-eyed, Amazon.

Her bone straight hair was pulled back into a tight ponytail and as their eyes made love, the mask that covered one side of her face allowed him the pleasure of taking in her Middle Eastern features.

"The Beauty was able to turn the Beast into a prince because she was able to recognize the man beyond the monster that everyone else saw." She smiled while extending her manicured fingers. *"Persia, my home and name,"* she smiled.

219

Messiah took her soft hand, before placing a soft kiss upon the top. "Messiah, my name and sometimes my title," he returned the smile.

As his eyes took her in, he wondered if she was a prop in the horror movie that his life had become. Her eyes fell to the necklace and as a curious expression etched into her features.

"Strange. What kind of trinket is this?" she asked before reaching out to touch it, but Messiah's hand became a blur, and before she could blink, he'd captured her wrist.

"Don't. It's nothing, Queen," he replied, before releasing her. The necklace was no longer aglow, and now merely resembled an expensive piece of jewelry. Persia studied it before assessing him.

"Maybe another time perhaps," she said, her smile returning.

She reached down and took one of the martinis off the cloth table, and glancing down into the clear cocktail, she used the small toothpick olive to stir it. "You want to know another beautiful element within the story of the Beauty and the Beast?" she proposed as her eyes lifted to study the red ruby in the center of his mask.

Messiah was all hood when he took up a bottle of Eau de Vie and sipped straight from it, before wiping his mouth with the back of his hand. "Listen, mama. I don't belong here. I'm just a nigga out of the slums of Oak Cliff that loves deeply. I don't give a fuck about the story of the Beauty and the—"

"Unless the Beauty is your wife, and the Beast is..." she cut him off, pointing to something behind him.

Messiah's eyes crawled over her before following her outstretched finger, confused until his vision landed on—

"Justice?" he whispered.

That's when shit got funky. Justice wore a mask that resembled the one Halle Berry wore as Cat Woman, yet, he'd know his wife regardless of the attire. And as his eyes turned to the man that held her by the arm, Messiah couldn't believe

what he saw. He was the only man there without a mask, but what confused him even more was Pimpin Maxwell was the only man who shouldn't have been there.
   Shit was about to pop off!

To Be Continued...

Son of a Dope Fiend 2
Coming to a hood near you!

Lock Down Publications and Ca$h Presents
Assisted Publishing Packages

BASIC PACKAGE	UPGRADED PACKAGE
$499	$800
Editing	Typing
Cover Design	Editing
Formatting	Cover Design
	Formatting
ADVANCE PACKAGE	**LDP SUPREME PACKAGE**
$1,200	$1,500
Typing	Typing
Editing	Editing
Cover Design	Cover Design
Formatting	Formatting
Copyright registration	Copyright registration
Proofreading	Proofreading
Upload book to Amazon	Set up Amazon account
	Upload book to Amazon
	Advertise on LDP, Amazon and Facebook Page

***Other services available upon request.
Additional charges may apply

Lock Down Publications
P.O. Box 944
Stockbridge, GA 30281-9998
Phone: 470 303-9761

Submission Guideline

Submit the first three chapters of your completed manuscript to ldpsubmissions@gmail.com. In the subject line add **Your Book's Title**. The manuscript must be in a Word Doc file and sent as an attachment. Document should be in Times New Roman, double spaced, and in size 12 font. Also, provide your synopsis and full contact information. If sending multiple submissions, they must each be in a separate email.

Have a story but no way to send it electronically? You can still submit to LDP/Ca$h Presents. Send in the first three chapters, written or typed, of your completed manuscript to:

LDP: Submissions Dept
P.O. Box 944
Stockbridge, GA 30281-9998

DO NOT send original manuscript. Must be a duplicate.
Provide your synopsis and a cover letter containing your full contact information.

Thanks for considering LDP and Ca$h Presents.

NEW RELEASES

BLOODLINE OF A SAVAGE **BY PRINCE A. TAUHID**

THE MURDER QUEENS 4 **BY MICHAEL GALLON**

THE BUTTERFLY MAFIA **BY FUMIYA PAYNE**

KING KILLA 2 **BY VINCENT "VITTO" HOLLOWAY**

BABY, I'M WINTERTIME COLD 3 **BY MEESHA**

THESE VICIOUS STREETS **BY PRINCE A. TAUHID**

TIL DEATH 2 **BY ARYANNA**

CITY OF SMOKE 2 **BY MOLOTTI**

STEPPERS **BY KING RIO**

THE LANE **BY KEN-KEN SPENCE**

MONEY GAME 2 **BY SMOOVE DOLLA**

THE BLACK DIAMOND CARTEL **BY SAYNOMORE**

CRIME BOSS 2 **BY PLAYA RAY**

THUG OF SPADES **BY COREY ROBINSON**

LOVE IN THE TRENCHES 2 **BY COREY ROBINSON**

TIL DEATH 3 **BY ARYANNA**

THE BIRTH OF A GANGSTER 4 **BY DELMONT PLAYER**

PRODUCT OF THE STREETS **BY DEMOND "MONEY" ANDERSON**

Coming Soon from Lock Down Publications/Ca$h Presents

BLOOD OF A BOSS VI
SHADOWS OF THE GAME II
TRAP BASTARD II
By **Askari**

LOYAL TO THE GAME IV
By **T.J. & Jelissa**

TRUE SAVAGE VIII
MIDNIGHT CARTEL IV
DOPE BOY MAGIC IV
CITY OF KINGZ III
NIGHTMARE ON SILENT AVE II
THE PLUG OF LIL MEXICO II
CLASSIC CITY II
By **Chris Green**

BLAST FOR ME III
A SAVAGE DOPEBOY III
CUTTHROAT MAFIA III
DUFFLE BAG CARTEL VII
HEARTLESS GOON VI
By **Ghost**

A HUSTLER'S DECEIT III
KILL ZONE II
BAE BELONGS TO ME III
TIL DEATH II
By **Aryanna**

KING OF THE TRAP III
By **T.J. Edwards**

GORILLAZ IN THE BAY V
3X KRAZY III
STRAIGHT BEAST MODE III
By **De'Kari**

KINGPIN KILLAZ IV
STREET KINGS III
PAID IN BLOOD III
CARTEL KILLAZ IV
DOPE GODS III
By **Hood Rich**

SINS OF A HUSTLA II
By **ASAD**

YAYO V
BRED IN THE GAME 2
By **S. Allen**

THE STREETS WILL TALK II
By **Yolanda Moore**

SON OF A DOPE FIEND III
HEAVEN GOT A GHETTO III
SKI MASK MONEY III
By **Renta**

LOYALTY AIN'T PROMISED III
By **Keith Williams**

I'M NOTHING WITHOUT HIS LOVE II
SINS OF A THUG II
TO THE THUG I LOVED BEFORE II
IN A HUSTLER I TRUST II
By **Monet Dragun**

QUIET MONEY IV
EXTENDED CLIP III
THUG LIFE IV
By **Trai'Quan**

THE STREETS MADE ME IV
By **Larry D. Wright**

IF YOU CROSS ME ONCE III
ANGEL V
By **Anthony Fields**

THE STREETS WILL NEVER CLOSE IV
By **K'ajji**

HARD AND RUTHLESS III
KILLA KOUNTY IV
By **Khufu**

MONEY GAME III
By **Smoove Dolla**

MURDA WAS THE CASE III
Elijah R. Freeman

AN UNFORESEEN LOVE IV
BABY, I'M WINTERTIME COLD III
By **Meesha**

QUEEN OF THE ZOO III
By **Black Migo**

CONFESSIONS OF A JACKBOY III
By **Nicholas Lock**

JACK BOYS VS DOPE BOYS IV
A GANGSTA'S QUR'AN V
COKE GIRLZ II
COKE BOYS II
LIFE OF A SAVAGE V
CHI'RAQ GANGSTAS V
SOSA GANG III
BRONX SAVAGES II
BODYMORE KINGPINS II
By **Romell Tukes**

KING KILLA II
By **Vincent "Vitto" Holloway**

BETRAYAL OF A THUG III
By **Fre$h**

THE MURDER QUEENS III
By **Michael Gallon**

THE BIRTH OF A GANGSTER III
By **Delmont Player**

TREAL LOVE II
By **Le'Monica Jackson**

FOR THE LOVE OF BLOOD III
By **Jamel Mitchell**

RAN OFF ON DA PLUG II
By **Paper Boi Rari**

HOOD CONSIGLIERE III
By **Keese**

PRETTY GIRLS DO NASTY THINGS II
By **Nicole Goosby**

PROTÉGÉ OF A LEGEND III
LOVE IN THE TRENCHES II
By **Corey Robinson**

IT'S JUST ME AND YOU II
By **Ah'Million**

FOREVER GANGSTA III
By **Adrian Dulan**

GORILLAZ IN THE TRENCHES II
By **SayNoMore**

THE COCAINE PRINCESS VIII
By **King Rio**

CRIME BOSS II
By **Playa Ray**

LOYALTY IS EVERYTHING III
By **Molotti**

HERE TODAY GONE TOMORROW II
By **Fly Rock**

REAL G'S MOVE IN SILENCE II
By **Von Diesel**

GRIMEY WAYS IV
By **Ray Vinci**

Available Now

RESTRAINING ORDER I & II
By **CA$H & Coffee**

LOVE KNOWS NO BOUNDARIES I II & III
By **Coffee**

RAISED AS A GOON I, II, III & IV
BRED BY THE SLUMS I, II, III
BLAST FOR ME I & II
ROTTEN TO THE CORE I II III
A BRONX TALE I, II, III
DUFFLE BAG CARTEL I II III IV V VI
HEARTLESS GOON I II III IV V
A SAVAGE DOPEBOY I II
DRUG LORDS I II III
CUTTHROAT MAFIA I II
KING OF THE TRENCHES
By **Ghost**

LAY IT DOWN I & II
LAST OF A DYING BREED I II
BLOOD STAINS OF A SHOTTA I & II III
By **Jamaica**

LOYAL TO THE GAME I II III
LIFE OF SIN I, II III
By **TJ & Jelissa**

IF LOVING HIM IS WRONG…I & II
LOVE ME EVEN WHEN IT HURTS I II III
By **Jelissa**

SON OF A DOPEFIEND | RENTA

BLOODY COMMAS I & II
SKI MASK CARTEL I, II & III
KING OF NEW YORK I II, III IV V
RISE TO POWER I II III
COKE KINGS I II III IV V
BORN HEARTLESS I II III IV
KING OF THE TRAP I II
By **T.J. Edwards**

WHEN THE STREETS CLAP BACK I & II III
THE HEART OF A SAVAGE I II III IV
MONEY MAFIA I II
LOYAL TO THE SOIL I II III
By **Jibril Williams**

A DISTINGUISHED THUG STOLE MY HEART I II &
III
LOVE SHOULDN'T HURT I II III IV
RENEGADE BOYS I II III IV
PAID IN KARMA I II III
SAVAGE STORMS I II III
AN UNFORESEEN LOVE I II III
BABY, I'M WINTERTIME COLD I II
By **Meesha**

A GANGSTER'S CODE I &, II III
A GANGSTER'S SYN I II III
THE SAVAGE LIFE I II III
CHAINED TO THE STREETS I II III
BLOOD ON THE MONEY I II III
A GANGSTA'S PAIN I II III
By **J-Blunt**

PUSH IT TO THE LIMIT
By **Bre' Hayes**

BLOOD OF A BOSS I, II, III, IV, V
SHADOWS OF THE GAME
TRAP BASTARD
By **Askari**

THE STREETS BLEED MURDER I, II & III
THE HEART OF A GANGSTA I II& III
By **Jerry Jackson**

CUM FOR ME I II III IV V VI VII VIII
An **LDP Erotica Collaboration**

BRIDE OF A HUSTLA I II & II
THE FETTI GIRLS I, II& III
CORRUPTED BY A GANGSTA I, II III, IV
BLINDED BY HIS LOVE
THE PRICE YOU PAY FOR LOVE I, II ,III
DOPE GIRL MAGIC I II III
By **Destiny Skai**

WHEN A GOOD GIRL GOES BAD
By **Adrienne**

A GANGSTER'S REVENGE I II III & IV
THE BOSS MAN'S DAUGHTERS I II III IV V
A SAVAGE LOVE I & II
BAE BELONGS TO ME I II
A HUSTLER'S DECEIT I, II, III
WHAT BAD BITCHES DO I, II, III
SOUL OF A MONSTER I II III
KILL ZONE
A DOPE BOY'S QUEEN I II III
TIL DEATH
By **Aryanna**

THE COST OF LOYALTY I II III
By Kweli

A KINGPIN'S AMBITION
A KINGPIN'S AMBITION **II**
I MURDER FOR THE DOUGH
By **Ambitious**

TRUE SAVAGE I II III IV V VI VII
DOPE BOY MAGIC I, II, III
MIDNIGHT CARTEL I II III
CITY OF KINGZ I II
NIGHTMARE ON SILENT AVE
THE PLUG OF LIL MEXICO II
CLASSIC CITY
By **Chris Green**

A DOPEBOY'S PRAYER
By **Eddie "Wolf" Lee**

THE KING CARTEL I, II & III
By **Frank Gresham**

THESE NIGGAS AIN'T LOYAL I, II & III
By **Nikki Tee**

GANGSTA SHYT I II &III
By **CATO**

THE ULTIMATE BETRAYAL
By **Phoenix**

BOSS'N UP I, II & III
By **Royal Nicole**

SON OF A DOPEFIEND | RENTA

I LOVE YOU TO DEATH
By **Destiny J**

I RIDE FOR MY HITTA
I STILL RIDE FOR MY HITTA
By **Misty Holt**

LOVE & CHASIN' PAPER
By **Qay Crockett**

TO DIE IN VAIN
SINS OF A HUSTLA
By **ASAD**

BROOKLYN HUSTLAZ
By **Boogsy Morina**

BROOKLYN ON LOCK I & II
By **Sonovia**

GANGSTA CITY
By **Teddy Duke**

A DRUG KING AND HIS DIAMOND I & II III
A DOPEMAN'S RICHES
HER MAN, MINE'S TOO I, II
CASH MONEY HO'S
THE WIFEY I USED TO BE I II
PRETTY GIRLS DO NASTY THINGS
By Nicole Goosby

LIPSTICK KILLAH I, II, III
CRIME OF PASSION I II & III
FRIEND OR FOE I II III
By **Mimi**

TRAPHOUSE KING I II & III
KINGPIN KILLAZ I II III
STREET KINGS I II
PAID IN BLOOD I II
CARTEL KILLAZ I II III
DOPE GODS I II
By **Hood Rich**

STEADY MOBBN' I, II, III
THE STREETS STAINED MY SOUL I II III
By **Marcellus Allen**

WHO SHOT YA I, II, III
SON OF A DOPE FIEND I II
HEAVEN GOT A GHETTO I II
SKI MASK MONEY I II
By **Renta**

GORILLAZ IN THE BAY I II III IV
TEARS OF A GANGSTA I II
3X KRAZY I II
STRAIGHT BEAST MODE I II
By **DE'KARI**

TRIGGADALE I II III
MURDA WAS THE CASE I II
By **Elijah R. Freeman**

THE STREETS ARE CALLING
By **Duquie Wilson**

SLAUGHTER GANG I II III
RUTHLESS HEART I II III
By **Willie Slaughter**

SON OF A DOPEFIEND | RENTA

GOD BLESS THE TRAPPERS I, II, III
THESE SCANDALOUS STREETS I, II, III
FEAR MY GANGSTA I, II, III IV, V
THESE STREETS DON'T LOVE NOBODY I, II
BURY ME A G I, II, III, IV, V
A GANGSTA'S EMPIRE I, II, III, IV
THE DOPEMAN'S BODYGAURD I II
THE REALEST KILLAZ I II III
THE LAST OF THE OGS I II III
By **Tranay Adams**

MARRIED TO A BOSS I II III
By **Destiny Skai & Chris Green**

KINGZ OF THE GAME I II III IV V VI VII
CRIME BOSS
By **Playa Ray**

FUK SHYT
By **Blakk Diamond**

DON'T F#CK WITH MY HEART I II
By **Linnea**

ADDICTED TO THE DRAMA I II III
IN THE ARM OF HIS BOSS II
By **Jamila**

YAYO I II III IV
A SHOOTER'S AMBITION I II
BRED IN THE GAME
By **S. Allen**

LOYALTY AIN'T PROMISED I II
By **Keith Williams**

237

TRAP GOD I II III
RICH $AVAGE I II III
MONEY IN THE GRAVE I II III
By **Martell Troublesome Bolden**

FOREVER GANGSTA I II
GLOCKS ON SATIN SHEETS I II
By **Adrian Dulan**

TOE TAGZ I II III IV
LEVELS TO THIS SHYT I II
IT'S JUST ME AND YOU
By **Ah'Million**

KINGPIN DREAMS I II III
RAN OFF ON DA PLUG
By **Paper Boi Rari**

CONFESSIONS OF A GANGSTA I II III IV
CONFESSIONS OF A JACKBOY I II
By **Nicholas Lock**

I'M NOTHING WITHOUT HIS LOVE
SINS OF A THUG
TO THE THUG I LOVED BEFORE
A GANGSTA SAVED XMAS
IN A HUSTLER I TRUST
By **Monet Dragun**

QUIET MONEY I II III
THUG LIFE I II III
EXTENDED CLIP I II
A GANGSTA'S PARADISE
By **Trai'Quan**

SON OF A DOPEFIEND | RENTA

CAUGHT UP IN THE LIFE I II III
THE STREETS NEVER LET GO I II III
By **Robert Baptiste**

NEW TO THE GAME I II III
MONEY, MURDER & MEMORIES I II III
By **Malik D. Rice**

CREAM I II III
THE STREETS WILL TALK
By **Yolanda Moore**

LIFE OF A SAVAGE I II III IV
A GANGSTA'S QUR'AN I II III IV
MURDA SEASON I II III
GANGLAND CARTEL I II III
CHI'RAQ GANGSTAS I II III IV
KILLERS ON ELM STREET I II III
JACK BOYZ N DA BRONX I II III
A DOPEBOY'S DREAM I II III
JACK BOYS VS DOPE BOYS I II III
COKE GIRLZ
COKE BOYS
SOSA GANG I II
BRONX SAVAGES
BODYMORE KINGPINS
By **Romell Tukes**

THE STREETS MADE ME I II III
By **Larry D. Wright**

CONCRETE KILLA I II III
VICIOUS LOYALTY I II III
By **Kingpen**

SON OF A DOPEFIEND | RENTA

THE ULTIMATE SACRIFICE I, II, III, IV, V, VI
KHADIFI
IF YOU CROSS ME ONCE I II
ANGEL I II III IV
IN THE BLINK OF AN EYE
By **Anthony Fields**

THE LIFE OF A HOOD STAR
By **Ca$h & Rashia Wilson**

THE STREETS WILL NEVER CLOSE I II III
By **K'ajji**

NIGHTMARES OF A HUSTLA I II III
By **King Dream**

HARD AND RUTHLESS I II
MOB TOWN 251
THE BILLIONAIRE BENTLEYS I II III
REAL G'S MOVE IN SILENCE
By **Von Diesel**

GHOST MOB
By **Stilloan Robinson**

MOB TIES I II III IV V VI
SOUL OF A HUSTLER, HEART OF A KILLER I II
GORILLAZ IN THE TRENCHES
By **SayNoMore**

BODYMORE MURDERLAND I II III
THE BIRTH OF A GANGSTER I II
By **Delmont Player**

SON OF A DOPEFIEND | RENTA

FOR THE LOVE OF A BOSS
By **C. D. Blue**

KILLA KOUNTY I II III IV
By Khufu

MOBBED UP I II III IV
THE BRICK MAN I II III IV V
THE COCAINE PRINCESS I II III IV V VI VII
By **King Rio**

MONEY GAME I II
By **Smoove Dolla**

A GANGSTA'S KARMA I II III
By **FLAME**

KING OF THE TRENCHES I II III
By **GHOST & TRANAY ADAMS**

QUEEN OF THE ZOO I II
By **Black Migo**

GRIMEY WAYS I II III
By **Ray Vinci**

XMAS WITH AN ATL SHOOTER
By **Ca$h & Destiny Skai**

KING KILLA
By **Vincent "Vitto" Holloway**

BETRAYAL OF A THUG I II
By **Fre$h**

SON OF A DOPEFIEND | RENTA

THE MURDER QUEENS I II
By **Michael Gallon**

TREAL LOVE
By **Le'Monica Jackson**

FOR THE LOVE OF BLOOD I II
By **Jamel Mitchell**

HOOD CONSIGLIERE I II
By **Keese**

PROTÉGÉ OF A LEGEND I II
LOVE IN THE TRENCHES
By **Corey Robinson**

BORN IN THE GRAVE I II III
By **Self Made Tay**

MOAN IN MY MOUTH
By **XTASY**

TORN BETWEEN A GANGSTER AND A
GENTLEMAN
By **J-BLUNT & Miss Kim**

LOYALTY IS EVERYTHING I II
By **Molotti**

HERE TODAY GONE TOMORROW
By **Fly Rock**

PILLOW PRINCESS
By **S. Hawkins**

SON OF A DOPEFIEND | RENTA

SANCTIFIED AND HORNY
by **XTASY**

THE PLUG OF LIL MEXICO 2
by **CHRIS GREEN**

THE BLACK DIAMOND CARTEL
by **SAYNOMORE**

THE BIRTH OF A GANGSTER 3
by **DELMONT PLAYER**

BOOKS BY LDP'S CEO, CA$H

TRUST IN NO MAN
TRUST IN NO MAN 2
TRUST IN NO MAN 3
BONDED BY BLOOD
SHORTY GOT A THUG
THUGS CRY
THUGS CRY 2
THUGS CRY 3
TRUST NO BITCH
TRUST NO BITCH 2
TRUST NO BITCH 3
TIL MY CASKET DROPS
RESTRAINING ORDER
RESTRAINING ORDER 2
IN LOVE WITH A CONVICT
LIFE OF A HOOD STAR
XMAS WITH AN ATL SHOOTER
BONDED BY BLOOD 2
BOW DOWN TO MY GANGSTA

www.ingramcontent.com/pod-product-compliance
Lightning Source LLC
Chambersburg PA
CBHW060549260626
47161CB00003B/1118